I saved his life . . . and I had much to demand in return.

When he washed up on shore, I knew my prayers had been answered, and that I, Lady Chelsea Campion, need no longer fear poverty and heartbreak. To secure my family's estate, all I needed was a child. Handsome, clearly noble-born, and with no memory of his previous life, the mysterious man was perfect. All I had to do was visit his bedchamber and seduce him. I had expected him to be a skillful, scandalously wonderful lover, but once in his arms I was over-come by something more than mere passion. I had fallen hopelessly, desperately in love.

My plan has gone shockingly awry. But I will not give up a man who makes me feel such wicked ecstasy. No matter his true identity, no matter the secrets he struggles to remember, I will do anything in this world to make this stranger love me.

WHEN A STRANGER LOVES ME

Julianne MacLean

AVON

An Imprint of HarperCollinsPublishers

AVON BOOKS
An Imprint of HarperCollins*Publishers*
10 East 53rd Street
New York, New York 10022-5299

Copyright © 2009 by Julianne MacLean
ISBN 978-0-06-145685-5
www.avonromance.com

First Avon Books paperback printing: February 2009

Avon Trademark Reg. U.S. Pat. Off. and in Other Countries, Marca Registrada, Hecho en U.S.A.
HarperCollins® is a registered trademark of HarperCollins Publishers.

Printed in the U.S.A.

10 9 8 7 6 5 4 3 2 1

Acknowledgments

Special thanks to my friend Tracey Taweel, for the memorable camping trip to "The Ovens" in Lunenburg, Nova Scotia, where the sea caves turned out to be a great inspiration for this book.

Thank you also to my cousin Michelle Phillips, for reading and critiquing, and for always being a great friend. And to Kelly Boyce, for constantly stepping up to the plate. You rock.

Finally, to my amazing husband, Stephen, for your work on the book videos we have so much fun with. (And all the other stuff, too.)

Prologue

The thunderous boom from a cannon shook the ground beneath his nude body and rumbled through the foggy haze in his head.

Who am I? I do not exist. I must be dead.

He lay on his stomach. Pebbles and rocks cut into his cold skin. A pain, sharp and searing, worse than death, shot through his abdomen.

Is there a musket ball in my gut? A knife? Was I run through by a bayonet?

He could not move. He was paralyzed. The agony was unimaginable.

But I am not dead.

Boom!

Another shot from the cannon startled him, sent his heart racing, but still his body would not answer his thoughts. Somehow he found the strength to lift his eyelids.

The noise from the cannon echoed off the glistening walls of a black cave. Witches were shrieking, flying in circles overhead, laughing and cackling at his demise. Would they take him to Hell? Or had he already arrived?

But this was no battlefield. Everything was wet and cold and dripping. Where in God's name was he?

Who was he?

That question, more than any other, was the most disturbing of all, for he did not know the answer. He did not even know his own name.

Chapter 1

Western tip of the Jersey Islands, 1874

My Dearest Lady Chelsea,

I shall presume this letter finds you well, or as well as can be expected under your unfortunate circumstances. It cannot be easy living in the manner in which you are forced to live—hidden away from the world on that cruel, remote island, like the lowliest of social offenders condemned to prison. It must be a bleak and lonely existence for you. How you must suffer day after day, alone and ashamed, unable to change your past or correct your mistakes, with no one to sit by your side and offer comfort, other than your aging, widowed mother.

My greatest wish is that I can relieve you of your misery, and provide you with some hope for what is presently a future without prospects. I shall be blunt. After ten years of marriage, your elder brother has not yet provided the family with an heir, and I have recently learned he has not been well. I was most distressed to hear it.

As I am sure you are aware, if he has no heir to succeed him, the Neufeld title shall pass to me, I will inherit all your late father's properties, and you and your mother will be without a home.

I realize I am many years your senior and that I am not the handsomest of men, but I am not without pity either. I believe in charity and forgiveness, and would therefore be prepared to overlook your disgrace and take you as a wife. You are a beautiful woman, Chelsea, and that shall be enough.

I will take the liberty of presuming that this generous offer has made you happy. I will await your prompt reply.

Sincerely,
Lord Jerome Carruthers

Lady Chelsea stood on the grassy edge of the cliff and stared at the letter while she contemplated her "bleak and lonely existence" on this cruel island prison where she was forced to live, then threw her head back and laughed.

"He cannot be serious."

Lowering the letter to her side, she looked out

at the raging sea below. A strong north wind whipped wildly at her skirts and tugged at her hat.

How fast, she wondered, would a letter, such as the one in her hand, fly through the air on a gusty morning like this?

She took a step forward, peered over the edge, and held the letter out. It flapped and fluttered between her fingers for a few desperate seconds, then the wind sucked it from her grasp. It soared upward, performed a few loop de loops, and swung down into the ferocious, oceanic abyss below.

"Quite fast indeed," she said as she stepped back from the edge, then retied her hat ribbons under her chin.

It was a violent morning—passionate and extreme. It seemed almost as if the ocean was ranting about the storm the night before. Waves crashed onto the coastline in magnificent explosions of spray and foam, and the sea roared its displeasure like an enraged lion.

It rather mirrored her mood, thanks to that exasperating letter, which suggested she was unhappy.

Chelsea breathed deeply of the fresh salty air and tried to push the letter from her mind. She looked up at the sky. There was not a single cloud in sight. The sun was shining and seabirds were

circling overhead, frolicking on the wind, shrieking and screeching as they swooped down to the
surging whitecaps below.

She envied those birds their freedom, their ability to float on the wind, or ride it straight down
fearlessly at unthinkable speeds. She wished she
could somehow soar like that.

But then she strove to remind herself that she
did not need to fly. She was not bored. Contrary
to what Lord Jerome had written, she loved it here
on the wild Jersey coast. It fired her spirit and inspired her imagination, gave her just the material
she needed to pour excitement and soul into her
stories.

And that was what mattered most to her. Her
writing. She did not need a husband to make her
happy, and certainly not Jerome. The men she
wrote about were far more handsome and exciting
than that, and she was fulfilled. Truly she was.

Prisoner, indeed. London society and her very
"generous" cousin could go to the devil for all she
cared.

The tide was on its way out, so she started down
the hill toward the beach, wondering if the storm
had washed some treasures ashore. She picked her
way down the rocky path and was soon walking
along the water's edge, dodging the foamy waves
as they rolled in and slid back out again. The surf
was deafening this morning. It was an incredible

day. She would write about it. She would put a shipwreck in her next story, with a dashing captain who is washed ashore and falls in love with the young maiden who cares for him. Then what would happen?

Something shiny on the beach interrupted her thoughts, however, as it reflected the sun's rays. She squinted and walked toward it, kneeling down to pick it up.

It was a gentleman's watch on a fine gold chain, in pristine condition, though the hands had stopped at three-forty.

She rose to her feet and turned toward the sea, shaded her eyes and looked in all directions, as if there would be some clue as to where the watch had come from.

There was none, of course. There was nothing but blue water and clear skies.

She turned the watch over in her hand and inspected the initials engraved on the back: B.H.S.

Slowly, she began strolling while she set the correct time at seven-thirty and wound the watch. She held it to her ear. *Tick, tick, tick.* It worked perfectly, and looked very fine. It was clean and shiny, without a trace of rust, which suggested it could not have been in the water long. She looked up at the tops of the cliffs, wondering if someone had simply dropped it while walking along this beach earlier that morning.

But who? Her family's summer mansion was the only house for miles.

Slipping the watch into her pocket, she started off toward the sea caves, walking briskly, enjoying the vigorous use of her body. By the time she arrived at the jagged outcropping and stepped gingerly over the rocks into the first cave, she was out of breath.

She stopped for a moment in the dark confines to allow her eyes to adjust to the reduced light, and breathed in the clean aroma. The walls of the cave glistened with wetness. The chilly air kissed her cheeks. She listened to the sound of water dripping from the shiny rocks.

Just on the other side of those thick cave walls was another narrower grotto called Cannon Cave, where the surf surged in and out in great, thunderous explosions. It never ceased to amaze her, especially on a tumultuous day like this one.

She delved a little deeper into the cave, looking down at her feet as she hopped over shallow tidewater pools, where tiny snails in shells clung to the rocks, and seaweed danced gracefully in the current.

When she looked up, she saw something farther in. She blinked a few times. Her heart beat a little faster.

Were her eyes playing tricks on her? No, they were not. She was looking at something . . .

A body.

Fear plunged into the pit of her stomach, and she froze on the spot.

It was a man. A naked man. Facedown on the rocks.

Instinct, rather than conscious thought, drove her forward, and she dropped to her knees in a puddle beside him. She touched her hand to his cold back and shook him hard.

"Sir! Sir!"

Was he alive? He couldn't be. He was as cold as the grave. He must be dead.

The thought terrified her. She did not want to believe it.

He gave no response, so she pressed the heels of her hands against the side of his rib cage and rolled him over onto his back. His heavy body was limp, but not stiff.

Her eyes darted quickly over his muscular body and focused briefly on his male anatomy. It was not something she had ever seen before, and she found herself momentarily arrested, eyes wide as she swallowed.

Her fascination vanished instantly, however, when she saw that he was wounded. He'd been impaled by something. Or stabbed? Had someone tried to murder him and left him here to die?

Chelsea leaned forward and pressed her ear to his chest. The weak sound of his heart revived her hopes, and she sat back on her heels. He was alive, but not for long if she didn't soon get him out of here.

She rose to her feet and turned to face the light at the cave entrance. *"Help! Someone! Help!"*

But it was no use to call out. Even if there were others on the beach, they would never hear her over the thunderous roar of the surf.

Whirling around, she looked down at the man, then quickly began to unbutton her cloak. She shrugged out of it, dropped to her knees and wrapped him up tight. Then struggling to her feet, she gathered her wet skirts in her fists and stumbled briefly before dashing out of the cave to fetch help.

Chapter 2

⌒◯⌒

Three hours later Chelsea sat in the breakfast room with her mother and tapped a finger on the white-clothed tabletop. They were waiting for the doctor to come and explain the mysterious man's condition, or at least to assure them that he was still alive.

Tap tap tap . . . She could not keep her finger still. Impatience was bounding around inside her brain like a rubber ball.

Her mother huffed and lowered her needlepoint to her lap. "Really, Chelsea. Must you do that? Can you not sit still?"

"Aren't you curious what the doctor has to say?" she replied. "Are you not wondering who the man is? Or where he came from?"

"We shall find out soon enough, as soon as he wakes." Her mother lifted her needlepoint and resumed her work. "*If* he wakes."

"Let us not lose hope."

They sat in silence for some time, then her mother cleared her throat to speak. She kept her eyes downcast, however, remaining focused on her stitching.

"Did you find time to read the letter from Lord Jerome?"

How light and casual her tone was. She could have been humming a happy tune.

Chelsea stilled her finger. "Yes, as a matter of fact I did."

"Well?"

"Well *what*, Mother?"

She set down the frame again. "He has written to me as well and informed me of his intentions with you. Surely you must realize, dear, that it is a very generous offer, and it is likely the only one you will ever receive."

For a long moment Chelsea stared at her, then she let out a derisive chuckle. "Thank you for the vote of confidence."

"It is no laughing matter." Her mother began stitching again. "I am disappointed, Chelsea. Clearly you have given up all hope for a happy future for yourself."

"A happy future for *me*? I think it is *your* future you are thinking of Mother, not mine. You know I am content here. I do not require the approval of London society, nor do I wish to receive invitations and calling cards from all those snobby nobles. To get dressed up and cart myself around a congested city to go to parties and balls, praying every night for a proposal from some handsome aristocrat. I prefer Jersey. I have my writing, and I am fulfilled." She sat back and waited uneasily for her mother's response.

Her mother began stitching at a faster pace. "You're being stubborn."

"Stubborn? How old is Lord Jerome? Fifty? Sixty? He is pompous and greedy, he mistreats his horses, he does not wash, and as a result his personal aroma is most offensive, and aside from that, all he wants is to preen with Sebastian's title. He is only proposing to me because no one else will have him, and he thinks I am desperate enough to say yes."

"You are young and beautiful, Chelsea. I am sure that has a great deal to do with it."

"But that is the point, you see. If I were to marry someone, it would be someone who values me for what I am on the inside, not the outside. I would want someone who appreciates me for my mind."

Her mother scoffed. "Like that handsome fortune hunter you ran off with seven years ago? I hardly think it was your mind that attracted *him*. Admit it, Chelsea. You were bamboozled by his looks and surface charm."

Chelsea ran her open hand over the tablecloth,

back and forth, trying to smooth out a ripple that refused to lie flat.

"I was only eighteen," she quietly explained, remembering that it was more than just the young man's surface charm. As a girl, she had always been an incurable romantic, dreaming of romance and fairy tales. She had wanted to be swept away by passion and love.

But it was something else, too—something deeper in the makeup of her character. Always, since she was a small child, she had a great need for independence. She wanted to make her own choices, even if it meant experimenting with mistakes, though she had not consciously understood it at the time.

The problem was, no one had ever let her make those mistakes, which was perhaps why she delivered such a spectacular rebellion. Someone was always standing by, warning her not to go near that bumblebee, or not to walk on that stone wall, lest she should fall—when all she wanted to do was explore.

Well, that was not exactly the whole story. She could not leave out Sebastian, the brother who was ten years older than she—and the only person who recognized and fed her curious spirit. When he came home from school, he would take her fishing and digging in the dirt for worms. He would flip a rock over so she could see all the extraordinary wriggling creatures in the cold damp soil beneath. She would touch them with a finger, and he'd share her fascination when a fuzzy caterpillar made its way across the back of her hand.

Sebastian had been gone for more than a year on his Grand Tour when she ran off with the fortune hunter. Looking back on it, she had probably gone a little mad from lack of mental exercise.

Her mother slammed the embroidery frame down on the table, stood up and spoke heatedly. "It was the scandal of the century, Chelsea. Your father was a very prominent member of the House with a great future ahead of him. He had many enemies who were more than ready to have an excuse to pull him down—so now here we are, ostracized. Exiled to this merciless, remote island on the edge of the Atlantic, pummeled by storms every other day, locked away from the world like traitors to the Crown."

Chelsea spoke firmly. "If you hate it so much, why don't you go back? Enough time has passed. I'm sure all has been forgotten. There have probably been dozens of scandals since then, far worse than mine. I would be perfectly fine here on my own. I enjoy the solitude."

She would not ever wish for more. She had given up her childish dreams of romance long ago. Now she found pleasure and excitement through her stories.

Her mother picked up her embroidery again and sat down. She began stitching with hands that shook. "Oh no. I could never show my face. I would be mortified."

Chelsea sighed heavily. "Well, that is your choice. As for me, I am content here. I do not need or want to marry just to get back into society's good graces." She cared nothing for society. It had done her no favors.

"It is not just for that," her mother argued. "What if something happens to your brother? What then? You and I would be at the mercy of Lord Jerome, which is why I wish you would not slight him."

Chelsea's stomach pitched and rolled. It was a truth she preferred not to confront, for Sebastian, throughout a ten-year marriage, had not provided the family with an heir.

He walked into the room just then and poured himself a cup of coffee. "Slight who?" His blue eyes narrowed with curiosity. "The murder victim upstairs?"

"No, of course not," Chelsea answered with growing uneasiness. "We are talking about Father's cousin, Lord Jerome."

"Ah, yes, our delightful cousin Jerome." He leaned back against the sideboard and wrapped his hands around the coffee cup to warm them. "He's not coming here, is he? Lord help us if he is. He'll empty our wine cellar in a day."

"And leave greasy smudge marks on all the mirrors," Chelsea agreed, without smiling.

"Did you know he's wearing a wig now?" Sebastian mentioned as he took a seat at the head of the table. "He thinks he has all the ladies fooled into believing it's his real hair."

"And do they actually believe it?"

He crinkled his nose and shook his head.

Their mother pushed her chair back and stood up. "That is enough, both of you. He is your father's cousin, and presently first in line to inherit your title, Sebastian. It is time you both gave this situation the attention it demands. It is no laughing matter."

Looking surprised at his mother's outburst, Sebastian lowered his cup to the table. "I understand that he is my heir, Mother, but I am young and healthy."

"You were ill last month."

"It was a bad case of the sniffles."

"You were on death's door," she argued. "We all knew it, and so did you. And even if you had not been ill, you could trip down the stairs tomorrow and kill yourself on the way to breakfast for all we know." She paused to calm herself. "The fact of the matter is, we do not know what the future holds for any of us, and we cannot go on drifting aimlessly through the years as if we have it all under control. I agree, Lord Jerome is a horrid, pompous—" She

stopped suddenly, as if she couldn't bring herself
to finish what she truly wanted to say. "The point
is, we must consider our future. We cannot afford
to be rude to him. We must keep all our ducks in
a row."

Sebastian leaned back in his chair and said
nothing for a long time, then met Chelsea's gaze.
"It's true, I suppose. You ought not to slight him,
and maybe you should at least consider it."

"Sebastian . . . " She couldn't believe she was
hearing this from him, of all people—the brother
who had always understood her independent
mind.

"Look, Chel," he said, "we all know I have not
been able to secure a future for you and Mother."
He raked a hand through his hair. "There's only
so much I can do. I worry about the two of you,
and Melissa's disappointment is—"

He stopped and shook his head.

Chelsea recognized his frustration, reached
across the table and covered his hand with her
own. "You cannot blame yourself for our situation. I did something very foolish seven years ago.
I am more to blame than you."

He reflected upon everything for a moment.
"There is no point casting blame. This is where
we are, and I take full responsibility for failing to
provide this family with an heir."

"He's right in at least one respect, Chelsea," her

mother said. "He does take on all the responsibility, when you have been nothing but a burden to this family. You have pulled us down, and now you refuse to do the one thing that could save us."

"But I don't love him," Chelsea said.

"*Love!*" Her mother laughed bitterly. "This is real life, Chelsea, not one of your childish stories. You of all people should know there is no hope for a happily ever after. Not for you. Any hope for that was dashed years ago when you ruined yourself, and now Lord Jerome is the only man in England who would ever make an offer, and he does so out of pity."

The butler entered the room and they all immediately fell silent. Their mother quickly sat down, picked up her needlepoint and resumed stitching. Chelsea fought to settle her distress.

"The doctor wishes to see you, my lord," Cartwright said.

Eager to hear some news of the man upstairs, Chelsea sat up.

Sebastian nodded. "Send him in. I am sure we would all like to hear his prognosis." As soon as the butler was out of earshot, he added under his breath, "And a change of subject would be a welcome diversion." He threw Chelsea a look filled with apology and regret.

A moment later the doctor entered the breakfast

room, but remained standing just inside the door. He bowed slightly at the waist. "Good morning, my lord. Ladies."

Sebastian stood. "How is the patient? Will he recover?"

"It is difficult to say. He has not yet regained consciousness. The good news is there was no sign of infection in the wound—at least not yet. Outside of that, he has a few bumps and bruises. His knuckles are badly cut up, which suggests he was . . . " He glanced uneasily at the ladies. "Well, I am sure it is not my place to speculate about what brought him here." He cleared his throat. "I've treated and dressed the wound. I've examined him. Now there is nothing to do but wait and pray."

Chelsea settled back in her chair and worked hard to hide the level of her anxiety. She had been craving information about the man's identity for the past three hours, and the waiting was excruciating. "He didn't wake at all while you were treating him? Not even for a moment? Long enough to tell you his name?"

"No, Lady Chelsea, I'm afraid not."

"So we still have no idea who he is, or how he came to be washed up on our beach?" she said.

"Without his clothes, no less," Sebastian added, sitting down and taking another sip of coffee.

The doctor pushed his glasses up the bridge of his nose. "Unusual circumstances, to be sure. I confess, I am rather curious myself."

Sebastian turned to Chelsea. "It's just like one of your stories."

She recalled her latest idea about a shipwreck and a handsome sea captain taken in by a young maiden. It was all very strange and extraordinary.

"He will be weak when he wakes," the doctor told them. "He will also be confused and disoriented. It might be helpful if someone was at his side at all times, keeping an eye on him and checking the wound for any infection that might still occur. Certainly if he develops a fever, send for me right away. And when he wakes . . . "

Chelsea sat forward. "Yes, Doctor?"

He shrugged. "Answer his questions, I suppose. Tell him who you are and where he is."

"I will sit with him." She pushed back her chair.

"You will do no such thing," her mother declared. "It would be highly improper."

Chelsea raised an eyebrow. "Are you worried about my reputation, Mother?"

An awkward silence ensued, and the doctor cleared his throat again. "Perhaps I should be on my way."

Sebastian stood. "Of course, Doctor. Thank you for coming so quickly. And rest assured, we'll keep a watchful eye on our guest."

As soon as the doctor was gone, Chelsea turned to her mother. "Have a maid chaperone me if you must, though I hardly think it's necessary. It's not as if the man is going to ravish me. He'd have to be at least *conscious* for that."

"Fine," her mother replied. "But when he wakes, you must fetch someone immediately. We don't know anything about him. He could be dangerous."

"If it will make you happy, Mother, I will do that." She stood and started to leave, but her mother stopped her.

"There is only one thing you can do to make me happy, Chelsea, and you know what that is."

Chelsea looked back and spoke over her shoulder. "Yes, Mother, I know."

"Promise me you will consider it, that you will not continue on this selfish path. If you marry Lord Jerome and bear him a son, your father's title will pass directly through you, and will at least remain in our family."

Chelsea nodded. "I understand what you are asking, Mother."

Then she left the room to go and sit at the mysterious stranger's bedside.

* * *

They had put the naked man in the blue guest chamber, a spacious, richly furnished room that overlooked the sea. The heavy velvet drapes were pulled open, and sunshine poured in, dazzling and balmy, while the thunderous noise of the surf kept any unwelcome silence at bay. One of the maids had placed a crystal vase of violets and bluebells on the desk, which brought the fresh scent of summer in from the outdoors.

Chelsea entered quietly and closed the door behind her with a soft click. She stood with her back to the door, eyes closed, while she contemplated her duty—marriage to Lord Jerome; a most repulsive future. She could not even bear to think of providing him with a son. That would mean she would have to let him touch her with those lecherous hands, kiss her with those thin, pitiless lips that curled over rancid, decaying teeth. She felt sick just thinking of it.

Opening her eyes, she looked at the stranger asleep in the bed. He lay flat on his back with his arms at his sides. The blue paisley coverlet was drawn up to his waist. Someone had dressed him in a white nightshirt.

She pushed away from the door and moved closer, both curious and tentative—and strangely, afraid. When she found him in the cave, she'd been frazzled and distraught. She hadn't noticed what his face looked like—though she did remember that his hair was jet black, shiny and wet.

She also remembered, very vividly, the image of his naked body. His legs were long and lean, his back and buttocks fit and muscular.

And when she'd rolled him over . . .

Well, suffice it to say, she'd never seen a man's private anatomy before, and in broad daylight no less. It had been a startling sight. She could not seem to push the image from her mind.

Not that she was trying very hard to do so. Truth be told, she hadn't been trying at all to forget it. She was thinking of it even now as she approached him. It helped her to forget everything else that weighed upon her mind today.

At last she stood beside the bed and took in the details of his face. He was handsome, there was no question of that, despite the fact that there was a deep gash across his left eyebrow and his bottom lip was split open and swollen. He had strong, dark features—long black eyelashes, a chiseled jaw, and full, soft-looking lips. She wondered if someone in the house had shaved him that morning, because he was surprisingly well groomed. Or perhaps he had shaved at a late hour the night before, which was why he was still presentable this morning, though that seemed unlikely, as still as he lay.

She looked down at his arm upon the covers. On his right hand he wore a large silver ring with a shiny black stone. An onyx perhaps. The knuckles on his other hand were bruised and bloodied.

What had happened to him? she wondered desperately, feeling unsettled at the sight of all his injuries. Had there been a shipwreck in the storm? Had he been hurt while clinging to the rigging as the boat went down, then tossed violently on the waves and flung like a child's toy up onto the jagged rocks by the unforgiving power of the sea?

Or perhaps that was too romantic a thought—the product of a reclusive writer's overactive imagination.

The more likely scenario was that he had been involved in a tavern brawl here on the island, was left for dead, then taken out on the water and tossed over the side of someone's fishing boat.

Chelsea reached out to touch his forearm, which was marked with abrasions, when a knock sounded at the door. She snatched her hand back.

Sebastian walked in. He moved around the foot of the bed and stood on the other side of it, looking down at their unconscious guest.

"Has he stirred?"

"No," she answered.

He glanced at the silver ring on the man's hand, then leaned over his face. "He's good-looking, I'll say that for him."

"Yes, he certainly is."

Sebastian raised an eyebrow at her. "Maybe he *is* your Prince Charming, Chel, and the fairy tale Mother mentioned earlier has finally begun. Wouldn't that be a nice change—for someone around here to be favored with a happy ending."

Chelsea knew he referred to Melissa, who longed so desperately to be a mother.

"Perhaps it will all work out somehow," she said, then leaned over the stranger's face and wondered what secrets were concealed behind those dark eyelids. She brushed a lock of hair away from his forehead. "Mother was right about one thing. We know nothing about him. He could be a dangerous criminal for all we know."

"You're intrigued, aren't you?" Sebastian said, studying her intently.

"Of course I am. I'm a writer."

"Be honest. It's more than that. A naked man washed up onto the beach. You must have gotten an eyeful before you came for help."

Chelsea picked up a decorative fringed pillow and biffed it at him.

He laughed, catching it in his hands. "Careful, you'll injure him again."

"Keep your voice down. And it's not funny. He might not ever recover. Then you'll regret joking about it, won't you?"

Sebastian tossed the pillow to the foot of the bed. "Are you going to stay here and watch him all day?"

"Probably. You heard what the doctor said. Someone should stay with him."

He glanced at Mary, the young maid, who was sitting in the corner, acting as chaperone. "I'm sure Melissa would be happy to sit with you. Then Mary could get back to work."

"That would be nice."

He started for the door. "I'll tell her to come and join you when she returns from her morning ride. She'll certainly be surprised to hear of all this."

He left the room, and Chelsea remained standing over the bed, looking again at the stranger's scarred forearms and large hands.

Something made her change her mind about touching him. She moved away from the bed with a strange feeling of trepidation.

Chelsea remained at her post in the blue guest chamber for the rest of the morning, sitting in the chair by the window with a book, or pacing around the bed, watching the man from what her mother would have regarded as a reasonably safe distance. He did not move or make a single sound.

He remained as still as a corpse, flat on his back with his arms at his sides, showing no signs of life or even a hint of future recovery.

A maid brought Chelsea lunch on a tray, and then her sister-in-law, Melissa, arrived and sat across from her by the window, dismissing the other maid.

Chelsea described how she found the man naked and wounded in the cave, and how distressed and frantic she'd been, running up the hill for help. They also talked about Lord Jerome and his proposal, and how she'd been told she had no choice in the matter, that she owed it to the family to secure their future.

Throughout the rest of the afternoon, Chelsea read a book while Melissa worked on her needlepoint, and when teatime rolled around, they ate scones with raspberry jam and butter, while they watched over the man in the bed, who still did not move a muscle or utter a single word.

A few hours later, when the sun went down and the dinner gong echoed through the corridors of the mansion, Melissa rose from her chair and stretched her arms over her head. "Are you coming?"

Chelsea glanced at the man in the bed. "I believe I will stay here, but perhaps you could have my dinner sent up. And send the maid back as well."

"Certainly, but promise you won't stay up too late."

"I won't."

"I'll come back before I retire and see if you need anything." With that, she left the room.

Chelsea sat for a long time, listening to the steady ticking of the clock on the mantel and the constant murmur of the sea. The sun had disappeared below the horizon, and outside the window, high in the sky, the stars appeared, one by one.

Rising to her feet, she strolled to the bedside, put a hand to her mouth to stifle a yawn, then leaned over the man. He would no doubt be very weak when he opened his eyes, perhaps too weak to even speak.

Feeling a sudden wave of compassion for his suffering, she laid her open hand upon his forearm. Gently, with the tip of her finger, she traced a path around all the little scrapes and cuts, as if she were following a maze. He was warm to her touch, but so very still and lifeless.

Her eyes traveled down the length of his body. She could see the outline of his firm torso and long legs, and remembered again his naked form in the cave. Her belly swirled with fascination and arousal, which shamed her for a moment, until she remembered that she was a flesh and blood woman—a woman who had once known passion and desire for a brief time before this seven-year exile. There was a time she'd wanted nothing more than to know a man's body, and to be made love to by someone she adored.

Suddenly, without warning, the man's arm snapped up. He grabbed her wrist.

Panic flared in her stomach. She gasped, but before she could even comprehend the pain in her arm, he was scrambling out of the bed like a wild animal, coming at her with raging fury in his eyes.

She screamed as he threw her to the floor. Her head hit the rug and she squeezed her eyes shut. All the air sailed out of her lungs.

The man pinned her down, tossed a leg over her hips and straddled her. When she opened her eyes, he was sitting on top of her, holding a brass candlestick over his head. It gleamed in the fire-light, just like the ferocity in his wild blue eyes.

"*Aaah!*" he yelled as he drew the weapon back and swung.

Chapter 3

C helsea held out her hands to deflect the blow. *"No!"* she cried. She braced herself and uttered a frantic prayer.

Nothing happened for a few seconds, so she cautiously opened her eyes. The man was still brandishing the candlestick over his head. He glared down at her with fire in his eyes.

"Who the hell are you?" he demanded.

"I'm Lady Chelsea Campion," she said breathlessly.

His brow furrowed with tension, and he drew his arm back again as if he had changed his mind and was going to bludgeon her to death after all.

"No! Please!" she cried. "I'm not your enemy!"

Again he hesitated.

Chelsea's frightened gaze dropped to his midsection. "You're bleeding."

He glanced down. He seemed to discover, only in that instant, that he was injured. Dropping the candlestick to the floor with a noisy clang, he doubled over in pain and covered his wound with both hands.

"Oh, God," he groaned.

He toppled over and landed on the floor beside her. Lying on his side, he brought his knees to his chest.

She scrambled to her feet. "I'll get someone. The doctor."

She made a dash for the bellpull.

"You're hurt," she tried to explain as she tugged hard on the velvet rope.

"Who did this to me?" He spoke through gritted teeth, with a deep, enraged snarl, glaring at her with loathing. "Was it you?"

"No. I don't know who did it."

He grimaced in pain.

Chelsea returned to his side, knelt down and touched his shoulder. His eyes were squeezed tightly shut, his face contorted in agony while he struggled to breathe.

"Try to calm down," she said. "Someone will be here soon." His blood was dripping onto the carpet. "You shouldn't have gotten out of bed."

"Bed?" he repeated, as if the word were completely foreign to him. He looked around in a panic. "Where am I? What am I doing here?"

"You were washed into a sea cave here on Jersey

Island, and that is where I found you," she explained. "You were hurt. We brought you here."

"Where's *here*? Who's *we*?"

Just then someone knocked on the door. *"Come in!"* Chelsea shouted. *"Hurry!"*

But it was only Mary, the youngest maid. She took one look at the man writhing in pain on the floor and her eyes flew open in horror, wide as saucers.

"Go and send for the doctor," Chelsea instructed. "And tell Lord Neufeld to come quickly!"

Mary dashed back out into the corridor.

As soon as she was gone, the man grabbed Chelsea by the throat and pulled her down. She fought for breath while he lifted his head off the floor and squeezed her neck in a viselike grip. Anger burned in his eyes like the flames of hell.

"Who am I?"

She gazed at him with confusion and fright. "I don't know," she rasped.

His hand fell away from her throat and he lowered his head to the floor.

Coughing and sputtering, her heart pounding with terror, Chelsea rolled over onto her back, while he blinked up at the ceiling in a daze.

"I don't know either," he said.

Then his hellish eyes fell closed and oblivion claimed him once more.

* * *

Sebastian, dressed in formal black and white dinner attire, came running into the room. "What the devil happened?"

Only then did Chelsea realize how badly she was shaking. Carefully, she rose to her feet. "He woke up and attacked me."

"Attacked you?" Her brother rushed forward and looked down at the man on the floor.

"He seemed confused and delirious," she tried to explain. "He thought I stabbed him. I think he was trying to defend himself."

Sebastian knelt down and placed two fingers on the man's neck. "My God, he's barely alive. He must have lost a great deal of blood."

"I assure you," she said, "he was quite alive and hot-blooded a few minutes ago. There was no shortage of fire racing through those veins."

Sebastian slipped both hands under the man's arms. "Help me get him back up on the bed. Take his ankles."

"Be careful," she said, struggling to help her brother lift him. "He might wake up again."

"I hope he does," Sebastian replied. "Because I'd like to knock his bloody block off for scaring you like that."

They maneuvered him back onto the bed.

Chelsea leaned over him. "Look how he's bleeding. He must have opened the wound."

"The doctor has been sent for."

"But we can't just sit here and wait." She climbed onto the wide bed, knelt beside the man and laid her hands upon his stomach where the blood had seeped through the nightshirt.

"*Chel,*" Sebastian said with a warning tone. "What are you doing?"

She felt for the dressing. "I'm going to press on the wound to slow the bleeding until the doctor gets here."

While she applied pressure to his lower abdomen, near his hipbone, she regarded the man's face and thought how peaceful he appeared now, compared to the fury she had witnessed a few minutes ago. Whatever happened to him to fill him with such rage?

"It would probably be best if you didn't tell Mother what I just told you," she said.

"Don't worry," her brother replied. "I know how she gets."

Chelsea pressed on the dressing for a number of minutes while the man remained asleep, unmoving, his arms splayed out upon the bed.

"I'm going to look at the stitches," she said. "Pass me that blanket."

Sebastian tossed the wool coverlet that was folded at the foot of the bed. She covered the man, then lifted his nightshirt to check under the bandage.

"Just as I thought. The stitches have come loose. How long do you think it will be before the doctor gets here? Can we wait?"

"Not if we want him to live, I suppose."

She sat back on her heels and considered her options, then knew what she had to do. "I'm going to require a needle and thread. Will you go and get that from Mrs. Hubley? And some warm water and a cloth. What else?"

"Brandy." He made a move to leave. "But you shouldn't be alone with him."

"I'll be fine," she replied. "I won't be caught off guard again. Besides, he's in no shape to do any damage now."

Sebastian nodded. "All right, but scream if he so much as blinks." He hastened from the room.

Chelsea reached for a clean section of the bandage and pressed it to the wound while she waited for Sebastian to return. The seconds ticked by on the clock like minutes—relentless and sluggish. Time seemed heavy and suffocating.

She touched the man's forehead and cheek. At least there was no sign of fever.

A moan escaped him. He turned his head into her palm.

"You're going to be all right," she said, holding his face in her hand, hoping to keep him calm. "You're safe here."

His eyes fluttered open and he stared up at the ceiling for a second or two, then his body jerked. He rose up on his elbows. Fire shot through her veins again and she stiffened, certain that he was going to leap up and lunge at her. His eyes flashed with panic and distrust.

"Who are you?" he asked for the second time, as if she had no right to be there.

"I am Lady Chelsea. You are in the care of my brother, Earl Neufeld. You were washed ashore here on Jersey Island, and that is where I found you, on the beach. Can you tell me your name and where you come from? Who is your family?"

He struggled to think. "I don't know. I don't know any of that."

"You don't even know your name?"

"No."

Chelsea wet her lips and urged him back down onto the pillow. "I am sure it is just the shock of what has happened to you. Give yourself some time. It will all come back."

He laid his head down and continued to watch her while she checked his wound.

She looked toward the door. Where was her brother? What was keeping him?

The man's jaw clenched with pain. He seemed to be holding back some colorful language.

"You've started to bleed again," she told him, "and I don't want to wait for the doctor. If he is on another call, it could be hours before he arrives, so I am going to stitch you up myself."

He looked down at her hands and spoke through clenched teeth. "All right."

Her gaze flicked up. Judging by the paleness of his face, she decided it would be best if she could keep him talking and distracted from his pain. "Are you always so agreeable? When you're not brandishing a candlestick, that is."

"I have no idea if I am or not." His eyes rolled back in his head and he writhed on the bed. "I attacked you before. Why did I do that?"

She was uncomfortably aware of the strength and power of his body. He was large and muscular, not like any gentleman she'd ever met before. "I don't know. You gave no warning. You just opened your eyes and threw me down."

He grunted. "My apologies, Lady Chelsea."

How strange it felt to be conversing with him this way. Was this really happening? "Apology accepted."

He lay still for a moment, focusing intently on one spot on the ceiling. "Do you have any brandy? Wine? Anything will do. Anything at all."

"My brother is on his way up with a bottle. He should be here any time now." She glanced impatiently at the door again. Where was he?

The man closed his eyes and nodded, while Chelsea sat beside him, looking at his dark lashes and the strong line of his jaw. He had a perfect face—well-proportioned and balanced, as if he'd been sculpted by an artist.

Aside from the scraped knuckles, his hands were well-groomed. He was a gentleman, and a very appealing one, there was no question of it. His speech and accent were impeccable, his tone of voice polite, especially when he'd apologized to her just now. There was something immensely confident and dignified about him, now that he was no longer trying to snuff the life out of her.

Heavy footsteps came marching down the hall. Her brother entered the room at a brisk pace, a bottle and glass in one hand, a needle—already threaded—in the other. "I have everything," he said, "and a maid is on her way up with a pitcher of water and more bandages."

The stranger opened his eyes. "Are you the earl?"

"Yes." Sebastian glanced curiously at Chelsea.

"Pass me the needle," she said, ignoring her brother's distress over her safety.

Sebastian hesitated. "Maybe I should do it."

"No. I know what to do, and besides, my hands are already covered in blood. Just give it to me."

With barely enough strength to blink, the gentleman turned his head toward her brother. "I think you had better do what the lady says. She seems very determined."

Sebastian passed the needle across the bed. Chelsea took hold of it between two blood-soaked fingers.

"Are you ready?"

The stranger nodded.

But *she* wasn't ready.

She paused. "Do you need something to bite down on?"

He shook his head. "No. Just do it."

Digging deep for courage and grit, she inched forward and began stitching him up. He watched the entire procedure in silence, without uttering a single oath, and for some reason she could not explain, his cold control unnerved her almost as much as the violence of his awakening.

Chapter 4

"You mean to tell me he doesn't know who he is? He doesn't even know his own name?"

Chelsea sat down in the drawing room, her head still spinning from the day's extraordinary events. "That's right, Mother."

The doctor had arrived an hour after she stitched the gentleman up, took one look at the wound and told her she'd just saved his life. He was now conducting a more thorough examination.

"Do you think perhaps he is an idiot?" her mother asked. "That he escaped from an asylum somewhere? That would certainly explain why he was naked. Maybe he thought he was in the bathtub."

Chelsea glanced at Melissa, who was seated across from her mother. "No, I don't believe he is from an asylum, although I suppose anything is possible. My feeling is that he suffered a blow to the head when he was washed up onto the rocks, and that it has dislodged his memory somehow."

"Dislodged his memory?" her mother said incredulously. "How absolutely ridiculous. I've never heard of any such thing."

"Well, either way," Chelsea continued, "the fact of the matter is—he doesn't know who he is, and I should think he must be feeling very lost, to say the least."

"Lost, indeed," Melissa added thoughtfully. "To not know who you are or where you come from, or whether or not you have a family . . . It would be most distressing. It would be a complete loss of your identity and all that you have become."

Chelsea nodded. "Exactly, which is why I believe that we must make him feel welcome and do all we can to help him."

"For how long?" her mother asked indignantly.

"Until he recovers his memory, I suppose," Chelsea replied, "or until someone comes to claim him."

"But no one knows he is here."

"We can inform the local magistrate," Melissa suggested helpfully, "as well as the London authorities and newspapers."

Chelsea gestured toward her sister-in-law with a hand. "Yes, that is an excellent idea, and if he comes from a good family, someone should be looking for him."

"What makes you think he comes from a good

family?" her mother asked. "As I said before, he could just as easily have escaped from a madhouse."

Chelsea shook her head. "I don't think so, Mother. He is well spoken and well groomed."

Melissa reached for her teacup. "For all we know, he could be a missing duke or even a prince. That's what Sebastian suggested."

"A missing duke indeed," her mother scoffed.

Sebastian entered the room and presented the doctor. "Dr. Melville, if you would be so kind as to share with the ladies your prognosis."

He took a seat across from Chelsea.

"Is our patient feeling any better?" she asked.

"I wouldn't go so far as to say that, but his vitals are strong—his heart, his breathing, and so on. You did a fine job with your stitching, Lady Chelsea. The wound looks as though it will heal nicely, as long as there is no infection looming on the horizon." His eyes smiled and he spoke with a touch of humor. "And providing he does not leap out of bed and attack you again. My word, you were lucky to have escaped with your life. Clearly he was not in his right mind, and I suspect that whatever brought him here was an ordeal of the very worst kind."

Though she did not turn and look at her mother, Chelsea could feel her shocked gaze boring into the side of her head.

"You exaggerate, Doctor. It wasn't nearly as bad as that. He was just a bit disoriented when he woke. He didn't know where he was."

"He tore his wound wide open and threw you to the floor," the doctor argued. "I'd hardly call that a mere state of confusion. It was a most violent awakening, which is why I think—"

"He threw you to the floor?" her mother asked. "Why did you not tell me this before?"

Chelsea sighed. "Because I knew it would upset you."

"It certainly has upset me. Good heavens . . . I think my nerves are failing. I cannot breathe." She placed her hand on her chest.

The doctor rose from his chair, picked up a book from the table and began to fan her face. "Perhaps a little brandy for your nerves, my lady."

Sebastian stood. "I'll get it." He left the room in a state of perfect calm, for he had fetched brandy for his mother more than a few times over the years, whenever her nerves decided to act up.

"Chelsea, you are not to go into that room again," her mother insisted. "Do you understand me? Clearly the man is insane."

"He is not insane." She wasn't exactly sure why she was defending him, however, when he had tried to brain her a few short hours ago. She looked at the doctor. "*You* don't think he's insane, do you?"

Dr. Melville glanced uneasily from Chelsea to her mother, who was pursing her lips at him. "Well," he stammered, "it is difficult to say . . . "

Sebastian returned with a glass of brandy and handed it to their mother.

She took a sip and moaned. "How shall I survive this? Sometimes, Chelsea, I am certain it is your goal in life to put me in an early grave, though why you should wish that, I've no idea."

"I wish for no such thing, Mother."

The doctor was still fanning her with the book. She flopped back against the sofa cushions. "Oh, yes, Dr. Melville, that is most helpful. You are such a fine medical man." She relaxed for a moment, then sat up abruptly and turned her attention back to Chelsea. "You are not to go in there again," she said. "Your brother will see to his needs, not you."

She pointed at Sebastian. "And make sure you are on your guard at all times. It wouldn't hurt to keep a pistol in your pocket. At the very least, we must keep the door to his room locked, at least until we know more about him. Oh," she sighed, lying back again, "I have a very bad feeling about this. He attacked my only daughter. What kind of animal have we brought into our home? I fear he brings disaster."

* * *

He woke to a high-pitched ringing in his ears and a rage so intense that he sat up and shouted into the darkness. He looked around with alarm, then became aware of the excruciating pain in his side. With a quiet oath through clenched teeth, he eased himself back down onto the pillow.

Agony vibrated through his body with the same relentless peal as the ringing in his ears, and a cold film of sweat covered his skin.

He was alone in the empty room, though he could recall a golden-haired beauty who had been there earlier and tried to explain things to him.

You were washed into a sea cave here on Jersey Island, and that is where I found you. She also told him that he was in the care of her brother, Earl Neufeld, in the family's summer home.

She had been sitting on the bed with him, and just the memory of her voice brought him some comfort. He remembered watching her skillful fingers stitch him back together with a needle and thread. He had watched her face, too, and her eyes were tense with concentration.

Lady Chelsea. That was her name.

There had also been a doctor asking him questions he could not answer.

What was his name?

Where did he come from?

How did he get here?

Placing a hand on his side where the bandage covered his wound, he shut his eyes and tried to remember where he had been before any of this. He tried to picture the place where he lived, but there were no images, no familiar thoughts or memories. It was as if he did not exist in the world before today, which was not possible, of course. He must have been a child once, for now he was a grown man, although he had no idea how old he was.

He looked at his hands, turned them over in front of his face, with nothing but the moonlight streaming in through the window to illuminate them. Twenty-five perhaps? Thirty? Thirty-five? He did not have the slightest idea. He knew nothing, except that he was alive and in the care of a noble family.

The clock on the mantel ticked steadily in the silence, and somewhere in the house another grandfather clock chimed—one, two, three, then four times. All fell quiet again, though he could hear the distant hiss of the sea outside the window. The waves were breaking onto the shore. They did not rest.

He must try to relax and go back to sleep. Perhaps in the morning his memory would return to him. Perhaps he only needed time to recover and regain his strength, as Lady Chelsea had suggested.

The pain in his side eventually subsided to a dull ache, and before long he drifted back into the deep, black void of slumber.

In the morning he opened his eyes to the distinctive sound of a key turning in a lock. The door creaked open.

The room was awash in sunlight, he discovered groggily, as he blinked up at the scrolled ceiling and then turned his head toward the window. The sky was clear and blue. It was the kind of day that should move a man to leap out of bed and accomplish a great number of tasks, but the only thing he felt at the moment was the same acute panic he had experienced the night before, when all his instincts told him to lash out and swing his fists.

A maid entered the room with a breakfast tray. There was a young man in the doorway as well—a footman, he presumed—standing there with his hand on the knob, watching intently. He felt rather like a freakish curiosity in a glass display case.

Without a word, without even lifting her eyes from the floor, the maid set the tray on the bed beside him, turned around and hastened from the room. The footman slammed the door shut behind her, and the key turned quickly in the lock.

He glanced suspiciously at the food, then back

at the door. The sound of the servants hurrying down the hall faded to silence. His eyes darted to the window. It was no doubt locked as well.

Was he a prisoner here? he wondered.

Working hard to subdue the urge to get out of bed and pound on the door for answers, he instead inched up against the pillows and headboard. It would do no good to get up too quickly and open his wound again. He should eat.

He reached for the steaming cup of coffee and held it to his lips, breathing in the pleasing aroma. The coffee was black. Did he like it black or with cream? He did not know. He took a sip to find out. It was fine as it was. He decided no cream was needed.

Next, he reached for the toast and devoured it in three large bites. The eggs and sausage . . . With those, he took his time, savoring each mouthful, while he was disturbingly aware of the thunderous roar outside the window—those relentless and impregnable waves crashing violently onto the rocks.

All at once he experienced a flash memory of waking up in the sea cave with the certain belief that he was dying. He also remembered the frustration of fighting the waves, thrashing about and sucking in water, and the pain of being dashed against the rocks. Other than those disturbing images, however, he could recall nothing.

His gut rolled with nausea, and he found himself unable to finish the breakfast. Quietly, he set down his fork, laid his head back on the pillow, and wished the lady would return.

Bang! Bang! Bang! The door rattled in its hinges.

"Is anyone there?" He pounded his fist against the blue painted door and shouted the question again.

Barely withstanding the pain in his side, he looked down to see if his wound was bleeding, but the bandage was still clean, even though it ached like the devil just from getting out of bed and crossing the room.

"I wish to be let out! Open the door, damn it!"

Bloody hell. Where in God's name was everyone?

Feeling dizzy and light-headed, he backed away and tried to calm his breathing. He turned around and made his way carefully to the window, holding onto the foot of the four-poster bed for support as he passed.

When at last he reached the window, he braced one hand on the sill, while he cupped his sore side with the other arm. Outside, the rough, white-capped ocean swelled and surged. He could see the white foamy spray, bursting forth onto the rocks along the coastline.

He towered above it all, however, here on the second floor of the earl's summer home, which stood on a steep cliff overlooking the sea. Just below, there was a green lawn enclosed by a thick hedge of bright pink roses that whipped in the wind—to keep one from falling over the edge, he supposed.

He was truly cut off from the world, trapped here on this remote island, where no one would ever find him if they were looking.

If he even mattered to anyone. He did not know.

His frustration mounted to new heights, and he returned to the door. *Bang, bang, bang.*

"For God's sake, open the damn door! Can anyone hear me?"

He continued to pound on it, cursing to himself until his fist was numb. Tipping his head forward against the oak panels, weary with defeat, he closed his eyes and rested a moment.

A key slipped into the lock.

He stepped back.

The lock clicked, the knob turned, and the door pushed open.

The golden-haired beauty—Lady Chelsea—stepped into the room. She wore a blue floral day dress with no jewelry or adornments, and her hair was pulled up into a simple, braided knot. Her lips were full and moist, a rich red color, her skin the color of cream, and he could barely think through his fascination and his relief that it was she who had answered his call, and no one else.

"I must ask you to control your language, sir," she said. "It is Sunday, after all."

"Why wouldn't anyone come?" he asked impatiently. "I've been pounding on that door for an hour. For that matter, why am I locked in here like a prisoner?"

"You are not a prisoner," she explained. "No one came because they are all attending the Sunday service. I am the only one here besides a few servants. And the door is locked because my mother learned of your conduct with the candlestick last night and has insisted upon it for our safety."

"The candlestick." He paused a moment and frowned. "I had forgotten. I've been forgetting a lot of things lately, it seems. Did I apologize to you?"

"Yes."

"Good. Nevertheless, I shall apologize again. It was unspeakably rude of me to threaten the life of such a lovely woman."

She seemed taken aback by the compliment, and glanced uneasily out into the corridor.

"I am not a danger to you," he assured her, stepping forward, sensing that she wished to leave. "I don't even know why I behaved that way."

He did not want her to go. He did not want

to be alone. He could not stand the stillness, the sense of nothingness.

"That may be true," she replied, "but surely you understand why we must be cautious. You are a stranger to us, and you presented yourself somewhat violently."

She was far too reasonable to squabble with, even though he felt very much like arguing. He was restless and agitated. He had so many questions that no one could answer. He had rather enjoyed pounding on the door just now.

She glanced down at his side. "How are you feeling this morning? Better, I presume, since you are out of bed and on your feet."

"I am not as well as I appear. I simply couldn't stand the boredom." He turned and hobbled back to the bed.

Lady Chelsea remained in the doorway with her hand on the knob, just as the footman had.

"You're quite safe," he told her, drawing up the covers. "Surely you can see I am in no condition to attack anyone."

"Yet you managed to attack the door quite impressively. I'm surprised you didn't pound a hole in it."

He sat up against the thick pillows, looking at her fathomless blue eyes while she stared back at him with equal measure. The surf exploded like thunder onto the cliffs outside.

"You're a writer, aren't you?" he said, curious about the details of her daily life.

She tilted her head to the side and frowned. "How would you know that? Did someone tell you?"

He shook his head. "No. No one mentioned it."

"Then how would you know?"

"You have that look about you," he replied. "It's in your eyes. There are all kinds of things going on inside your mind that you don't share with anyone."

She wet her lips. Her hand fell away from the doorknob and she strolled into the room, stopping at the foot of the bed, looking at him curiously.

God, he couldn't take his eyes off her. She was stunning.

"I didn't realize I was such an open book," she said.

For the longest time he could do nothing but admire her beauty—the soft curves of her face, her clear, dewy skin, and her charming, inquisitive expression.

But after a time, he could not bring himself to keep up the charade.

"I am toying with you," he confessed. "The evidence is right there on your right hand. I don't recall ever seeing a lady's fingers stained with quite so much ink." He glanced at the window and chuckled somewhat bitterly. "That is a good sign, I suppose. At least I remember what I do *not* recall."

She laughed as well, very softly, while she lowered her gaze. It was an attractive mannerism. He found her very appealing, especially when he felt so incredibly alone.

"Why are *you* not at church?" he asked, curious all of a sudden.

"I worship at home." Then she lowered her gaze again in that adorably shy manner, which somehow eased the pain in his side. "I just realized how odd that must sound."

"It is rather unconventional," he said. "Why wouldn't you be welcome there?"

She stood with her hands behind her back, looking at the window, pondering her answer, then turned her eyes toward him again. The shyness was gone now. She appeared almost confrontational. Devilish and daring.

"Because I have a reputation," she said, lifting her chin. "I am a notoriously wicked woman."

His head drew back. "Indeed."

She laughed. "Indeed. No need to hide the fact. It is no secret. I am almost famous. Maybe you've even heard of me. *Before.*"

"Before . . . " He squinted at her, searching for understanding. "Before I lost my memories, you mean."

"Yes. If you reside in London, you look to be about the right age of someone who would have heard the gossip when the scandal broke."

"And what age do I look to you?"

She studied his face. Her luminous eyes traveled down the length of his body, which was concealed under the heavy covers, thank God, for he felt himself becoming aroused just by the movement of her eyes.

"You're roughly the same age as I am," she said. "I would estimate twenty-five."

He nodded. "Good to know. And what was the scandal, if you don't mind my asking?"

"I eloped with a fortune hunter," she promptly answered, "and made it across the border to Scotland before my father overtook our carriage and dragged me home in tears."

"So you never married the man."

"No, but we were gone long enough for the world to presume that the damage was done."

"And was it?" he boldly asked.

"Absolutely." She shrugged a shoulder. "As I told you before, I am ruined—and lavishly famous for it."

He chuckled and glanced at the door. "Well, now that we have *that* out in the open . . . "

"As I said, it's no secret. You would have heard it eventually from someone."

Suddenly she jumped, as if she just remembered something of vital importance. "Oh, I have an item that might belong to you." She reached into her pocket. "I found this on the beach shortly before I found you in the cave." She moved around the bed and handed him a shiny gold watch on a chain. It was set to the correct time and ticking steadily. "Does it look familiar?"

He examined it carefully—it was very fine— then turned it over and noticed the initials engraved on the back: B.H.S.

He shook his head and held it out to her. "No, I don't recognize it. But that doesn't really mean anything."

"You should keep it," she said, returning to the foot of the bed. "It's probably yours, and when you remember who you are, you might be glad to have it. Perhaps it has some sentimental value."

They said nothing for a moment or two, then his lovely nursemaid wandered casually to the window and looked out at the water. "Can I get you anything? A book? Something to eat or drink?"

"Your enchanting company is all I require at the moment."

She did not seem the least bit fazed by his flirtatious tone. "You know, when you attacked me last night," she said, "I thought you were going to kill me. You looked angry enough to do it."

"I wish I could explain why. All I know is that I *was* angry enough to kill. I still am, for some reason."

She faced him. "How do you mean?"

"I woke up in the middle of the night and wanted to fight someone, and just now, pounding on the door . . . I feel rather like a stick of dynamite, ready to blow. It's like my insides are bound up with ropes and something in me is thrashing around, trying to get loose."

"That's strange." She moved closer. "Do you think it's because of what happened to you? Perhaps you were fighting with someone before you ended up in the ocean. Do you think someone tied you up?"

"I don't know."

She walked to the bed, rested her temple on the ornately carved post and spoke wistfully. "I am very sorry you were hurt, and that you feel so out of sorts."

"I appreciate your concern."

"It's strange," she continued. "I am in full possession of my memories, yet sometimes I feel like a stick of dynamite myself. It's a general day-to-day frustration, I suppose."

"With what?"

"My life. Someone suggested recently that I am living in a prison here, and though I've always loved this house and the beach and I enjoy myself most of the time—because I've always been free to do as I please and write what I want—I can't help wondering if it is true in many ways that I am *not* free, because of the geography of this place. I walk to the edge of the cliff and cannot go any farther. Sometimes I do become bored. And now, my family wants me to do my *duty* for them . . . " She accentuated the word with an indication of spite. "So the freedom I once knew will soon be gone."

"What duty?" he asked, frowning. An unexpected aversion poured through him at the mere mention of the word.

He heard a commotion downstairs then, and Chelsea stepped back. "They've returned. I must go." She hurried to the door, but turned to him before she walked out. "If you don't mind, keep this visit to yourself. My mother doesn't need to know I was here. She tends to worry over things."

"Your secret is safe with me."

She hurried out and shut the door behind her. The key slipped into the lock and turned with a profound *click*, then he was alone again, listening to the sound of Lady Chelsea's footsteps tapping down the hall.

The room fell quiet, until another wave crashed onto the rocks outside the window and caused him to jump. Willing his heart to slow down, he settled back onto the soft bed and wondered how it was possible that while he was as good as a prisoner on this island, all he could do was marvel at the beauty of the woman who was keeping him locked up, and wonder when she would return.

Chapter 5

C helsea did not return to the gentleman's bed-chamber that day, for her mother insisted she spend time with Melissa outdoors, and after lunch she sent her on a long errand to deliver bread to two different neighbors who lived quite a distance apart from each other in opposite di-rections. Clearly it was a scheme to keep her oc-cupied, so she would not sit at the man's bedside all day, because he was, according to her mother, a crazy person.

The maids took charge of bringing his meals, and the doctor returned in the evening to reex-amine him and change his dressing. Dr. Melville informed the family just before dinner that the patient was doing well. He was gaining strength and would soon be up and around.

For that reason, Chelsea's mother reiterated the importance of keeping him locked in the bed-chamber, for they still could not be sure that he was not a raving lunatic. What would they do if he came at them at night brandishing another candlestick? Or worse, a kitchen knife?

Chelsea did not argue with her. She certainly did not mention the fact that he told her he still woke up wanting to kill someone.

That night in bed she lay on her back staring up at the ceiling, thinking of the conversation she'd had with him earlier that day while everyone was at church.

It was a strange thing, talking to a beautiful man with no name or identity. It was almost as if he did not exist, as if he were a fictional character from one her stories. A figment of her richly textured imagination.

He was not, of course. He was a flesh-and-blood man, and a handsome one, at that, with broad shoulders and dark, silky hair. She couldn't have invented anyone better to play the part of a handsome hero, and when she'd stood in his room earlier, looking down at him in the bed while he paid her compliments, she felt almost intoxicated by sexuality.

If this *were* a story born from her imagination, what would happen next? she wondered. How would she write it?

She tucked an arm under her head and smiled. She knew exactly how she would plot it. He would become her secret lover. They would enjoy each other until they were satisfied, and no one would be the wiser. No one would ever know she had secretly experienced scandalous sexual pleasures with a nameless stranger in a locked bedchamber. It would be as if it never happened, and Lord Jerome would never know the difference. He already presumed, like the rest of the world, that she was not a virgin, and he would not expect to see blood on the sheets on their wedding night. So what would it matter? She felt no high, moral desire to save herself for him. Why should she? She was already sacrificing everything else.

She rolled onto her side, rested her cheek on the back of her hand, and imagined what it would be like to let the nameless guest seduce her, or better yet, for her to seduce him. But that was veering a little too far into the world of fiction, because she wouldn't have a clue how to go about that. She had no experience. Despite what the world thought, she was a virgin, pure as fresh fallen snow.

Chelsea smiled. She certainly did have a vivid imagination. But that, unfortunately, was how it would remain, because if she were to do something so wild and reckless in real life, she would, with her luck, end up at the altar to marry Lord Jerome already carrying another man's child in her womb, and wouldn't that be a fine ball of wax?

She blinked a few times, then sat up.

What if she did seduce the man whose life she had saved? What if she *did* become pregnant?

Her heart began to race. Who would ever have to know? And more importantly, who would ever know it was not Sebastian's and Melissa's baby?

Overcome with curiosity—could such a plan really work?—she tossed the covers aside, hopped out of bed, and reached for her wrapper. She flew out of the room to go and wake her brother.

Ten minutes later Chelsea was sitting in the library with Sebastian and Melissa, by the light of a single kerosene lamp.

"Have you lost your mind?" her brother asked. "Honestly, Chel, I think you need to get off this island. You've been here too long. You're starting to believe in your own inventions."

Melissa sat quietly on the sofa, her lips parted, her eyes wide with astonishment.

Sebastian paced around the room. "This is my fault. I spoiled you too much when you were a child. I should have been more strict like Father, instead of feeding your imagination and letting you do whatever you damn well pleased."

"That is not true," she said. "You kept me from going mad all those years ago. It was because of Father that I ran away and eloped. I knew he wanted to marry me off to a man of his choosing to further his political career, and I couldn't do it. I valued my freedom too much."

"Just like you value it now," Sebastian said. "Quite selfishly, I might add, when this family's future is at stake."

She sat forward. "But what I am suggesting will secure our future. Can you not see that?"

He stopped pacing and faced her. "All I see is my far too creative sister concocting a lunatic plan to escape the duty which is being pressed upon her. Just like the last time."

She paused and sat back. "Yes, I suppose I must concede that that is correct."

"But did you learn nothing from that?" he asked incredulously. "You were ousted from society, for pity's sake!"

But Chelsea was not yet ready to retreat. She could not bear to think of the dismal life she would lead if she did not make an attempt at this alternative. "I've been very happy as an outcast. I have my freedom. I can write and live as I please. I enjoy my solitude."

"But if you had a child for us," Melissa interjected, "you would be sacrificing your own future. At present you have a chance to be married and have children of your own. Not secretly, but legally and without shame."

Chelsea looked down at her hands in her lap. "I'm afraid, for me, that would be a far greater sacrifice, Melissa, for I cannot imagine bearing Lord Jerome's children." She shivered with revulsion at the thought. "Try to imagine how unhappy I would be. Truly, Sebastian, I don't think I could survive my wedding night. I would drown myself in my bathtub before he knocked on my door. Or worse, drown *him* before he had a chance to kick off his slippers."

"Would it really be so bad?" her brother asked, stopping in the middle of the room and frowning down at her with concern.

"Honestly? I don't think I can possibly convey in words the despair I would feel as I became nothing more than a breeding factory for such a vile and repulsive man. He is not kind. You know that about him. I would rather not have children at all than allow him to be a father to them. And I have no doubt he would be cruel to me if I ever denied him his husbandly rights. Try to understand that, Sebastian. I could not bear it. I wish only for a way out, no matter how preposterous it might seem to you."

Her brother sank into a chair beside her and cupped his forehead in a hand. For a long time he sat in silence with his eyes closed, then at last he spoke. His voice was quiet and resigned.

"I'm sorry, Chelsea," he said. "I've been so wrapped up in my own responsibilities and failures that I have not stopped to think about what it would be like for you. What it would *really* be like. I should have considered your happiness before I took Mother's side today. It was wrong of me to push you to marry our cousin. I hope you can forgive me."

She lifted her gaze, and thought of all the days on the lake with Sebastian when she was a little girl, no more than five years old—casting a line, swinging a fish into the boat, laughing and learning. He had been the one person who understood her need to be free in a soulful way—to connect with nature, to explore the natural world.

"But I still do not think this is the solution," he said nevertheless.

They were all quiet for a long time, then Chelsea stood and walked to the window. "Mother said I have dragged you all down, and for that reason, she believes I have a debt to pay. You must believe me when I tell you that this would at least be a debt I would *enjoy* paying."

"Are you saying you wish to do this for your own pleasure?" her brother asked with utter disbelief.

Melissa rose and joined Chelsea at the window. She spoke quietly. "How can you be sure you would enjoy it, Chelsea? We know nothing about this man. You are forgetting that he attacked you last night."

"No, I am not forgetting. He apologized for that, and I believe he was sincere."

"Well, he is definitely more attractive than Lord Jerome," Melissa said after some consideration.

"That is hardly the point, darling," Sebastian said.

"I think it has some bearing on it," his wife argued.

Chelsea interjected. "She's right. It does indeed have some bearing. I am not going to deny it. A few nights with that handsome stranger would be far preferable to a lifetime of the equivalent with our despicable cousin."

That was putting it mildly. She had already entertained a number of exotic dreams about this particular stranger's hands on her body.

"That man down the hall is not a stud for hire," Sebastian said with a slight scolding tone. "And what happens when he remembers who he is? Have either of you considered that? If he is a gentleman, as you believe he is, he may want to do the honorable thing and marry you, whether you are with child or not."

Chelsea shook her head. "No. As far as he is concerned, it would be nothing more than a few wild nights of debauchery, and he would be long gone by the time my belly grew round. I doubt he would suspect anything if I seduced him. He already knows I am ruined."

"How does he know that?" Sebastian asked.

"I told him so."

"Just like that. You told him. Out of the blue, you said, 'By the way, I am soiled goods.'"

She nodded. "Yes, that's quite accurate."

Sebastian rose to his feet and strolled to the window. "It is a risky plan."

Melissa went to him and took his hand in hers. "But it could work, darling. You could have an heir—a Neufeld heir. And I could be a mother."

"But the child would not be a legitimate issue," he said. "The title cannot pass through a daughter."

"But no one would know," Melissa repeated.

"It is dishonest," he said.

"The dishonesty you are referring to is a legal matter, and an unfair law in my opinion, that a title cannot pass through a daughter. Family blood is family blood, but that is another debate." She squeezed Sebastian's hand. "In our *hearts* the child would be legitimate. He or she would have your father's blood running through his veins, in a direct line through Chelsea. We are a married couple. We have been so for ten years. If we are blessed with a boy, he would be our son, without question, both in our eyes and in the eyes of the world. Why shouldn't he inherit your title?"

Sebastian touched her cheek and kissed her tenderly on the forehead.

"It might just as easily be a daughter," he reminded her.

"He is right," Chelsea said from the sofa, where she now sat. "It is important that we are prepared for such an outcome."

Melissa turned to her. "I hear that if you eat asparagus, it increases the likelihood of a boy."

"Then I shall tell Cook to serve it tomorrow."

Sebastian turned his gaze to her. "So you have decided, then. You are determined to do this? There is nothing I can say to change your mind?"

"And decide I would prefer to marry Lord Jerome after all? Believe me, I shall never choose that option. This way, I will have done my duty for you and Mother, and I shall not have to worry about her trying to marry me off ever again."

"But what if it could be someone you loved?" he pressed. "What if you fall in love with *this* man?"

"That is a very distinct possibility," Melissa abruptly said, not having thought of it before. "What would you do?"

Chelsea considered it for a moment. "I shall make every effort to prevent that from happening. I will not let my heart become engaged. But even if it did, I would simply be broken-hearted, which is nothing I haven't experienced before, so I know I would get over it eventually. At least this time there would be a silver lining, because you and Sebastian would have a child. It is worth a few tears."

Melissa gave a melancholy sigh, then her expression grew forlorn. "But what will your mother think?"

Sebastian went to pour himself a drink. "Does she even have to know?"

Chelsea looked at him with dismay. "How in the world would we keep it from her?"

He took a sip of his brandy and set down the glass. "The same way most English ladies keep their illegitimate children secret. We would hide your condition for as long as possible, then the three of us would go on an extended holiday."

Melissa's eyes lit up with anticipation. "Switzerland. I would love to see the Alps."

Chelsea moved forward, took hold of her sister-in-law's hands and gazed at her with affection. "Then that is where we will go."

Chapter 6

On that fateful night in the library, Chelsea, Sebastian, and Melissa stayed up until dawn discussing methods and strategies to bring their plan to fruition.

Melissa was a romantic. She suggested that Chelsea spend time with the convalescing gentleman over the next few days, reading to him and charming him, until his heart was won and he would initiate a tryst.

Though Chelsea, too, was a romantic, she was against this course of action. She argued that they were already being dishonest enough as it was about far too many things. To woo him that way, romantically, when she had only one thing in mind, only increased their deceptions.

She explained that while she was willing to use her feminine powers to swindle the English legal system—which, in her opinion, favored men unfairly when it came to inheritance laws—she was less inclined to trick the stranger into believing she was falling in love with him. It would be best, she insisted, to be straightforward about what she wanted. A few nights of coupling, nothing more. Men did that sort of thing all the time, didn't they? Surely he would take what she was offering without believing it ever had to lead to something more.

In the end they decided she was right. They would give the man two days to recover from his ordeal and gain his strength back—because he would definitely need his strength, Melissa whispered to her privately—then Chelsea would enter his bedchamber when the household was asleep and offer her body to him.

It was a simple, perfect plan, just like a scene she would write in one of her stories.

The following night Melissa was kind enough to share with Chelsea all she knew about the marriage act and how to arouse a man's desires. She was straightforward and explicit, and described various activities in clear, colorful detail. She even suggested what to say, and how a woman could use her mouth for more stimulating purposes than simply talking and kissing.

Chelsea was both shocked and inspired. She had already seen the man naked, so not everything Melissa described came as a surprise.

What did surprise her, however, was how fearless and eager she felt, and how impatient she was to get under way. Seven years had passed since her passionate elopement with the fortune hunter, and since then she had been alone without the company or affections of a man—a spinster without prospects—though she had not forgotten the pleasures of kissing a man and feeling his hands on her body through her clothes.

As she sat in Melissa's bedchamber remembering all the sensations that had been promised to her but were never delivered—for her father had intervened before the marriage could take place—she felt certain that she was going to succeed most spectacularly.

By the time the night of her deflowering arrived, Chelsea was more than prepared to embark upon her wild escapade. In the hours leading up to it, she spent the whole of the evening getting ready. She took a bath in rose-scented water and scrubbed her hair into a thick, sweet-smelling lather. After she rinsed, she laid her head back upon the rim of the tub and dreamed about the mysterious man in the bedchamber—about his naked body in the sea cave, the fire in his eyes when he woke and threw her violently to the floor, with great hulking strength.

And his hands . . . those strong, manly hands. She imagined them sliding up her bare legs, touching her face, kneading her breasts. She pictured herself naked on the bed beside him, and felt warm and relaxed in the tub, almost too weak to rise and get out.

She managed it, however, and stepped out dripping wet. She sat by the fire with a glass of brandy, completely naked, while her hair and body dried in the heat. Then, without the assistance of her maid, she combed and curled her hair so it fell in loose, shiny waves down her back.

Earlier in the day Melissa had come to her room and presented her with an exquisite silk dressing gown and her most expensive perfume, and Chelsea put everything on in a leisurely manner, taking her time to make sure all the details were perfect. She applied a balm to her lips to make them soft, and applied powder to her face and neck and arms, so that she smelled of roses.

When the clock in the hall finally chimed midnight, she was ready. She left her bedchamber with a bottle of wine and two glasses and tiptoed barefoot down the corridor to the gentleman's room.

Finally, there she stood, outside his door, arrested on the spot by the sudden beating of her heart, while she fought a howling storm of apprehension inside her belly, which seemed to have come out of nowhere.

It was real now, she supposed, no longer a story

playing out in her imagination. If her seduction was successful, he would kiss her and touch her and have sexual intercourse with her.

She took a deep, shaky breath and felt a sudden urge to return to her room.

But no. She could not do that. She'd made a decision and would not withdraw now. She *wanted* to do this. It was only natural to feel nervous, for no man had ever seen her in her dressing gown before, or even with her hair down, for that matter. She was not even wearing stockings. And this was nothing compared to what would occur once she was on the other side of this door.

Closing her eyes and wetting her lips, she reminded herself of all the reasons she was doing this and resolved to be brave. She reached for the key in her pocket and slipped it into the lock.

A few tempestuous heartbeats later she was inside the moonlit room, quietly locking the door behind her. She turned around and looked at the man asleep in the bed.

Her trembling breaths came faster and faster. Perhaps she should just pull off her nightdress, move straight to the bed, and slip silently under the covers. She could touch him, and if what Melissa said was true, he would be instantly aroused. She might not even need to say a word. He might simply roll over, couple with her, and it would be concluded, just like that.

"Where were you the past two days?" a gruff voice asked.

The question caused her to jump, for she hadn't realized the man was awake. Suddenly unable to speak, she almost turned around and dashed out, but the sound and sight of the covers rustling over his legs as he sat up in the bed kept her fixed to her spot.

"I asked you a question," he said. Anger darkened his voice, made him sound threatening. "Where have you been? I wanted to see you, but the maids ignored my requests."

Not quite sure how to answer him, she pushed away from the door and walked around the foot of the bed. A square of moonlight shone in through the window, illuminating the covers.

He watched her in silence. She could see only the dark outline of his head and shoulders, but could feel his masculine presence in the room like a low rumble of thunder, reverberating off the walls, quivering through her bones.

"I'm sorry," she said. "My mother kept me busy. Intentionally, I think."

"To keep you safe from the wild beast who attacked you a few nights ago?"

"Yes."

"And she's keeping the beast in a cage for good measure," he added broodingly. His resentment chilled her skin.

"I suppose that's right."

"You *suppose*?" His tone was menacing. "I don't appreciate being locked up."

"But you haven't complained," she anxiously replied. "I mean, I haven't heard you banging on the door since the other morning."

He tilted his head. "That's because your doctor has been drugging me. Laudanum. Put in my wine."

"What?" She couldn't believe it. "Perhaps it was just to help you with the pain."

"No. I was demanding to be let out on Sunday. The next thing I know, it's Tuesday."

She looked at the bottle of wine in her hand. "I'm very sorry, and I assure you, I had nothing to do with it. I didn't even know what went on here on Sunday. As I told you before, my mother has been keeping me busy. She sent me on an errand."

He watched her intently. "I didn't drink the wine today. I'm only now just coming around."

She set the bottle and glasses on the table by the window. "Then perhaps you don't wish to drink what I brought."

"Quite the contrary. I'm desperate for a taste of something. As long as it's not laced with sleeping potion."

She shook her head. "No, I snuck it out of the wine cellar myself."

"Snuck it out. So you were a rebel today, were you?"

"I suppose you could say that." She poured two glasses and approached the bed, handed him one, then backed away.

He slowly sipped the wine, then rested his handsome head on the pillows and regarded her directly. Oh, she was truly out of her depth. She had no idea how to proceed from here.

"How are you feeling otherwise?" she asked, making every effort to appear confident and at ease. "Is your wound any better?"

Because Melissa told her that he would have to be reasonably recovered in order to move about during their coupling. Evidently, he was going to work up a sweat.

"Much better," he replied. "Your stitches were flawless." He took another deep swig of the wine. "But why are you here, Lady Chelsea? According to the grandfather clock in the hall, it's past midnight. You can hardly call this a proper time for a call, not to mention your state of dress."

He looked her up and down slowly.

She was inclined to gather her dressing gown in a fist and pull it tight about her neck, but resisted. She could not forget that she was here to seduce him. She had to play the part of a coquette—a woman who knew what she wanted and how to go about getting it.

She gulped down half her wine, then spoke in a smooth and silky tone. "I was feeling lonely."

"I see." He finished his own wine and laid the empty glass down on the bed. "Then let me guess. You are here to seduce me."

Feeling her cheeks flush red, Chelsea quickly smothered her shock and managed instead a sly grin. "It seems you find me a very easy book to read."

He glanced down at her body again. "So I've hit the mark a second time. How clever of me."

"No need to be smug. I should think it's rather obvious. I've come to your bedchamber in the middle of the night wearing a dressing gown and enough perfume to make the room smell like a brothel. Why else would I be here?"

He looked at her with dark desire, then peeled back the covers beside him. For a full minute he reclined upon the fluffy pillows and waited.

Chelsea struggled to breathe steadily in and out. This was proving to be far more straightforward than she had imagined. And she had imagined quite a few interesting scenarios.

Making her way alluringly along the side of the bed, she paused a moment to finish her wine, then set the glass on the bedside table.

"Do you do this often with women you barely know?" she asked, fully aware that she was stalling.

"I have no idea. And I apologize in advance if I am inept at pleasing you. I don't know if I'm any good or not. I could be a virgin for all I know."

"I doubt that," she said sardonically.

"So do I."

Heart racing, she removed the silk wrapper and let it fall in a light, downy heap to the floor.

Well, it might have been light and downy, if not for the key in her pocket, which made a heavy *clunk* when it hit.

Her prospective lover paid it no mind, however. He simply sat there, his heated gaze roaming over her body.

It was time to climb onto the bed and slide beneath the covers.

Or perhaps she should remove her nightdress first . . .

Wetting her lips, she glanced away toward the window, wishing her stomach would stop swirling like a child's top. But how could she stop it? She barely knew this man. How could she do all the things she had imagined herself doing with him? And *to* him?

This was very different from her private imaginings by the fire. It was real, and it was terrifying.

"Maybe this was a mistake," she heard herself say before she could convince herself otherwise. Then she started for the door.

The man tossed the covers aside. He flew across the room in a flash. Chelsea halted in front of the door, but just as she grabbed for the knob, he smacked his hand against the door to keep it shut.

Not that she could have opened it anyway, because the key was still in the pocket of her wrapper, which was lying on the floor on the other side of the bed.

"What's the hurry?" he asked teasingly, his long arm stretched out, braced hard up against the door. "I thought you came here to seduce me."

Her breath caught in her throat. "But now it seems that *you* are the one initiating the seduction."

He chuckled. "I'd hardly call chasing you around the bed a seduction. To tell you the truth, I'm not sure what I'd call it. I may not remember much about my life, but I don't think this sort of thing is my usual style."

Laboring to stay calm, she lowered her hand from the doorknob and turned around. He took a step to the side and braced both arms on either side of her head. His nose touched hers.

"And what is your usual style?" she asked.

"I can't be absolutely sure, but I have a feeling I am a very depraved man who enjoys equally depraved women. Women who don't make me chase them."

She cleared her throat. "Then I apologize for getting you out of bed."

He smiled devilishly. "No apologies necessary. I rather enjoyed it. It was like being on a hunt and leaping over a fence. In case you're wondering, you're the fox."

He leaned closer and gently nuzzled her cheek, sending a torrent of gooseflesh tingling down the entire left side of her body.

"So you hunt," she said breathlessly. "Does that qualify as a memory?"

His head drew back slightly. "I don't recall anything specific, but you're right. I suppose it does."

"There. It tells me something about you."

"And what's that?"

"That it is likely you are not a butcher or a farmer."

"A gentleman, you think."

She nodded.

"*Hm.*" He continued to nuzzle her cheek, and ran his lips down the side of her neck. "Well, if I am a gentleman . . . " His hot, moist breath made her skin tingle. " . . . I suspect I am a terribly idle one who is irresponsible and hedonistic, because all I want to do at the present time is forget that I am being held captive, and settle myself between your luscious pink thighs and have my way with you."

A wild mixture of excitement and terror surged

through her body and shocked her with an unexpected shiver of delight. She was aroused by his audacity, she couldn't deny it, but she could not allow herself to forget why she was doing this. She was not here to seek thrills. She was here because a secret child in her womb could relieve her of her duty to her family, and guarantee her future independence.

She strove to recapture her courage and stay focused. "Perhaps that's what I want, too."

"Is that why you have me locked up, then?" he whispered in her ear. "So you can keep me as your private slave?"

"Yes, that's it exactly. Perhaps when we are finished here, you wouldn't mind sweeping out the grate in my bedchamber?"

He chuckled. "That would be a senseless waste of my talents, don't you think?"

"I have yet to see proof of your talents, sir."

He looked at her with a mixture of amusement and admiration, then stepped back and lowered his arms to his sides. "Take off your nightdress."

She swallowed. "You're not even going to kiss me first?"

"Do you want me to?"

She tried, but could not get her voice to work.

"I'll kiss you if you like," he said after a few intense seconds, "but I think I would do a better job at it if you were naked."

Her legs were shaking. She willed them to stop, but of course they wouldn't. All she could do was hope and pray that he would not see her knees quaking when the nightdress was on the floor.

"Would you like some help with the buttons?" he asked.

"No, thank you," she replied, bending down and gathering the fine silk fabric in her hands, then pulling it over her head.

Tossing it to the floor, she kept her eyes lowered, and trembled at the sensation of the cool air wafting over her bare skin. When at last she lifted her gaze, she discovered he was not looking at her eyes. He was looking at her body.

He took her by the hand and led her to the bed. "Sit."

She did as he told her to do, because despite everything Melissa had shared with her, she had no idea how to take charge of this.

"Now lie back."

She did that, too, while her legs, which dangled over the edge of the mattress, continued to shake.

The stranger stood before her and removed his nightshirt. The blue moonlight shone in through the window to illuminate his magnificent nude body, which was still scarred from being hurled onto the rocks a few days ago. His muscular torso was wrapped in a clean white bandage. His shoulders were broad, his arms bent slightly at the elbows. His hair was a thick, dark, wavy mane of temptation.

"Tell me something," he said, stepping forward to stand above her. He placed both hands on the tops of her thighs. "The other day you told me you had a duty to fulfill. What was it?"

She was finding it difficult to concentrate on his question when he was poised before her, in all his masculine glory.

"My mother wants me to marry my father's cousin," she answered plainly, "who will one day inherit my brother's title. He is very old."

"Your brother has no son of his own to inherit?"

"No, he does not."

Her lover frowned, and she wondered if he was remembering something. "You are being forced to marry someone you do not want, in order to keep your mother happy?"

"Yes."

Still standing, he positioned himself between her thighs. "Is that why you are here? To assert yourself and seek your own pleasures before you are carted off into the nightmare of your future?"

"Yes, that's exactly it."

"A fine reason, indeed," he replied. "I would probably do the same thing if I were in your shoes. So, in that case, I shall be happy to oblige you." He touched her breast with his thumb, and her nipples grew hard like pebbles. With the tip of a finger, he lightly stroked the length of her quivering belly, down to her navel.

She sucked in a breath of anticipation. "I thought you were going to kiss me first."

He paused. "Ah, yes. I did promise that, didn't I?"

Stepping back, he wrapped his arms around her backside, lifted her to the edge of the bed, then knelt down on both knees.

She had never in her life felt more exposed, while he stroked her calf, then dropped wet kisses along her inner thigh, suckling her sensitive skin until he arrived at the juncture between her legs.

To her utter shock and bewilderment, he began kissing her there, more passionately than she had ever imagined being kissed on the mouth before.

She writhed wildly on the bed, too stunned at first to enjoy it, until the initial few seconds passed and she was able to close her eyes and relax her body. Sensations like she had never known surged through her insides like the powerful undulations of the ocean. The wet sounds he made with his mouth inflamed her senses, and her hips began jerking urgently as she clutched his broad shoulders to pull him closer. She cried out in pleasure.

He drew back and wiped his wrist across his mouth. "I told you I had very specific talents."

"You weren't lying." She spoke in a breathy sigh, wanting desperately to kiss his soft, wet lips.

But still he did not kiss her on the mouth. He rose to his full height, then narrowed his lust-filled eyes and toyed with a lock of her hair, while her insides burned with a mixture of desire and trepidation.

It was going to hurt. Melissa had warned her . . .

He wiggled his hips into place and rested a hand on her flat belly. It was the hand on which he wore the silver onyx, which she had thought about so many times when she was alone earlier, planning how she was going to seduce him. He ran a finger up between her breasts and touched the cleft of her chin.

"Doesn't it bother you that you don't know my name?" he asked.

She shook her head. "That is part of the allure, I believe."

"Perhaps it is part of the allure for me as well, not knowing who I am or what duties I carry. There is absolutely nothing to distract me tonight, while I am making love to you."

She placed both her hands on his hips.

Inching closer to him, she closed her eyes.

She was surprised when he leaned forward and his mouth touched hers. The kiss was tender, but soon grew more passionate, as his lips parted and his tongue slipped into her mouth.

Chelsea cupped his head in her hands and kissed him deeply, overwhelmed by her desire to devour him. She had come here with a specific purpose in mind, but the only thing she cared about now was the complete fulfillment of her body's desires. She wanted him with every measure of her womanhood, every thread of her existence, every wild, raw inkling of sensation.

Reaching down with a hand, he guided himself into position, and she prepared herself for the invasion into her body. She could barely think through the urgency of her desires. She'd never imagined the anticipation would be so deeply electrifying.

At last he began to push.

Held back by the resistance of her maidenhead, however, he paused, then pushed again, gently but firmly. She felt him enter partway, and squeezed her eyes shut at the pain.

He went still and rose up on both arms above her. His feet were still on the floor. "You're a virgin."

She nodded, and blinked a tear from her eye, for the pain had not abated. "Yes."

"You told me you were ruined."

"I am, in the eyes of the world." She was finding it difficult to breathe.

"That is not the same thing, and you know it."

"What does it matter?" she asked, feeling

angry all of a sudden, not at him, but at the abrupt intrusion of reality, which disrupted her passions. "The man my mother wants me to marry does not expect a virgin. He expects the opposite."

He paused, looking down at her, half inside her, breathing heavily, and squeezed his eyes shut. He seemed engaged in a battle with his conscience.

Please do not let him change his mind now, she silently pleaded. Not when I have come so far, and am so close to success . . .

"I thought you were depraved," she reminded him. "You said you like depraved women."

"Depraved women are not usually virgins," he replied, holding very still. The moonlight shone on his face, illuminating a vein throbbing visibly at his forehead.

Thankfully, he seemed unable to completely control his desires, and with a slight groan pushed again, but only a small distance. Nevertheless, Chelsea winced at another burst of pain, for he was very thick.

Hesitating, he shook his head.

Not wanting him to stop now, she reached up and laid a hand on his cheek. "You said you would be happy to oblige me. Keep in mind that the man I am marrying will not make me happy. It is not a future I have chosen for myself. So please, just give me this one night."

He looked her in the eye. "I understand your need to defy your mother," he said huskily, "because I know all about duty and responsibility. I don't know why, but I do."

"So you will give me this, then?"

Slowly and gently, he drove his hips forward the rest of the way, and broke through what remained of her maidenhead.

Chelsea arched her back and gasped at the final thrust of pain, which began to subside as soon as she was able to fully comprehend the slick sensation of his presence inside her. It was exquisite, erotic, and filled her with an even greater yearning she was desperate to fulfill.

He gave her a moment to become accustomed to his size, then began moving with firm, long strokes, plunging slowly at first, then faster, until an incomprehensible pressure flooded through her body and demanded release. She wrapped her legs around his hips and lifted hers in response, to pull him deeper inside. She drove up hard against each of his firm, powerful thrusts. Soon an astonishing frenzy of lust racked her body, and a tremendous orgasm shuddered through her, causing her to convulse and cry out.

He bent forward and covered her mouth with his own, silencing her cries, then put a hand to his wound.

"Are you in pain?" she asked.

"Yes."

"Do you want to stop?"

"No." Then he groaned with both pleasure and pain, and drove hard with such force that he shoved her into the center of the bed and gave her what she had come for. She held him close and reeled with ecstasy at the wonderful, white-hot gush of his semen shooting mightily into her womb. Then at last she collapsed into a mind-numbing haze of total, incomprehensible bliss.

Chapter 7

Pembroke Palace
Berkshire, England

Seven English bloodhounds, barely restrained by their leads, barked and yowled as they scrambled through the wet forest, leading the search party to the river. The spring weather had been unforgiving in recent weeks, and after a brief interlude of clear skies and sunshine, the heavy rains had returned with an unholy vengeance. The fields were sodden, flooding again, and the estate roads were mired in muck.

This day offered no reprieve. The driving rain came down in horizontal sheets, battering the trees and drenching the moss-covered ground.

Devon Sinclair, Lord Hawthorne, heir to the eminent Duke of Pembroke, rode high atop a black charger. He galloped through the woods, ahead of the search party, comprised of able-bodied servants and loyal tenant farmers, all soaked to the skin under the cold, incessant downpour.

Reining in his mount at the river's edge, he turned in the saddle to address his brother Vincent, who rode up behind him.

"He wouldn't stand a chance in this!" he shouted above the roar of the white-water current.

Vincent's horse whinnied anxiously. "I still think this is a useless effort. He wouldn't have walked from the station, if he even took the train to begin with. We're not going to find him here."

"We have to start somewhere," Devon replied.

The keen hounds approached, staunchly committed to the task of sniffing out a body. The horses grew restless.

"We can't continue to remain at the palace doing nothing," Devon said, "while simply waiting for his arrival, or some news of him in the papers."

The barking hounds caught up to them, and the search party split in two, one heading upriver, the other down.

"We'd be better off searching in London," Vincent said as the wind whipped the tails of his riding cloak.

"If he were in London, he would have returned to the house in Mayfair," Devon said, "for a change of clothes at the very least. No one has seen him in over a week."

Vincent looked at his brother with concern. "You don't think he might have run off, do you? Because he doesn't want to marry?"

"And left us in the lurch?"

Devon was referring to their father's insane demand that all four of his sons marry by Christmas, or they would all be disinherited.

Devon had already fulfilled his duty by taking a wife straight away, and Vincent had done the same a week ago. Now there were only two brothers left to satisfy the terms of the will—Garrett and Blake.

Garrett, at the present time, was ignoring their pleas to return from Greece, because he was—in the eyes of most—a careless, thoughtless son of a bitch.

Blake, the responsible one, was missing.

Devon's horse stepped sideways and tossed his head. "Absolutely not," he said. "Blake is the most dutiful of us all. He has always put his responsibilities first, without complaint. If any act of rebellion is going to occur, it will be Garrett, who is still sailing around the sultry Mediterranean without a care in the world. Even you or I would have been more likely than Blake to refuse Father, and we have already surrendered and become husbands."

Vincent looked out at the raging river. "But we were difficult to press."

"Yes, but we did it, didn't we? Not only for our own inheritances, but for each other. Blake, on the other hand, would never resist Father's wishes, whether or not his inheritance was at stake. He has always done his duty, and with a great sense of satisfaction. He is the most calm, reasonable, level-headed man I've ever known, and he is not . . . " Devon paused, searching for the right word to describe his brother's agreeable disposition. "He is not selfish."

Vincent nodded. "Which is exactly what has Mother so worried. She knows he would never disappear intentionally. She asked me last night if I thought he was dead."

Devon glanced at him warily. "And what was your reply?"

A gust of wind blew across the river, sweeping spray up into the air.

"I suppose he could be lying in an alley somewhere," Vincent answered truthfully, "robbed and beaten. Or he could have been tossed into the Thames by drunken thugs, all for the sake of a few stolen shillings."

"Damn it, Vincent."

The two brothers, similar in their dark features and proud stature, high upon their thorough-breds, said nothing for a long moment.

"We cannot let this situation take a turn for the worse," Devon said at last. "Our family has been through enough tragedy in the past few years, and now, with Father's madness . . . " He did not finish the thought. "We must find our brother."

Vincent nodded. "The last time I saw him, he was in a foul mood after a long night drinking and gambling with a young buck he met, whose father was involved with the Horticultural Society. He also mentioned the young man's sister, who had caught his eye—a woman he believed Father would approve of."

"That will at least get us started. We will go to London today and find out who and where they are. With any luck, he has fallen head over heels in love and has simply forgotten to send word."

"Love can make a man forget a lot of things," Vincent said, referring to his own recent marital bliss.

They turned their horses away from the river.

"But in case that is *not* what has occurred," Vincent said, "I will search all the usual dens of debauchery in London where a man can lose sight of himself. I know where they are because I've been to every last one of them. I will leave no stone unturned."

"Good. While you're doing that, I will contact the police and check the clubs. He can't have fallen off the face of the earth, Vincent. Surely we will hear something from someone eventually."

"God willing."

They urged their horses into a gallop and made off for the palace.

Chelsea's eyes fluttered open as the warm light of dawn poured softly onto the bed. She lay on her stomach, naked, the bed linens tangled about her legs. It was at that moment she realized she was still in her lover's bedchamber and had fallen asleep and remained there all night. He was not, however, beside her.

With a sudden gasp, she whipped around and sat up, and was both relieved and disconcerted to see him sitting leisurely in the chair by the window, also naked, staring at her.

"Good morning," he casually said.

She swallowed nervously, grabbed for the sheet and tugged it hard to cover herself.

"It's always something," he said, "how the light of day can cause the most adventurous women to suddenly withdraw into a charming cocoon of shyness."

She became instantly defensive. "I'm not shy. But it is . . . " Pausing, she glanced around the room and spotted her nightdress in a heap by the door. "It is morning. People will be up. I should go."

She wrapped the sheet around herself and awkwardly inched her way to the edge of the bed, which seemed unnecessarily large all of a sudden, and difficult to maneuver across. She swung her legs to the floor and reached down for her wrapper, while fumbling to hold the sheet in place.

Quickly and efficiently, she slipped her arms into the silk sleeves and let the sheet fall to the floor, then turned her back on her nameless lover while she buttoned her wrapper from top to bottom.

Finally, in a more decent order, she turned. "Thank you for last night. It was very nice."

He sat with an elbow resting on the arm of the chair, a finger at his temple, watching her with amusement.

She nodded politely at him and tried not to blush or look down at his magnificent nude body as she started for the door. When she reached it, she bent to pick up her nightdress, not sure if it would be wise to walk back to her own bedchamber carrying it in her hands. What if she bumped into a servant?

Deciding to take her chances, she reached into her pocket for the key, but the pocket was empty.

Momentarily flustered, she hurried back around the bed to search the floor, while her lover in the chair did nothing but watch. She didn't spot the key right away, so she got down on hands and knees and checked under the bed.

It was not there.

With an irritated huff, she stood up and faced him. "Give it to me, please."

He raised an eyebrow. "Why should I?"

Her temper flared. "Because the sun is up, and I don't want to be caught in your bedroom with my hair in a tangled mess and my lips swollen from . . ."

"From what?"

"From a night of self-indulgence," she replied.

He grinned wickedly. "Is that was it was?"

She took a few steps closer. "Where is it?"

"I've hidden it, but you're welcome to search my person if you like." He spread his arms wide.

She couldn't help but look down at his legs and hips and the very arresting cluster of manhood growing larger and firmer by the minute.

"I am not going to put my hands on you," she said. "It's morning, and I have to go. Just give me the key."

"Find it yourself."

She pressed her lips together in a thin line. "Is it truly on you, or under you? Tell me that at least."

"It might be."

Riled by his teasing tone when she did not have time for this, she turned her head to the side, bent forward and slid her hands under his legs and buttocks. When she did not find what she was looking for, she checked along the sides and back of the cushion, leaning over him, shoving her hands straight down into the upholstery.

Her gaze was still averted, and she could feel his hot, moist breath upon her cheek while she searched. For a fleeting second she considered putting her hands on him after all, for her desires were beginning to flicker, but she ruled against it and straightened.

"You obviously don't have it," she said, "which was a most ungentlemanly trick."

"We both enjoyed it. What's the harm?"

"The harm is that I might be seen here by a servant, and my reputation is already in tatters. There is no need to see those tatters go up in flames as well."

He considered that, and relaxed his shoulders. "All right. I'll tell you where it is, but for a price."

"Name it."

"I want my life back."

Her composure—which until now had been mostly steadfast—was blown off its course. She had not expected him to say that.

"I would very much like to give you your life back," she said, "but it is not in my power. As far as finding out who you are, we have sent word to the magistrate here on the island, as well as the London authorities and newspapers. It might take some time, that's all."

He wet his lips, as if he were thinking of a way to negotiate for something more immediate. "You could at least let me out of this room and allow me to live like a normal human being. It's hard to say what might revive my memory—a face, a conversation . . . "

"I suppose I could try to arrange that."

"And no more laudanum."

"I will speak to the doctor," she said, "and also to my brother."

"And mother," he insisted.

"She won't be pleased, nor easy to convince that you won't brain us all in our sleep. She is like a brick wall sometimes." She heard a noise in the hall, and her heart squeezed with panic. "Give me the key, if you please. I must get back to my own room."

"I need some clothes," he flatly said. "Right away, as soon as you leave here, you will bring me something."

Her temper flared again. "I am simply supposed to do your bidding? I'll need time to talk to my brother," she tried to explain.

"Do you want the key or not?" He pulled a curtain open, and Chelsea squinted at the sudden light in the room. The servants would soon be bringing up a breakfast tray.

"You're a tyrant."

"Me!" He laughed. "I'm the one who's locked up, remember?"

"That is not the case at the moment. You are the one with the key."

"Yes, and it doesn't feel very nice, does it? To be at the mercy of a complete stranger?"

Recalling what they'd done the night before, she felt obliged to correct him. "We're hardly strangers now," she said. "For one thing, you're naked."

"Yes, I am, which is why I want you to bring me some clothes before my breakfast tray arrives. I've had enough of that nightshirt. Will you agree?"

She hesitated.

He pulled the other curtain wide open. The sky grew brighter. It was overcast—pure white with low hanging clouds.

"All right, I'll do it," she quickly said. "I'll find something of Sebastian's. You look about the same size. Now the key, please." She held out her hand.

He made no move. "How do I know I can trust you? Maybe I'd be better off keeping it and making a run for the back door, naked or not."

"And where would you go?" she asked without humor. "You have no money, no home, no family to go to."

The amusement faded from his eyes, and he looked at her with displeasure.

"I'm sorry," she said. "I shouldn't have said that. I'm sure you are more than aware—"

"Indeed I am, which is why I have no choice but to trust you to bring me what I need and make my convalescence here a bit more comfortable. You are the only person in the world I know. Except for the doctor, who wants to turn me into an opium addict."

She spoke quickly. "I will make sure he refrains from prescribing anything else. Now the key, please."

The desperation in her voice was palpable.

At last he stood up and walked to the clock on the mantel. He lifted it with one hand, and there was the key beneath it in a very simple hiding place.

He held it out to her. "As I said before, I am trusting you. Today, I would like to go for a walk in the garden, and I wish also to dine with your family."

She took the key from him. "I will do my best." She started for the door.

"And if you do a good job," he said in a low, husky voice that sent shivers through her body as she slipped the key into the lock, "I will do something for you in return."

"And what, pray tell, will that be?"

He approached and whispered in her ear, "I will satisfy your midnight desires again this evening."

The eroticism of his words trembled through

her, and she stopped breathing for a moment as she slipped out of the room.

It was exactly what she wanted. She could not deny it. The only problem was that it had nothing to do with duty or strategy—and everything to do with the heady taste of wicked pleasures and the promise of more to come.

Chapter 8

"**H**ere you are at last," Melissa said quietly to Chelsea in the breakfast room, before she had a chance to serve herself a plate from the sideboard. Melissa gave her a few seconds to pour a cup of coffee, then led her to the window at the far end of the room. "I went to your bedchamber this morning," she whispered, "but you weren't there."

Chelsea glanced uneasily at her mother, feasting on a mountain of eggs, toast, and ham at the far end of the table. "I wasn't there because I've been running around the house, trying to do all the things he's asked me to do. The unruly scoundrel stole the key from me, and wouldn't let me out of the room this morning until I promised him."

"Promised him what?"

She sighed. "Oh, nothing immoral. In fact, I must admit, it was quite reasonable. He only wants to be let out of his room, to be free to move about the house like a normal person. I had to find clothes for him and speak to Sebastian. I expect our guest will be walking into this very room looking for breakfast in the next little while. He wants to recover his memory, and says he can't do that if he's staring at the same four walls day after day."

"I suppose he has a point," Melissa said. "Does your mother know?"

"Not yet, but she will soon enough."

They both looked at Lady Neufeld across the room, content while shoveling forkfuls of food into her mouth. She seemed completely oblivious to their soft-spoken conversation.

Melissa leaned a little closer. "You haven't told me yet. How did it go?"

They casually moved around the table so Chelsea could serve herself a plate from the sideboard. "It went perfectly according to plan," she replied. "I arrived at midnight, and the task was completed within the first hour."

Although that hardly described what really went on, all of which she intended to keep to herself. It was far too intimate and personal, too erotic to put into words. She wasn't even sure words existed to express what she felt about what they did together in the darkness. She could barely comprehend it in her own mind—the way he made her quiver with desire and fulfillment when his lips touched her body. This morning it all seemed like a dream, like she had been floating in some strange turquoise paradise of pleasure.

Melissa sipped her coffee. "Well done, Chelsea. Well done, indeed. You must have been very proficient."

Proficient . . . It was not the right word. Not in the least.

Chelsea spooned up some eggs. "I suppose one could pronounce me victorious, though in the end it was *he* who was more in charge of what went on. I simply did what he told me to do." She glanced over her shoulder at her mother. "The prey became the predator."

"But you enticed him into the role, which was half the battle." Melissa reached out a hand and held Chelsea back from approaching the table. "So did he . . . ? You know . . . "

Chelsea was famished, but knew she would have to satisfy Melissa's curiosity before she could sit down and eat in peace.

"Did he give me the material I require for our Machiavellian plan?" she plainly asked.

Melissa waited with bated breath for her reply. "Well? Did he?"

"Yes. Four times, to be exact. And I'm starved."

Her mother sneezed.

They both looked her way and said, "God bless you," at the same time, then gazed back at each other and resisted a collective urge to laugh.

"It appears our visitor is on the mend," Melissa whispered ●lose in her ear, "which is very nice, but quantity is not the only thing a woman requires. How was it otherwise? Was he . . . " She paused. " . . . *clever?*"

"*Clever* . . . I'm not quite sure what you mean, because I have no experience in such matters outside of last night, and therefore have nothing to compare it to. All I can say is that I enjoyed it even more than I imagined I would. He was . . . "

She glanced toward the window, recalling how he used his hands to bewitch her, making her feel beautiful and desirable and adored. It had been the most erotic night of her life.

She met her sister-in-law's gaze. "He was perfect."

And who should walk into the breakfast room at that moment, but her perfect, handsome, nameless lover, in the flesh, looking self-assured in Sebastian's black morning jacket and forest green waistcoat, his hair combed back in thick, shiny waves that played upon his shoulders in attractive disarray.

He was well groomed and clean-shaven, and carried himself like someone of stature. He looked like a king—or at the very least, an English lord.

Was he? she wondered suddenly. Had she just made love to a duke or a marquess?

"Good morning," he said with cool reserve, bowing at the waist.

Chelsea's mother looked up from her breakfast plate and nearly spit out her coffee. One look at him, however, in all his stately magnificence was all it took for her to be won over instantly, right there on the spot.

"Good morning," she replied, reaching quickly for her napkin and wiping the corner of her mouth. She appeared stunned. "How wonderful to see you up and around."

She seemed also to conveniently forget that she had insisted on locking him up a few days ago, and had suggested he was a madman, escaped from an asylum. Presently, she appeared dumbstruck by his good looks.

Chelsea could hardly blame her. She did not believe there had ever been a man so handsome inside the walls of this house. Ever.

"Good morning," Melissa said graciously, throwing a veil over the awkward silence by approaching their guest with an outstretched hand. "I am Lady Neufeld. It is such a pleasure to meet you at last. I am so sorry for what has happened to you, and I hope you've been comfortable here. We wish to do all we can to help you get well and recover your place in the world."

"Thank you, Lady Neufeld." He inclined his head and shook her hand, but still seemed suspicious of his hosts.

It did not take a fool to see that Melissa, like their mother, was frazzled as well. Her cheeks were flushed and her eyes were beaming.

"And this is my mother-in-law, Miriam, the dowager countess of Neufeld," she said.

Chelsea's mother held out her hand. "How wonderful to meet you, sir."

He bent forward and laid a kiss on her plump knuckles. "Not nearly as wonderful for you, madam, as it is for me. How can I ever repay you for your many kindnesses? I am in your debt."

For the laudanum? Chelsea thought scornfully.

But he was enough of a gentleman not to mention it.

Her mother struggled to behave courteously. "Oh, no sir. It was the least we could do. Truly. Would you care for some breakfast?"

How quickly the man could go from tyrant to charmer. Chelsea's head was spinning.

He frowned at her on his way to the sideboard, and as he passed her by, paused and leaned close. "You said she was a brick wall."

He moved on, and with Melissa's chattering company, helped himself to a plate of food.

At least he was inclined to keep up his strength, Chelsea thought. He would need it for tonight, she decided, as she finally sat down across from her mother and dug into her breakfast.

"You won't run off, will you?" Chelsea asked her lover as she escorted him to the front door later that morning. He had mentioned at breakfast that he would benefit from some fresh air and a walk around the gardens, and no one was inclined to refuse him. Both Melissa and her mother had been completely besotted by his looks. They would have said yes to anything.

He stopped in the entrance hall and faced her with a puckered brow. "Run off? Good God, woman. I'm not your lapdog."

"No, of course you are not."

But in all honesty, she did not want him to go off alone. What if he did not come back?

"Besides," he continued, "where would I go? I have no friends or acquaintances here, at least none that I know of. Even if I did recover all my faculties while wandering the grounds, I have no money, no means of support, nor any way to transport myself back to my home, wherever it may be."

"It was a silly thing to say," she replied.

He seemed to be studying her expression, reading all the thoughts and feelings she was trying so hard to keep hidden—like the fact that she wanted to go with him on his walk. There was no explanation for it except that she, too, was besotted. How could she not be? He was as handsome as the day was long, and the night before, he had taken her to places she had not known existed. Beautiful places. Erotic places that made her quiver even now just thinking about them.

She clutched her notebook to her chest.

"Would you like to come with me?" he asked. "You could show me the lay of the land and make sure I don't step off the edge of a cliff."

Chelsea hesitated, for she was not quite sure it would be wise—not because she did not trust him or that she feared being alone with him, but rather because she did not want her feelings to become more intense than they already were. She had thought about him this morning far too much as it was.

He gestured toward her notebook. "You had plans to write?"

"Yes. I thought I would sit in the library."

"Can you write outdoors?" he asked. "Because I would like to find a place to sit as well, to rest and do nothing. I promise I won't disturb you." When she continued to hesitate, he lowered his voice. "I've spent enough time alone over the past few days. I would appreciate the company and conversation. The stimulation of my mind might help me remember things."

She turned toward the door. "I suppose I could benefit from some fresh air as well."

They walked onto the wide steps and he turned to look up at the front of the house. "Quite an impressive structure," he said, referring to the sheer majesty of the home, designed in the classic Palladian style.

"The fifth Earl Neufeld had it built as a summer retreat, but Mother and I live here year 'round. My brother spends the winters at our country estate in Lincolnshire, though of course he resides in London when the House is in session."

"You don't find it too remote in the winter?" he asked. "The winds off the Atlantic must be fierce."

"They are," she replied. "We have no choice but to spend much time indoors during the winter months, but there are enough mild days to enjoy a walk or a sleigh ride in the snow."

They turned to descend the steps and headed out across the breezy lawn to look out at the gray sea, dotted with angry whitecaps. The clouds in the overcast sky seemed just out of reach.

Chelsea watched his profile as he looked out over the water. He seemed to be searching for something he might recognize, probing his mind for a recollection or an explanation as to why he had been out swimming in the frigid English Channel a few nights ago.

"There was a storm that night," she told him. "The winds were severe, and it was raining. It would have been a challenge for any vessel to stay afloat, especially if it ran up against the rocks. The morning I found you, the waves were still crashing up onto the shore with a fury I can barely describe."

"There have been no reports of a lost ship in the area? No other people washed ashore?"

"Not that we are aware of," she answered. "As I mentioned, Sebastian has given an account of your situation to the local authorities and he has sent word to London as well, so perhaps in time someone will come for you. And then you will know who you are."

"And so will you." He turned to face her. "In the meantime, you must call me something. A name. We must invent one."

She lowered her notebook to her side. "What kind of name do you feel would suit you? Do you feel like a Tom or a George?"

"No, neither of those. Come now, you're a writer. Pretend I am a character in one of your stories. What would you call me?"

She smiled at the challenge. "I often look to ancient mythology for inspiration, but in your case . . . "

"I am not a god to you?" he asked, perplexed.

"In some ways perhaps," she replied with a

laugh, "but heaven forbid anyone should find out I named you Zeus or Apollo."

"Indeed. What shall it be, then? Robert? Jack? Yes, that's it. Jack. For some reason that name seems to fit like a comfortable old shoe."

"Maybe it's your real name."

"If it is, I will be pleased."

"But the watch I found on the beach suggests a name that begins with B."

He shook his head. "I don't feel like a Bob or a Buckley."

"Bartholomew," she put forward. "Basil? Bernard."

He chuckled. "I don't think so."

"Byron? Bruce. What about Burt?"

"No."

They started along the rosebushes toward the sandy, meandering path that led to the beach, and picked their way down over the loose stones. Once or twice "Jack" stopped and turned to offer his hand to her at a particularly difficult spot on the trail, and even though she had negotiated this trek hundreds of times on her own, she allowed him to play the chivalrous gentleman, and could not deny that she enjoyed it.

Down on the pebbly beach the surf seemed almost deafening, so they walked side by side in silence—slowly, as Jack was not yet fully recovered.

They soon came to a flat outcropping where Chelsea often sat and wrote. It would be different today, however, for she was not alone. She was not certain she would be able to lose herself enough, in order to concentrate and make the words come.

She gestured to the spot with her notebook. "This is where I usually sit when I write."

"Then we shall adhere to your routine." He stepped up onto the wide rock and turned to offer his hand again. The wind blew a part in his wavy, dark hair, and his shirt collar whipped in the fresh breezes.

She couldn't help thinking that he looked almost like a natural piece of this rugged coastline. He seemed to belong here—for he was wild and unpredictable, and he excited her, just like the tempestuous sea.

Slipping her hand into his, she allowed him to pull her up the sloping boulders to the top. Gulls soared over their heads and called out to one another against the white sky. On the horizon, the clouds loomed darker. She hoped the rain would stay away for at least a little while longer.

They sat down together in a spot where they could rest their backs on some rocks, and Chelsea opened her notebook. She looked down at the pages she had already filled with sentences and paragraphs, as well as the blank pages ahead, and wondered at once if this had been a ridiculous idea. How in the world was she supposed to concentrate with such a handsome man sitting beside her—a man with whom she had been naked the night before?

The very man who had claimed her virginity and would possess it forever.

"How much paper do you have?" he asked. "Could you spare some?"

She looked up. "Do you want to write something?"

"No, but if you have an extra pencil, I would like to draw."

Her eyebrows lifted. "Really. Are you an artist?"

"I don't know. Let's find out."

Intrigued, she tore a sheet out of her book and passed it to him, then reached into her pocket for an extra pencil.

He used his raised knee to lay the paper upon, and began sketching something small in the corner of the page. He spent some time on it, examined it carefully, turned the page sideways, upside down, then began drawing again with broad, sweeping pencil strokes.

"Just go ahead and write," he said. "Don't let me distract you."

Easier said than done, she thought as she turned her gaze down to her own notebook.

It took great effort, but finally she was able to settle her mind into her character's world, and the words began to flow from her imagination to her hand and down onto the paper. She wrote about the young impoverished lady from Yorkshire who became a governess in the home of a handsome French aristocrat who lost his wife in the revolution.

After about twenty minutes she lifted her eyes and watched Jack hard at work on his drawing. He was shading something. His hand was moving back and forth very quickly.

He glanced up. His eyes were dark, his expression brooding as he looked at her. When he noticed she was staring back at him, he said curtly, "Look down, please."

Realizing he was drawing *her*, she felt her lips curl into a smile, lowered her lashes and continued to write.

A short while later his hand moved slower, more gracefully, over the page. She was acutely aware of it, as well as the sound of the pencil scraping over the heavy paper, even though she kept her eyes trained on her own notebook, looking up only occasionally to ponder a different word or phrase.

He stopped and breathed deeply, then rose to his feet. Chelsea looked up at him, dark and striking against the pure white sky.

"What do you think?" He handed the picture to her.

She reached out, took it from him, and beheld

her own likeness through his eyes. Clearly, he possessed not only a raw and wonderful talent, but a skillful, trained hand as well. The picture had an almost dreamlike quality, yet it was realistic.

"You *are* an artist," she said, "and a very talented one at that. I would ask where you learned to draw like this, but . . . " She let her voice trail off.

Looking at the picture again, she noticed the small shape in the corner, like an emblem of some kind—a simple flower perhaps. "What's this?" she asked, pointing at it.

He frowned. "I have no idea. It's just something I keep seeing in my mind. Does it look familiar to you?"

"No, I've never seen it before."

"Perhaps it will come to me eventually." He turned and faced the sea. "I quite enjoyed sketching you. I feel rejuvenated."

"I am pleased to hear it."

"I am going to take a walk along the beach by myself," he said, stepping carefully down the sloping rocks, "to ponder the universe and leave you to your art. If it's all right with you, I shall come back later and fetch you, and we can walk back to the house together."

"I won't move from this spot."

He pressed a hand to the wound at his side and paused a moment. "Where was it, exactly, that I was found?"

Chelsea wet her lips and pointed. "There is a cove on the other side of that cliff. You can't reach it from here. We would have to go back up the path, cross our property to reach the road, then take a different, more challenging path down the other side."

He did not yet have the strength for such a hike. She knew it and so did he.

"Another day perhaps," he said.

"Yes."

She watched him head to the water's edge and stroll leisurely along the beach, stopping every so often to stand with his hands behind his back and stare out at the sea.

An hour later Jack returned. "I would like to go back now," he said, with a hand pressed to his side. "I was too ambitious. I must rest."

Chelsea closed her notebook and stood. "Are you feeling unwell? Will you be able to make it up the hill?"

"Yes, but I'll pay a price. I doubt I'll be dining with your family this evening. A tray brought to my room would be most appreciated." He continued to hold onto his side. Tension darkened his brow.

"Of course. I'll see to it personally." She stepped down the sloping rocks and came to stand beside him.

"Can I trust you to keep the laudanum out of my wine?" he asked with a touch of humor, despite his discomfort.

"There won't be a single drop. I promise."

She could see the pain in his eyes as he offered his arm. Slowly, they started up the beach.

Chelsea leaned toward him. "If you are not feeling well, I don't want you to feel obligated to keep our . . . *appointment* tonight."

She would be disappointed, to be sure, but the last thing she wanted was to cause him more pain or hinder his recovery.

"In that regard, there is something I want to discuss with you," he said soberly, and a shadow of dread moved through her. She sensed a hint of remorse in his tone. Was he going to tell her that he had changed his mind?

"It is one thing," he said, "for me to send you off to your wedding bed as an experienced woman. It is quite another to send you there with a seed already planted in your womb. If we are going to make love again, we must take precautions."

But that was precisely why she had gone to his bed in the first place—to conceive a child for Sebastian and Melissa and secure a way out of a marriage to a man she would despise. It would be rather pointless, wouldn't it, to go to his bed if he was going take steps to prevent such an event?

Well, perhaps not entirely pointless . . .

"What kind of precautions?" she asked warily.

"I will withdraw at the right time."

She looked at him uncertainly. "But we would still . . . *enjoy* each other, wouldn't we? Would you still . . . ?" She didn't know quite how to put it.

"Yes," he replied. "It is just a matter of geography. I shall enjoy myself outside of your body, instead of inside it."

She cleared her throat. "How strange it is, to be discussing these things."

"Why?" He looked down at her. "Are you becoming shy again?"

"Perhaps a little."

They reached the path. She gathered her skirts in her fists to follow him up the steep slope.

"Last night," she said, speaking in a louder voice so he could hear her over the thunderous surf, "you claimed you were depraved, yet this morning I am seeing some evidence of honor."

He said nothing for a time as he climbed the hill, then at last he responded. "Maybe I don't want to end up beaten to a pulp by an outraged husband. Or handed a dueling pistol. Perhaps that very thing has happened to me before."

"Do you think that is what brought you here?" she asked. "A fight over a woman?"

She did not like the idea of it—of another woman being a part of his life. Not when she was presently enjoying the total exclusivity of his attentions.

But she could certainly see dozens of women vying for those same attentions, married or no. She knew she would be naive to think otherwise, no matter what kind of life he lived.

"Who knows?" he replied.

They did not converse the rest of the way, for Chelsea could hear the strain in his voice. He was weary and in considerable pain.

They reached the top of the path and started toward the house.

"So shall I come tonight?" she asked hesitantly, before they reached the door.

"Yes," he replied. "On one condition."

"And that is . . . ?"

He leaned close and whispered, "You must be on top."

She had not expected him to say anything so specific, and her flesh tingled at the sensation of his hot breath in her ear. "But I've never—"

"I'll help you figure it out." With that, he climbed the steps, leaving her to wonder why she should even be going to his bed tonight, when her initial objectives had just been routed.

But there was no point deluding herself. Those dutiful objectives had very little to do with anything at the moment—especially when she was watching his beautiful male form climb the stairs, one slow step at a time, and feeling almost feverish with lust.

Chapter 9

"**I** beg your pardon?" Melissa sat down on a chintz chair in her boudoir.

"He wants to take precautions," Chelsea repeated. She had gone to see her sister-in-law immediately after entering the house.

"But why?" Melissa asked. "You offered yourself to him freely. I was hoping that after all he'd been through, he would be in a somewhat . . . *selfish* mood."

"He was, I believe—very much so, in fact. Last night he behaved like an absolute libertine, with little care for any consequences that might arise. I felt like I had walked into the den of a hungry lion who wanted only to devour me. But then . . . " She paused.

"But then . . . *what*?"

"He said a few things that contradicted my initial impression. He said he understood my need to defy Mother, because he knew all about duty. He didn't know *why* he knew, for he could not relate it to his own life. He simply knew."

"So perhaps he is a responsible man after all, who is bitter about the burdens he carries."

"But why would he believe something about himself—that he is reckless and wild—when the opposite is true? Is it possible that an ordeal such as the one he experienced could not only erase one's memories, but cause a complete personality change?"

Melissa stood and rang for tea. "Maybe it isn't a change. Maybe he behaves one way in his own life, when that does not match who he really is on the inside. Many people wear masks."

"So which is the real Jack?" Chelsea asked. "The rake who is reckless, or the gentleman who is honorable?"

"Both, perhaps."

"But which is the mask? The rake or the honorable gentleman?"

"We'll know the answer to that," she said, "only when he remembers his life."

And what would happen when he did remember it?

Feeling a pang of trepidation for what lay ahead, Chelsea changed the subject. "All that aside, what am I to do, now that he does not want to risk a pregnancy? Should we simply pray that last night did the trick and put an end to this?"

Melissa studied her carefully. "Would you like to put an end to it?"

Looking down at her hands, Chelsea shook her head. "Not really."

"I didn't think so."

"But this is wrong, isn't it? My purpose was to provide you and Sebastian with the child you've always longed for, but if I am only going to his bed to enjoy myself . . . "

Melissa shook her head. "First of all, you have every right to enjoy yourself, considering what your mother has asked you to do. On top of that, there is still a chance you might conceive, even if he does take precautions. Nothing is ever fail-safe. Think of all the accidental pregnancies that have occurred throughout the ages—all the il-legitimate children of monarchs and aristocrats, even servants and unmarried women."

"So even if he does not take his pleasure inside of me, I could still conceive?"

"Yes, I think so, and certainly, if you are pleas-ing him, he might lose his head in the heat of the moment and forget to withdraw. You could en-courage that, in a discreet way."

She sighed. "That would feel very conniving."

"And you don't think going to his room last night fit into that category? It is no different."

"Yes, but last night he was a stranger. Today he has a name—an invented one, mind you, but still . . . And this morning I saw traces of a man who was not careless. An artistic man who wanted to do the right thing." She recalled, however, what he'd said on the path. "Although he did mention not wanting to get beaten to a pulp by an angry husband."

"Well, he won't have to worry about that," Melissa said, "because you won't be marrying Lord Jerome."

"No—or anyone else, for that matter," she replied with a twinge of regret for all the girlhood dreams she had left behind years ago. "Not in real life."

"You say 'real life' as if this were a scene out of one of your stories."

"It feels that way. It feels like a dream."

"Well, it's not, Chelsea. It's real—*very* real—and if the Fates rule in our favor, in nine months' time you will feel that more than anyone."

"I suppose."

"You must continue on," Melissa said. "*Please*, continue on. For your brother's sake, and mine."

The tea arrived, steaming hot.

"I should think about it," Chelsea said, glancing up at the maid and whispering. "Because suddenly it is becoming a bit more complicated than I imagined it would be."

And she was feeling a strong, instinctive urge to protect herself.

* * *

Chelsea certainly did think about Jack and their prearranged midnight rendezvous—all day in fact. While she took measures to have his dinner sent to his room, she imagined him getting out of bed to sit at the table and eat by the window. She pictured his hands holding the knife and fork, slicing the meat. She thought about his lips on the glass of red wine, his disheveled hair falling into his eyes, his cravat loosened and his collar open as he leaned forward over the plate.

It was enough to cause her desires to flood through her body so thoroughly, it made her belly swirl with an almost obsessive anticipation.

Later in the day, she sat in the library with her notebook, hopelessly inept at putting even two sentences together as she fantasized about making love with him again. She sat with an elbow perched on the desktop, her cheek resting on a hand. Her brain went all fuzzy and lazy, and her body melted into something that resembled a thick blob of chocolate pudding.

By dinnertime she grew increasingly disturbed by her inability to purge Jack from her mind, even for the briefest of moments. He was in her thoughts constantly, and her emotions were caught up in the mix as well, filling her heart with thrills and joys, but mostly doubts and fears.

It was more than clear to her by now that her desires had nothing to do with her duty to her family. What started out as a simple act of goodwill—and an escape from her marriage to Lord Jerome—had exploded into something far more ferocious. For she might very well be growing infatuated with Jack, after knowing him only a few days, and still not knowing who he was or where he came from.

Presently, her mother still believed she would marry Lord Jerome, yet here she was, attempting to become pregnant with another man's child. Dealing with that alone was going to be enough of a problem, without throwing a broken heart into the mix.

She slapped her hands over her face. *Stop, Chelsea. Stop. You are losing control. You cannot let yourself enjoy this too much. You must keep your head and exert great caution. You cannot fall in love, or you will end up doing something foolish and rash, just like the last time. And that did not end well.*

That night, Jack lay in the darkness, listening to the waves crash and boom onto the shore outside the window. He had slept for most of the day, and as a result was awake now and extremely alert. He felt robust and invigorated, and for that reason was able to anticipate Chelsea's arrival with great enthusiasm.

He watched the hand on the mantel clock tick one second at a time.

Tick . . .

Tick . . .

Tick . . .

He felt energetic. It would be good tonight. He would make sure she was well pleasured. He would have the strength and vigor to go on for quite some time.

At last the hands struck twelve. Out in the hall the chiming of the grandfather clock began like a royal announcement. Already basking in a pleasant state of arousal, he lay back and watched the door . . .

One hour later he was pacing around the room like a caged tiger, irritated and angry, his frustration roaring like a monster inside his head. A monster he could not conquer.

There was nothing in his mind with which to wage a battle, he supposed. That was the problem. He had no past or future to think about—no experiences, problems, no projects to complete that might distract him from his frustration over Chelsea's failure to arrive.

There were no thoughts of people who meant something to him—no friends or relations who might provide some reassurance that he actually mattered, let alone existed. Chelsea was all he had, and she had failed to come. He could not sleep, so there was nothing for him to do now but continue to wait for her, and grapple with this incredible, consuming emptiness.

He continued to pace the room, clenching his fist to keep from hitting something, for apart from his frustration over Chelsea, he couldn't bear any more of this incessant waiting for his life to begin. She was a welcome diversion, to be sure, but he could not go on depending upon her to fill the gouged out hole inside of him—to make him feel as if he existed. No single person should have that much power.

He stopped in his tracks and decided that he needed to *do* something—to get out of this house, to get off this island, and search for his identity. But where would he begin?

Just then a quick knock sounded at the door. Before he had a chance to answer, the knob turned, the door opened, and Chelsea hurried inside. She shut the door behind her and leaned up against it, seeming out of breath.

He said nothing. He just stood in the center of the dark room, also breathing hard. The muscles in his stomach clenched tightly.

"I wasn't going to come," she explained. Her tone was frantic, as if someone had chased her down the hall.

"If you had kept me waiting another minute, woman, I might be strangling you right now."

She was not wearing her silk wrapper. She wore only the plain linen nightdress. Her hair hung loose upon her shoulders. Her cheeks were flushed. The effect was both sweet and seductive.

"Why?" she asked.

It was too complicated a question. "Because I wanted you here sooner," he answered.

She took a step away from the door. "And do you always get what you want?"

"I have no idea." He paused, thinking about it. "But I doubt it. Why are you late?"

Her eyebrows pulled together in a frown. "Why are you so angry?"

He was still breathing hard, while he strove to curb the frustration boiling up and over the rim of his existence. "Because I wanted to see you."

"I wanted to see you, too," she replied, seeming to feed off his anger. Her voice was laced with resentment, as if she were holding back the urge to yell at him. "A little too much, I dare say. I couldn't concentrate on anything this afternoon. I felt like I was losing my mind. I spent the entire night trying to convince myself that I could resist coming here. That it was only the desires of my body that were making me insane." She looked away. "And I am in control of that, aren't I? At least I should be."

"I'm not," he said. "I have no control whatso-ever over anything. I feel like a bloody volcano."

She stared at him for a long time in the darkness, then her voice gentled to a shaky, uneasy sigh. "So do I, and I don't want to feel that way. Not about you, when I know so little about who you are."

He stood very still, immobilized by her reply, and by the tension in his loins, as their mutual desires vibrated in the air between them.

"Come here," he said.

She moved toward him.

For a moment they stood facing each other, then he pulled her close, buried his face in the sweet, heavenly warmth of her neck, and held her firmly in his arms.

An astonishing sense of relief washed over him as her arms curled around his rib cage, her chin rested on his shoulder, and her soft breasts pressed into his chest. He could have wept from the flood of emotions running through him at that moment—mostly gratefulness. He felt like dropping to his knees and thanking God that she had come.

She smelled clean, like soap and flowers. He held her tight for a long time, and somehow, miraculously, she made all the emptiness disappear. Desire took its place, so he sought out her beautiful mouth and crushed his lips to hers.

Very quickly he remembered that he was not only a lost soul, but a sexual being with unruly urges for this exquisite creature in his arms, and the embrace, however fulfilling, was not going to be enough to satisfy him.

With the strength and vigor of a man who had not recently been at death's door, he swept her into his arms and carried her to the bed. Standing back, he pulled his nightshirt off over his head while she did the same with her gown, then quickly he was on top of her, settling himself between her soft, pink thighs and sliding into her heated depths.

"I thought you wanted me on top tonight," she said in a breathless sigh while wrapping her legs around his hips.

"Later. For now, I must have you my own way."

He kissed her again, and thrust deeper inside, pushing with all his might as far as he could into the warm, welcoming haven of her body. Rising up on both arms, he looked down at her in the moonlight pouring in through the window, and made love to her for a long time—both generously and greedily.

"You're the most beautiful woman I've ever seen," he said, conscious of the fact that he remembered none of the women in his life. But it didn't matter. No man could ever feel more awestruck by a woman, no matter who he was.

With a passionate jolt, she cried out, and he

drove into her faster, with a force that left them both gasping for air. Before long he felt the rapid throbbing of her womanhood, and she arched her back beneath him, digging her nails into his hips. She took in a sharp breath, and he plunged his face down onto her soft breast and sucked on a hard nipple while she convulsed and quivered around him.

A moment later his own body began to quicken, and he poured into her freely, without concern for his vow earlier that day, when he had promised to withdraw at the proper time. But there was nothing proper about this. He could not withdraw because he wanted her with blinding fury, and his climax was so powerful, it had overcome his passions and completely baked his brain.

With a groan of release, he gave one final thrust, then let his body sink to rest upon hers. "God," he whispered. "I don't think I'll ever be able to move again."

He was still inside her.

"You don't have to," she replied, wrapping her arms and legs around him. "I would keep you here inside me forever if I could."

This was what he had needed earlier—this closeness. It made everything that was lost to him seem unimportant, and when he'd believed he would not have this tonight, he had nearly gone mad.

They lay together, drained and exhausted, until he peeled his sticky body from hers and rolled onto his back.

"I'm done for," he said. He turned his head on the pillow. "You'll definitely get your chance to be on top next time."

"And when will that be?" She grinned mischievously.

"Give me a half hour to recuperate," he said with a smile. "Then I will be all yours, to do with as you please."

She rolled onto her side to face him and rested her cheek on a hand. "Then I shall simply lie here patiently, and wait until you are ready."

Chapter 10

"**Y**ou're all I have," Jack said later, after he made love to Chelsea a third time that night.

She was completely satisfied and joyful beyond any imagining. Rolling off him, she lay on her side and rested her head on his shoulder. He pulled the covers up and held her close.

"How do you mean?" she asked.

He stared up at the ceiling and ran his thumb over her bare shoulder. "I mean that from my vantage point, there is no one else in the world who cares anything for me. I have no thoughts of any loved ones to give me a sense of importance. I feel as if I could draw my last breath tomorrow, and no one would notice or care. Except for you."

She leaned up on one elbow. "But that is not true. I would not be the only one. That is only what you feel because you cannot recall any of those people who care for you. In reality, they *do* exist and are probably sick with worry and searching for you this very moment. You just don't know it."

She kissed him tenderly on the mouth, then lay back down again, thinking about all the friends and acquaintances he must have, the siblings and cousins, uncles and aunts and parents.

Somewhere in a hidden place inside her, jealousy surfaced, because those people would know so much more about him than she did—for she knew nothing, only that he could be whisked away from her tomorrow, like a leaf on the wind, if someone arrived to claim him.

But that was selfish, she knew. It was wrong to think such things, to resent those people in his life, so she closed her eyes and strove to strengthen her heart just a little and enjoy this without feeling too deeply, for she did not know how long it would last.

"I want to remember my life," he said, still stroking her shoulder, "but at the same time I do not. What if I don't like it? What if I am vindictive or dishonest, or at odds with a family I despise? What if I am married to a woman I hate?"

She leaned up on her elbow again and listened to his fears with secret apprehensions of her own.

"Or a woman you love," she added.

His expression stilled and grew serious. "That almost seems like a worse possibility."

"Because you would always have to live with the knowledge that you were unfaithful to her."

Because of me, and this thing I have done. She grew uneasy.

"Yes."

"But you don't behave like a married man," she reminded him, hoping to ease his mind, as well as her own—for what would she do if he *did* have a wife? She had taken that possibility very lightly before, when she decided to enter into this affair. She had stuck her head in the sand, shutting her eyes against all the possible consequences that might cause pain in the future.

She had not wanted to face any of that. All she'd wanted was to become this beautiful stranger's lover and therefore escape her marriage to Lord Jerome. Clearly she had been superficial in her thinking. She had not known how profound or vulnerable her emotions would become in such a short time.

"No, that's right," he replied as he raised his hand to rub at his forehead. "Nor do I feel like a married man. But I am quite certain I do have responsibilities. Just in the last few minutes, I've begun to feel some concern, as if I am supposed to be somewhere or be doing something, and that it might be urgent."

She frowned. "Last night you said you understood about duties and responsibilities, and you were happy to help me defy my mother. Perhaps you have been avoiding this urgent thing for the same reason—because you do not want to do it."

"I suppose only time will provide the answers to those questions. Otherwise," he said with a more lighthearted sigh, "you will be stuck with me."

She kissed him on the chest and smiled, and let her heart fall open, just for a moment. One moment, that was all. "I can think of worse things."

But as she lay her head back down on his shoulder, her mind fluttered with anxiety, because this was the first time he had shown any signs of recollection. He was suspicious that there was an urgent duty he must attend to. It weighed upon his conscience.

If that was so, and he remembered what it was and felt compelled to leave, it would mean the abrupt end of their affair.

But that was not all. There was also the unalterable fact that she had already given her word to Sebastian and Melissa that if she became pregnant with this man's child, she would send him away without ever telling him, and give the child up to be raised by them.

She had been very wrong to think that this plan would be straightforward or easy. It was nothing of the sort. Her emotions were involved, as well as her conscience, and she suspected that in the coming weeks she was going to have a very difficult time with this plan she had concocted. She would have to think very carefully about how best to resolve it. Or back away from it completely.

Just before dawn, Chelsea woke to the sound of a bird chirping outside the window, and knew she would soon have to leave and return to her own room before the servants were up and about.

She did not want to leave. She wanted to remain here in her lover's arms, and make love with him all day until they couldn't breathe, move, or even think anymore.

Despite her fears and apprehensions—or perhaps because of them—last night had been the most incredible night of her life, surpassing even the previous one, which seemed, at the time, the summit of all pleasures. The first night had been the end of her virginity, after all, and therefore changed her life forever.

But last night she'd immersed herself more deeply in her emotions, for she did not know how long this would last and wanted to experience everything more fully. There were no words to describe the rapture she had known, not only when they were making love, but also while they were talking or simply holding each other, listening to the waves outside the window.

She had been consumed not only by pleasure and desire, but by a profound mixture of joy and sorrow that made her realize how much of life she'd been missing. She had not known it was possible to *feel* so much, to want to laugh and cry, all at the same time, and despite her fears and regrets, her self-reproach and misgivings, she was grateful for this emotional experience. Last night she finally realized how dead she had been over these past seven years, living through the characters in her stories, and this morning she felt reborn.

She was also feeling shamelessly aroused—*again*—and could not resist the pull to touch Jack. She slid her hand across to where he lay stretched out on his back, gorgeously nude under the sheet. He appeared to be in a deep slumber, for he was breathing softly, so she began to stroke him.

At the first light touch of her hand, he turned his head slightly on the pillow and let out a quiet, low moan. Chelsea continued to toy with his impressive masculine anatomy, which was increasing in size and stiffness with every devoted caress she offered.

His hand came up, cupped her head and guided her down across his chest, pushing gently on her shoulder until her lips were almost touching the place where he was most eager for her attentions.

Recalling how he had kissed and tongued her the first night and driven her to the highest peaks of human ecstasy, she took him in her mouth and slid her tongue down the length of his erection.

Eyes closed, still drowsy in sleep, he moaned again.

"Elizabeth . . . "

Chelsea's eyes flew open and she sat bolt upright. "What did you say?"

He jerked violently awake and sat up, too, not unlike the first night when he had regained consciousness and thrown her to the floor like a madman.

"What's going on?" he asked, glaring at her, then glancing down at his erection.

"I was . . . I was kissing you." She did not have the courage to tell him where, exactly, she had been kissing him, or how much he seemed to be enjoying it. "And you just called me Elizabeth."

"Who's Elizabeth?"

The flame in her heart blew out. Jack was experiencing an unconscious memory from his real life. A sexual memory. He had not been thinking of her in his sleep. He'd been dreaming of someone else.

Somehow she managed to speak calmly and sensibly, while on the inside all her dreams and joys were sinking into a dark, dread-filled abyss. "I don't know. I was hoping you'd be able to tell *me*."

He sat up on the pillows and lowered his forehead into a hand.

Chapter 11

~~~OC~~~

Jack had not been able to tell Chelsea who Elizabeth was because he had no idea. Despite great efforts, he could not place the name. Nothing about it rang a single bell in his mind, and in the end he concluded that Elizabeth was probably a recent lover.

"Your wife, perhaps?" Chelsea pressed, her insides squeezing with angst. "Or a fiancée?"

He got out of bed and quickly yanked on his trousers. "I don't know."

His voice was curt, almost angry, as he kept his back to her and hastily fastened the buttons and searched for his shirt.

"I wonder how many lovers you've had," she said distantly, struggling not to be hurt by this. She had to push such feelings away.

But of course he could not answer that question either. She therefore had no choice but to accept his explanation—and his apology for calling her by another woman's name at a most inopportune time.

That did not mean she could forget it, however, for the awkward incident reestablished that self-protective instinct she had felt the day before, and reminded her how important it was to keep her heart out of this, no matter how glorious and romantic these days seemed. Because it was very likely that one day she, too, would be regarded as a recent lover. He would go back to where he came from and rejoin the people who were his friends and family. Perhaps he would say *her* name when he was with another, and remember this bizarre, abnormal experience with a sense of guilt and remorse.

Thus, she could not forget that none of this was real and it would not last long. No matter how intimately they behaved with each other, no matter how romantic and fanciful it all seemed, he would eventually return to his life, and she, in turn, would be required to keep secrets from him.

So, if she was going to succeed with this plan, she must remember to stay detached, because when all was said and done, all contact between them would be severed.

Chelsea's mother decided to serve lunch outdoors that day, for it was a calm, clear afternoon. The servants carried white-clothed tables onto the lawn, adorned them with flowers and fruit in large pewter bowls, and the family enjoyed an extravagant feast of cold meats and fresh vegetables, with frosted pound cake for dessert.

All the while, Chelsea failed completely at remaining detached.

After the meal, Melissa took her by the arm to walk with her across the lawn to the rosebushes, where they could look out at the sea.

"What's wrong?" she asked. "You look miserable."

"I don't think I can do this anymore," Chelsea flatly replied.

There was an echo of surprise in Melissa's voice. "Why not?"

"It's not as simple as I thought it would be. I was so cavalier about it before, but now I'm having so many thoughts and feelings. I'm thinking about the future—*his* future—and I fear he might have a lover or even a wife. He called me by another woman's name this morning when we were in bed."

"Oh dear. Did he remember anything? Could he tell you who she was?"

"No, and still, he remembers nothing. He was half asleep when he said it. But aside from that, I am finding the guilt over this deception to be worse than I imagined it would be. I thought I could be matter-of-fact about it all, and I am trying very hard to keep my heart out of it, but I am not sure I can be the mercenary soldier I wanted to be. If there is a child, I don't know how I will be able to keep it from him. It will be the worst lie of my life. Why did I not think of this before? Why did I think it would be simple?"

"Are you falling in love with him? Is that the problem?"

She looked up at the sky. "I think maybe . . . yes, a little. I'm not sure. But whatever my feelings are, they are making everything very complicated."

Melissa touched her arm. "I was afraid this would happen. It's not easy to be intimate with a man and keep your heart covered up. It goes against our natures as women."

Chelsea withdrew, but continued to hold Melissa's hands. "Not for all women. What about the ones who sell their bodies to strangers? Surely they don't fall in love every night. Why can't I be like them?"

She had never imagined she would wish for such a thing, but there it was.

Melissa considered it. "That would be a very different experience from this. You have yourself a handsome and charming gentleman who appears—from what I can see—to be more than a little enamored with you."

"Do you think so?" She glanced uneasily at Jack, who was sitting at the table with her mother, engaged in conversation.

They said nothing for a long time, then Melissa spoke with compassion. "We will not ask you to continue this if you are not comfortable, Chelsea. I will be honest and tell you that Sebastian would be greatly relieved if you ended it. He is not handling any of this well. It has taken all my energies to keep him from intervening, and I am not always sure I am doing the right thing."

Chelsea took a deep breath and let it out. "Sometimes when I think about giving up the plan, I also think of the alternative—marrying Lord Jerome. But mostly I think about how impossible it will be for me to say goodbye to Jack, when all I want to do is be with him."

"I promise, if you find yourself with child, Sebastian and I will be here for you, no matter what you decide to do. And if we go ahead with things as planned, we will be in your debt forever. We will spend the rest of our days making sure that you get the happiness you deserve."

She looked at her sister-in-law. "I wasn't doing this just for my own happiness," she confessed. "*Your* happiness means a great deal to me as well. I know how badly you want to be a mother. I wanted to do this for you."

Melissa pulled her into her arms and held her. "You are my best friend," she said.

"And you are mine."

Which made all of this so very, very difficult.

* * *

"You've been distant today," Jack said, offering his arm to Chelsea as they strolled along the row of azaleas on the sunny side of the house. "Is it because of what happened this morning?"

Chelsea tried to find a way to explain how she felt, without sounding wounded or heartbroken. She tried also to remember what she and Melissa had just been discussing. She had not entered into this to fall in love. She'd had a very specific purpose. She must think of her fate with Lord Jerome, and try to stay rational.

"Yes," she said matter-of-factly. "Your calling me by another woman's name was a healthy dose of reality, don't you think?"

So much for staying rational. She'd just spoken harshly. Her breaking heart had revealed itself.

"It introduced nothing we did not already know."

"It introduced another woman," she corrected him.

He stopped and tilted his head to the side, and with a slight scowl in his dark features, studied her expression.

"Yes," he said, a clear note of warning in his voice, "but the notion of my having a past is hardly unexpected or out of the ordinary. I am a grown man, Chelsea, and you know my situation here. Of course, I would have had lovers, and you and I are hardly committed to each other. You are betrothed to another. You came to me for one thing, and one thing only, and I played my part. I have not misled you or taken advantage of you. And correct me if I am wrong, but you've been enjoying yourself, so I will not stand here and be treated as if I have betrayed you."

"No, of course not," she said, kicking herself for behaving in such a way when she had just resolved to be level-headed. "I did not mean to imply that."

They walked on in silence for a moment.

"You are right," she said, laboring to convince herself more than him. "We are not committed to each other. I am not your wife, or even your mistress. For all we know, you may be gone from here tomorrow, and if that is the case, we shall part as friends. And I will be grateful for the time we have spent together and all that you have taught me about the marriage bed. It has been wonderful."

There. She had said all the right things.

"Well," he said coolly, "that sounds very . . . *expedient* for both of us. No strings, no duties. How perfectly decadent."

"Yes, exactly." She began walking again, and tried to behave like the carefree lover she wanted to be. "Because clearly we both have an aversion toward the duties we must fulfill. We shall therefore be happy to know that we have each rebelled in this very enjoyable way, by seeking pleasure for pleasure's sake while we had the chance."

They walked around the house to look out at the sea, which sparkled brightly like thousands of diamonds in the sun.

"And yet," Jack said, his voice becoming quiet and low, "there is a part of me that will not want to say goodbye to you."

The remark did nothing to help her stay focused on her purpose, or to remain detached. Instead, it caused her heart to tremble ever so cautiously with hope.

For the longest time she said nothing. She simply stood at the edge of the property with these unwelcome emotions flooding through her. She thought about her life and everything she wanted, as well as everything that had hurt her in the past.

She had not been lucky in love. She had made poor decisions. For years she'd been a social outcast, yet never felt alone or unhappy. Why? Because she'd always had her imagination and her writing. She could create fictional worlds and live vicariously through her characters, without ever risking her own heart.

In addition, she had her family. There was her mother, who no one would deny could be beastly sometimes, but she never meant any harm. And she had Sebastian and Melissa, who were both so dear to her.

Despite everything, she had achieved a certain kind of happiness in recent years. She had learned to rely on herself, and though she could not deny being somewhat bored on certain occasions, she'd become content here on the island, with her solitary life.

But everything was different now, since Jack had washed up onto her shore. Her contentment was slipping away. She was aware now of what she'd been missing, and she almost wished that she had never discovered it.

She wished Jack—or whatever his real name was—had never come here.

"Let me guess," she said, responding to his subtle declaration of affection. "You will not want to say goodbye to me because I am all you have."

He needed her because he felt alone. That was all it was. She was the last woman on earth, so to speak.

"It's a heavy responsibility," she added, "to be the sole provider of your happiness."

She spoke with bite, cognizant of the fact that she was trying to push him away. She wanted to pick a fight. She did not want to be in love, and she certainly did not want to feel jealous of whoever had made love to him before she had.

"You may not like it," he replied, frowning at

her, "but until I remember my old life, or begin a new one, you are my everything."

' "Until I remember my old life,' " she repeated, trying desperately to focus on those words, instead of the way it made her feel to know that at the moment she was his everything. "It is something we would both do well to remember, Jack, because as soon as you venture out into the world, you will no longer need me, and this will be over."

He would replace her with other friends, other activities, and other women, because right now he was just using her to fill his sense of emptiness. He had told her so more than once.

But she was using him, too, she realized, and for far more deceitful purposes, and therefore had no right to be arguing with him or punishing him. She had started all this, so she would have to cope with the chaos of her emotions. She could not take it out on him.

"If you will excuse me," she said, deciding it was not a good day for coping, and that it would be best to end the conversation. "I am feeling tired, and I don't really want to talk about this anymore."

He bowed his head politely, and did not object to her departure. She crossed the lawn, walked around the house, and nearly collided head-on with her mother.

"What have you been up to, Chelsea?" she asked accusingly.

"Nothing, Mother."

Chelsea did not stop to elaborate. She continued on, but felt her mother's disapproving gaze burning a hole into the back of her head as she entered the house.

Ten minutes later a knock sounded at her door, but before she had a chance to respond, her mother barged in.

"I am not a fool," she said, slamming the door behind her. "What is going on?"

"Nothing," Chelsea replied, feeling as if she were six years old again, taking a scolding for climbing trees. But then she remembered she was a grown woman, and lifted her chin. "I don't appreciate being interrupted like this, Mother. You cannot just walk in here as if these were your rooms."

She quickly picked up her pencil to give the impression that she had been writing, though she hadn't. She'd been staring at the wall.

Her mother strode closer. "You're not fancying yourself in love with him, are you? He is handsome and charming, no doubt about it, but we still don't know anything about him, and you have a responsibility to this family. You are as good as promised to Lord Jerome, and I will not tolerate a repeat performance of the last time, when you ran off with an unsuitable young man because he knew how to flatter you and you became infatuated."

Chelsea strove to keep her voice under control. "How many times must I repeat this? The performance you are referring to happened when I was eighteen. I was young and foolish. Since then I have been living here in exile with you, without complaint, for seven years. I have not once asked for anything for my own happiness. I have been dutifully paying the price for my mistakes. Does that not count for anything?"

"I tried to talk to Melissa just now," her mother said, ignoring everything Chelsea had just said, "and she was hiding something. I could see it in her eyes. You're not scheming to make him fall in love with you and propose, are you? So that you might get out of marrying Lord Jerome?"

"Of course not." But then her back went up, for she was tired of paying for that mistake she made all those years ago, and wanted her mother to know it. "But what if I were? And what if he *did* propose to me? If I wanted to marry him, I would."

Good Lord, what was she saying?

Her mother's face went white as stone. "You insolent girl. Clearly you have not learned a thing. You have no sense at all."

"Why? Because I might want some joy for myself? It is not fair what you ask me to do. Lord Jerome is more than twice my age, and he is a horrid, self-regarding, repulsive man."

"You must do your duty, as we all must."

"You might speak differently if it was *you* who had to marry him."

"He doesn't want me," she said. "He wants you, because you will be able to give him heirs."

Chelsea recoiled in disgust at the thought of sharing a bed with him, especially now that she knew what would occur—and when she knew how enjoyable lovemaking could be with a man like Jack.

"I will be miserable, Mother."

Her mother scoffed. "Well, if you think the handsome stranger in our midst has just washed ashore to save you from your fate, you are a fool. He could be a fish merchant for all we know, in which case a match would be completely inappropriate. You are the daughter of an earl. You will not marry beneath you."

"*Beneath* me? I am the lowliest of the low, according to you."

Her mother said nothing to refute her claim, which only incensed Chelsea further.

"And you must know he is not a fish merchant," she argued. "He may even be a duke or a prince.

Surely you would not oppose it then. Or *would* you? Just to see me miserable?"

Her mother's eyes narrowed. "If he is a duke or a prince, you are even more a fool than I thought, to think that he would propose. Tsk tsk, Chelsea. You forget sometimes that you are ruined. No man of such eminence would ever have you as a wife. You would be lucky if he were inclined to use you as a mistress, which would never happen, of course, because I would not permit it. That is why you must settle for Lord Jerome."

"Settle? Like you did?"

Her mother pressed her lips into a hard line. "I loved your father."

"You loved that he was an earl. That's what you settled for. You resigned yourself to a marriage without love, and therefore a life without joy or laughter or passion."

"Passion fades. A title does not."

"So while you were married, you had a title and what else? Boredom? Resentment? Contempt, even? That's what I remember most about you and Father, which is why I ran away with that 'unsuitable' man in the first place, and why I would do it again in a heartbeat—with that equally unsuitable man outside in the garden."

There. She had said it. The truth.

Her mother's cheeks flushed with fury. "You just say these things to spite me."

Then she walked out and slammed the door behind her.

For a fleeting second Chelsea thought she was off the hook—until a key slipped into the lock and turned.

She gasped. Leaping out of her chair, she ran to the door, grabbed hold of the knob and rattled it frantically. "Let me out of here, Mother! You're behaving like a child!"

"You are the child, Chelsea, not me," her mother said from the other side. "I will not let you run off again and leave us all here to rot. I am writing to Lord Jerome today, and I will tell him to come and collect you as soon as he is able."

"But you won't rot!" she shouted, suddenly desperate to save her future by any means possible. "I have a plan. I am trying very hard to do my duty at this moment. I might have already succeeded." But she would not know for sure for at least a few weeks.

There was a long silence on the other side of the door. "What plan?"

Chelsea let go of the knob and took a step back, certain that if she tried to explain, it would come out all wrong, and her mother would faint out there in the hall, or worse—do exactly what she said she was going to do and tell Lord Jerome to come right away.

"Why don't you talk to Sebastian?" Chelsea suggested. "He will tell you everything."

"Sebastian knows?"

"Yes."

There was another long silence on the other side of the door.

"Go and see him, Mother, I beg of you," Chelsea pleaded.

The only response was the sound of her mother's shoes, treading heavily down the hall to the stairs.

Chapter 12

An hour later Chelsea woke to the sound of a key turning in her lock. Groggy from a nap, she sat up and watched the door, curious to see who would come in to talk sense to her next.

The door opened. Her brother peeked his head in. "Don't throw anything. It's only me."

She rose from the bed and smoothed out her hair, tucking the loose strands back into place. "Did Mother talk to you? Am I to be shipped off to Lord Jerome in the morning?"

He entered the room and reached into his pocket. "She said to give you this."

"What is it?"

He handed her a tiny bottle.

"It's her favorite perfume," Chelsea said.

"She wanted me to tell you that you had to wear it tonight. Clearly, it's her way of letting you know that she is consenting to your idea—by delivering a command of her own."

Slow to comprehend what he was saying because she was having a hard time believing it, Chelsea opened the bottle and sniffed it. "You're telling me she liked the plan. Was she intoxicated?"

He let out a melancholy sigh. "No, but I think it was just underhanded enough to appeal to her controlling side, which we both know so well." He strolled to the bed and sat down. "After she got over the initial shock, I believe she wished she'd thought of it herself. Although she did suggest that it would have been simpler to send Melissa to him, instead of you, just in case it is my fault there is no heir."

Chelsea smothered a gasp. "What did you say?"

"I told her hell would freeze over first. I love my wife, Chel, and no other man will ever put his hands on her—*ever* —not as long as I have breath in my body. It's difficult enough as it is for me to let *you* go through with this. My own sister. I must tell you that there have been moments when I wanted to bash down his door and throw him out on his ear. I have not been sleeping well."

Chelsea touched his arm. "I'm sorry it's been difficult for you, but perhaps it will give you some comfort to know that he has been very good to me. It has not been unpleasant. Not at all. And if this saves me from having to marry Lord Jerome, I will forever be in your debt for allowing me to do this. You will be saving me from a terrible fate."

He did not look up, and she could see that her words were doing little to console him.

She decided to take a different tack, to try and lighten his mood. "Besides, if we did send Melissa and she conceived, the child would not be of Father's bloodline, and we do have *some* scruples."

"Not many," he said quietly.

Still hoping to ease his conscience, she crossed the room to her dressing table and began to comb her hair. "So Mother will not write to Lord Jerome today?"

"That's right."

Ever hopeful, she turned to face her brother. "Does this mean I will not have to marry him? *Ever*?"

"Don't get too excited," Sebastian replied. "There will have to be a male issue before she lets go of that safety net. I suspect she will write to him and string him along until you give birth." His eyes were streaked with red as he regarded her. "If things work out, that is, and you find yourself with child." He paused. "Were you being honest with me, Chelsea? Is he good to you? Does he treat you well, because if not—"

She interrupted him. "He is lovely, Sebastian. Truly. If things were different, I could see myself falling quite head over heels."

They were the words her brother needed to hear.

"Well," he said awkwardly, clearing his throat, "I hope you know how grateful we are for what you are doing. Melissa is overjoyed. Truth be told, it wouldn't matter to her if it was a girl or a boy, or a donkey for that matter. She is just so happy, Chel."

In some ways, Chelsea was pleased to hear it, yet at the same time, she could not bear to think of it. She did not want to imagine a baby growing in her womb—perhaps a boy, who would grow up to be tall and handsome, with dark, wavy hair, a strong, confident disposition, and creative, like both his parents . . .

"So where is Jack now?" she asked, thrusting those thoughts from her mind.

"In his guest chamber. He mentioned feeling tired. I don't think he's fully recovered yet."

She looked at herself in the mirror and dabbed some perfume behind each ear.

Her brother watched her for a moment, then glanced uncomfortably toward her desk. "I suppose I should leave you to your letters."

That was not why he was leaving, and they both knew it.

Chelsea finally met his gaze in the mirror's reflection. "Thank you, Sebastian, for speaking to Mother," she said, "and for buying me time."

He merely nodded at her, then walked out and closed the door.

She picked up her brush and continued to comb out her hair, ignoring the pain from the knots that had tangled while she slept.

"So you've forgiven me, then?" Jack asked as he withdrew from the sweet, honeyed depths of Chelsea's irresistible body and refastened his trousers.

They had made love standing up against the door of his bedchamber, thumping away like rabbits. She had not seemed to mind the base carnality of it, nor suggested they move to a quieter spot on the bed. Perhaps she knew there was no one nearby to hear, for clearly she'd come here with one thing on her mind, and they got down to business without any of the usual genteel preliminaries.

He nuzzled her cheek and stepped back, realizing only then that he had not withdrawn at the proper time—*again*—and he wondered why he was inclined to take these risks, when he still had no idea what lay in his future. Or his past.

Next time, he promised himself . . . Next time he would be more careful.

She dropped her skirts and pushed away from the door. "We already agreed that there is nothing to forgive," she said. "You were right when we spoke outside earlier today. You have not kept anything from me. I knew what I was getting myself into when I came to you the other night, and I have indeed been more than satisfied."

He watched her for a strange moment, as she walked seductively to the window.

"But there is something different about you," he said, narrowing his eyes. "You're closed off. You're not acting like yourself."

"That's ridiculous."

"Is it? I think you are still angry about what happened in bed this morning." He hesitated. "Or perhaps . . . *hurt*."

"I am neither," she quickly asserted as she pulled the curtain aside with one finger and looked out. "I am simply trying to be realistic."

"How so?"

She faced him. He had the distinct impression she was giving a great deal of consideration to her answer, almost as if she were plotting one of her stories, deciding upon the most effective piece of dialogue for her protagonist.

"I don't want to become too attached to you," she said at last.

He studied her eyes and saw a hint of vulnerability there, mixed possibly with some melancholy.

But it was an honest answer—at least he believed it to be so—and it gave him some reassurance that he had not lost her completely. She was still being open with him.

He approached her. "And is there a danger of you becoming too attached?"

"There is a danger of anything. You are very pleasant to be around. *Most* of the time," she added playfully.

"When I am not calling you by other women's names, I suppose."

"Precisely."

"I'll try not to do it again."

"I would appreciate that."

For a moment more they stood without talking, merely looking at each other while the waves rolled up onto the shoreline outside the window. Here in the room, the clock ticked steadily on the mantel.

Jack noticed the heavy beat of his heart. He felt restless, filled with a yearning that seemed to have no cure—for he could not close the space between them. How could he, when he did not know who he was, or if he was even free to care for her the way he wanted to?

Then, for some unknown reason, he remembered the urgency he'd felt the night before, and felt again that he was letting someone down. The feeling dropped into his stomach like a stone. Someone needed him. Of that, he was certain. There was a duty he was expected to fulfill.

God, *was* there a wife?

He looked down at the floor.

"So until we know more about you," Chelsea said, her voice more forceful now, almost as if she had read his thoughts, "I will simply keep my heart out of it, as you should do as well."

"That's probably wise," he heard himself saying, without looking up, because he was not in a position to offer his heart, or any kind of promise that involved the future. As things stood, he could offer Chelsea nothing, and she knew it.

Pembroke House, Mayfair

"He *has* left us in the lurch," Vincent said to Devon as he walked into the library at four in the morning. He had just come back from an extensive search of his old stomping grounds—the whorehouses, gambling dens, and all the places where vice and greed were practiced without reserve. "I searched everywhere, and no one has seen him."

"He wouldn't desert us like this," Devon told him. "Not intentionally. I know our brother. He is as dependable as they come."

Vincent went to pour himself a drink. "Did you hear any mention of him at the club? Has anyone heard from him?"

"Not since that night you referred to, when he came back to the palace talking about a night at the tables with a certain wild young buck with a pretty sister. The gentleman's father, George

Fenton, Baron Ridgeley, is the director of the London Horticultural Society."

Vincent blinked. "Father's beneficiary if we don't all marry by Christmas?"

"The very same," Devon replied.

"Have you gone to see this man?"

"I went to his house here in London, but there was no one there, except for a butler who informed me that the family was in France, which leads me to suspect—"

"That Blake went off with them without telling us."

"It's possible," Devon said, "though not typical of him, unless a message became lost on its way to us. In fact, I hope that is the case. It would certainly be preferable to our brother lying in an alley somewhere with his pockets emptied, or at the bottom of the Thames because of a disagreement over a card game."

"I can't argue with that," Vincent said. "So tomorrow . . . "

"Tomorrow we try to discover where the family has traveled to in France, and get word to them."

"At least now we have something to pin our hopes on," Vincent said. "Mother will be pleased to hear it."

"I won't be pleased until we have him in our sights."

"Indeed."

They each downed their brandy.

"Do you think he was courting that girl?" Vincent asked.

"The sister? It is entirely possible, and just like Blake to do his duty without a fuss."

"Well, if that is the case," Vincent raised his glass again, "we shall be one step closer to securing our inheritances, with three brothers taken care of, and only one left to tame."

"To marital bliss," Devon said, holding up his glass.

Clink. "To marital bliss."

Chapter 13

$\sim\!\!\!\curvearrowright\!\!\!\curvearrowright\!\!\!\sim$

"**M**aybe I am a magistrate," Jack said casually while they lay naked in bed a week later, after making love all afternoon. "Or a solicitor."

Chelsea bent her knee and draped her leg across his thighs. "What makes you say that?"

"I don't know. I think I must *do* something, and I doubt I am a laborer. My hands are not rough enough."

"An artist?"

He glanced over at the pile of drawings strewn across the table by the window, then shook his head. "No, I think I enjoy sketching too much. I can't imagine using it to earn a living."

She sat up and rested her chin on the back of her hand. "If you ask me, I think you are a gentleman of some stature—and an idle one at that. You spend your days reading the paper, riding around your country estate, hunting, going to balls, sipping brandy at your club . . . that sort of thing."

He flicked his eyebrows and nodded, accepting that it was entirely possible he led such a life.

"Would I be happy doing that, do you think?"

Chelsea watched him for a moment. "No, I think you'd be bored."

He nodded. "Yes, I believe you're right."

The following afternoon they waited for the tide to move out, then walked down the wooded lane to reach the steep sandy path that led to the sea caves.

Picking their way down the trail, they talked of Chelsea's stories, and Jack offered some interesting suggestions for future ones. He also helped her come up with a solution to a problem she was having with the current one—about the governess and the widowed French aristocrat.

"I quite enjoy talking about your stories," he said when they reached the bottom of the path and started along the pebbled beach. "I only wish you would let me read one."

"You can read one if I ever find the courage to send anything to a publisher, and if that publisher deems it fit to be printed."

"Will you write under your own name?"

"Definitely not. I am far too notorious."

"Maybe you should use that to your advantage, since you are writing scandalous yarns."

She smiled. "Now there's a thought."

They came to the end of the beach and Chelsea stopped. "Here we must climb over these rocks, and beyond them we will come to the sea caves."

He looked up at the steep face of the cliff. At the top, weathered pines bowed over the edge, clinging by their gnarled, exposed roots to the eroding rock.

"Those trees will be gone in a few years," Chelsea said wistfully as she lifted her skirts and stepped onto the rocks. "The ground beneath them will slowly fall away, and one by one they'll topple into the sea."

"Which is a most unforgiving force of nature," he said, following her.

"If anyone can vouch for that," she said, "it would be you."

They hopped down from the rocks, walked across the short beach, and entered the cave. Inside, water dripped incessantly from the damp, shiny walls. A chill touched their faces.

"You can't come in here when the tide is in," Chelsea told him as she stepped over the slippery rocks and tidewater puddles. "In twelve hours all of this will be submerged."

She pointed toward a narrow area, deeper inside. "That's where I found you, on that high section. You were lying on your stomach, wearing not a stitch of clothing."

"You must have gotten the shock of your life

when you discovered a naked man in your cave."

She puckered her brows at him. "Don't joke. When I first touched you, your skin was as frigid as the sea. I thought you were dead."

He was quiet for a time, then walked to the place she indicated. He looked down at the ground, then up at the walls. "I remember waking up and not knowing where I was. At first I thought I was lying on a battlefield with cannons going off all around me."

"Beyond that wall," she said, pointing, "is another cave called Cannon Cave. They named it that because of the noise it makes on a rough day. The surf pours in through a narrow cavity, and each wave echoes off that inside wall. It's quite miraculous, and it was booming like a cannon that day, to be sure."

"But it's quiet now," he said.

"Yes. The tide is out, and everything is calm."

When he said nothing more, she asked, "Do you remember anything else? Does this help you to recall where you were the night before?"

He shook his head. "No."

She followed him back to the cave entrance and they went outside, climbed over the rocks, and returned to the main beach.

"I find it a bit odd," he said, strolling close to the water's edge, "that your mother says nothing to you about the time we've been spending together. You come to my bed in the afternoons, and you've become increasingly daring about the time you leave in the morning, as if you don't care if anyone sees you or guesses where you've been. Are you truly that cavalier about your reputation? Have you given up on it completely?"

An ambitious wave slid up the flat beach. "Watch yourself." Jack took her by the arm to pull her out of the way.

"First of all," she answered, as they recovered their leisurely pace, walking side by side, "my mother did say something to me last week, after we had lunch outdoors and she saw us go off together. She came to my room and warned me not to think anything would ever come of this, and that it wouldn't free me from marrying my cousin."

"And what did you say to that?" he asked.

She hesitated. "I told her I would do as I please."

"Ah." He smiled. "You are indeed a rebel. I think it is what I admire most about you."

"Well," she said, "if I am going to be forced to be miserable for the rest of my life while I do my duty for this family, I shall bloody well enjoy myself while I can, since there is nothing to lose. As I said before, my elderly cousin is not expecting a virgin bride, and Mother knows that."

He narrowed his eyes at her. "Are you telling

me she is aware of what we are doing and is turning a blind eye?"

She shrugged and looked down at her shoes.
"Let us not talk of this anymore. I want to be
lighthearted today. Your wounds are healing, and
here we are, on this beautiful beach." She stopped,
closed her eyes and breathed in deeply through
her nose. "Smell the air. It's fresh and clean. Isn't
it wonderful?"

"Smells like rain," he said, stopping to watch
her in the afternoon light.

She looked up at the overcast sky. "Yes, perhaps
so. The smell of it must be blowing over from the
mainland." She looked at him. "Have you been
reading the papers? The south of England has had
the wettest spring in over a century. Evidently
there have been all sorts of bridges collapsing and
fields are flooding."

He saw it in his mind suddenly—green fields
and mist and muddy roads. Mud everywhere.
Holes in the ground filling with rainwater . . .

Chelsea stopped. "What is it? Do you remember something?"

He looked out at the sea. "I don't know. Your
description of the rain made me see images. I'm
not sure if you could call them memories. Perhaps
it's just my imagination, picturing what it must
look like."

"What did you see?"

"I saw mud, and puddles, and holes in the ground. A statue . . . No wait . . . a fountain in the middle of a garden. But there are no flowers. It's a depressing image. It makes no sense to me."

"Perhaps you saw this statue before you went missing. Or maybe it is on the property where you live."

He turned to her. "Has it been very bad here? Has there been flooding?"

"No, we've been fortunate. It hasn't been nearly as bad as that."

They walked on for a time.

"The statue and garden must be something from your life," she suggested, "which is a good thing. If you remember that, you might soon begin to remember other things as well. The memories must still be there. You simply cannot access them at the moment."

Chelsea stopped and looked out at the water. Jack stood before her, not wanting to think about muddy gardens and depressing statues—images that only frustrated him, for he could not make sense of them.

He wanted only to admire the curve of her neck and the sweet contours of her chin, and her full, moist lips, reflecting the light. Her complexion was like rich cream, her slender figure sensuous and alluring. He let his eyes roam appreciatively from those perfect, well-rounded breasts to that tiny waist and down over her shapely hips, and hungered to unbutton that tight bodice she was wearing and free those ample pink breasts to his attentions.

"Your spirit is contagious," he said.

She opened her eyes and smiled at him.

"Shall we head back?" he asked in a low voice. "I saw a nice little patch of grass under a weeping willow along the side of the lane. It looked rather secluded."

A sensual huskiness deepened her tone. "That sounds rather lovely."

He held out his hand and led her back to the path, and as soon as they reached the narrow lane at the top, she laughed and took off in a run. Jack immediately chased after her, ripping his jacket off as he went.

Over the past days and nights it had become the custom not only for Jack to spend time with Chelsea in various private capacities, both indoors and out, but to dine formally with the family. Each evening he played a competitive game of whist with the dowager in the drawing room, while the others looked on with interest and amusement.

As it happened, Chelsea's mother was an excellent card player and seemed to greatly enjoy strategizing. Since she was Jack's hostess and was now treating him exceedingly well, he had no wish to refuse her nightly invitations to the table, and also found the activity beneficial to his mind in a way that he hoped might eventually spark a memory. *Any* memory.

Sometimes, just looking at the cards in his hands and flipping them to different positions felt familiar and exciting, as if everything might come flooding back to him at any moment. It was like having a word on the tip of one's tongue and waiting for it to suddenly spill out.

But on one particular night—after he'd spent the bulk of the day with Chelsea, riding on horseback down to the sea and enjoying a picnic in a quiet glen that smelled of pinecones—he was not in the mood to play cards. He was weary, both in mind and body, and needed time alone.

After dinner, as rain began to fall outside, he delivered his apologies to the dowager and bid the family good-night. He was on his way to the stairs when he passed by the open door of the library. There was no one in the room, but a warm fire was blazing in the hearth, keeping out the dampness, so he decided a brandy in the big leather chair might be just the thing.

He walked into the oak-paneled room and poured himself a drink, then took a seat by the fire. His thoughts went immediately to Chelsea and the fine day they had spent together, and he wondered what the devil he was going to do about the inconvenient fact that—despite all his efforts to prevent it—he was falling in love with her.

Yes, there it was, out in the open, in the clear meadows of his mind. He loved her. *Love.* He did not care one whit if he ever remembered the man he once was. He would never want to leave her for another life, even if he discovered he was King of England, Spain, and France.

All that mattered was the life he knew now, here on this beautiful, sea-swept island, and that he loved the woman who had found him in a cave and saved his life. He loved her!

But therein lay the problem, he reminded himself as he took a sip of his brandy and watched the fire dance in the grate, the wind gusting down the chimney.

His time here was not all that mattered. The future mattered, too, because he wanted Chelsea for the rest of his life, till death do them part, and beyond. If he could, he would steal her away in order to prevent her from marrying that lecherous old man she did not love.

Because he believed she loved *him*. Hell, he was certain of it, even though she was doing her best to prevent and deny it, for they had no idea who he was or if he was free to propose to her. They had both been taking great pains not to talk about the future or his other life, and were therefore living only in the present. One day at a time. Making love whenever they chose. Laughing and seeking joy at every opportunity.

So what was he to do?

The answer was obvious. He could not steal her away. He had no money or means of support. In order to do this properly, without guilt or regret, he would have to leave this place and search for his identity, and pray to God he was someone worthy enough to return and offer her marriage.

No, it had to be better than that, he thought as he rose from the chair to pour himself another drink. He could not simply be "worthy enough." He had to be *more* worthy than the man who was her brother's heir—a future peer of the realm, the man her mother wanted for her.

Bloody hell, he was not going to lie to himself. Of that, the chances were slim. They were not odds that would persuade a strategizing mother to allow her daughter to wait, Lord knew how long, for a possible proposal from a man who could be a bloody nobody.

Damn this situation. It was torture.

He sat down by the fire again to think on it some more, while the wind and rain outside battered the windowpanes.

Chelsea sat in the drawing room sipping tea and staring at the wall. *I cannot continue with this,* she thought. *It is too difficult. I love him. I am in love with him* . . . She felt frazzled and dizzy, as if she were being sucked into a vortex of disaster.

Her mother stood up from the piano, crossed the room and sat down beside her on the sofa. "How are you feeling tonight, Chelsea?"

"Fine, thank you," she answered flatly.

"Do you still have the perfume I sent to you last week, or have you used all of it?"

"No, I still have some. And thank you. That was very generous."

But she was not in the mood to talk to anyone, least of all her mother. She wanted to be alone and think about what she was doing and how she was going to survive this. There were choices to be made, and she feared that if she did not soon make a change of some kind, these passions were going to overwhelm her, and she would spoil everything and let her family down by disappearing into oblivion with a man who had no resources, no family, or even a name.

If he asked her to, that is. She was not even sure he shared her feelings. He had never told her that he loved her. They never talked about the future. How could they?

Her mother leaned closer and spoke softly. "Did *he* like the fragrance?"

Good God. She had to get out of here.

"If you will excuse me, Mother, I'm rather tired . . . "

Setting down her teacup, she made a move to stand, but her mother grabbed hold of her wrist. "You are not to go yet, Chelsea. I want to talk to you."

Chelsea strove to keep her breathing steady, while frantic emotions swirled around inside her brain like little hurricanes. "About what?"

"I have not yet written to Lord Jerome," her mother informed her. "I am waiting to see how things progress here."

"They are going well, Mother. I can assure you of that."

Her mother glanced over her shoulder to make sure there were no servants lurking about. "When did you last have your courses?"

"Must we talk about this?"

"Yes. I am not going to pick up my pen and spoil our chances with Lord Jerome until I am sure you know exactly what you are doing."

She laughed bitterly. "It's not that difficult, Mother. In fact, I have discovered, to my absolute delight, that it comes quite naturally."

Chelsea received, without surprise, a sharp slap across the face. She had deserved it, no question, and was, quite frankly, surprised it had not happened sooner.

"I am not talking about that," her mother said. "I am referring to the times during the month when you are most fertile. Did he have you today?"

Chelsea swallowed over the sour taste in her mouth. "What?"

"Did he *have* you? And did he take his pleasure inside of you?"

"I don't want to discuss this."

"Answer the question."

She paused. "No, we did not make love today." Although the day was not over yet.

"No? Why not? You were gone for six hours and alone the entire time. What were you doing?"

"That is none of your business."

"Yes, it is, if you want me to continue to agree to this plan."

"We went riding," she reluctantly explained. "It was the first time he'd been on a horse since he came here. He discovered he was quite an accomplished horseman."

"Surely you were not on horseback the entire time," her mother said.

"No, we had lunch and we talked and he sketched, and . . . " She swallowed again. "I wrote in my notebook, and then . . . we had a nap."

"You had a nap? Good God, child. And still, he did not have you?"

"Mother, must you speak of it this way? It's private."

"It most certainly is not. You have offered this family an heir, and it is a matter of great importance. When did you last have your courses?" she asked again.

Chelsea thought about it. "I finished a few weeks ago, just before he arrived."

Her mother's eyes darkened, then she took hold of Chelsea's wrist again and pulled her off the sofa.

"What are you doing?" She fought to pry her mother's bony fingers off her arm as she was dragged brutally out of the room.

"This is your most fertile time, Chelsea, and since he did not have you today, he must have you tonight. At least once. Twice if you can manage it."

Chelsea was near to breaking into sobs of fury. She did not want to go to him tonight. She couldn't bear it anymore. It was killing her. She needed time to think about what she was doing. "Mother!"

But her mother ignored her pleas and dragged her roughly and ruthlessly out of the drawing room toward the stairs.

Jack looked up when he heard a commotion in the hall. Rising from his chair, he crossed quietly to the door just as Chelsea and her mother scuffled by.

"You are going to his bed now," Lady Neufeld insisted, "whether you like it or not."

What the bloody hell . . . ?

He stepped into the doorway and watched them.

"Please, Mother, not tonight." Chelsea was practically sobbing, thrashing about and struggling against her mother's grip on her arm. "I don't want to! I *can't!*"

"You don't have a choice. He must have you when you are most fertile."

They started up the stairs, fighting maliciously against each other. Lady Neufeld stopped halfway. "You impudent child! You have a duty to this family and you are going up there. I'll drag you by the hair if I have to."

Jack took a step forward to intervene, but something held him back.

Chelsea broke free and pushed her mother against the wall. "No! I am not going to his bed tonight, and you cannot make me! I am not your pawn! And if you try to drag me anywhere like that one more time, Mother, I swear to God I will leave here forever and you will never see me again. You can forget about your precious Neufeld heir and rot on this island forever, for all I care."

She picked up her skirts, turned and dashed up the rest of the stairs.

Jack took a step back into the shadows, while he peered around the doorjamb at Lady Neufeld, who stood with her back to the wall, her cheeks flushed with fury as she stared after her daughter.

A moment or two later she recovered her composure and started up the stairs as well, stomping hard, her eyes narrowed with frustration. Jack remained inside the library until he heard her heels click down the corridor, then fade to silence as she entered her own bedchamber.

For a long time he stood with his back up against the wall, looking down at his brandy, swirling it around in the glass, contemplating what he had just seen.

He must have you when you are most fertile . . .

You can forget about your precious Neufeld heir . . .

His stomach began to churn. He felt like he was going to be sick.

He set his glass down on a table.

Slowly, with dark and sober resolve, he left the library. He started up the stairs, taking one step at a time, deciding that he was going to have a very frank word or two with his bed partner, who he now knew was not the defiant rebel he thought. In fact, she was the exact opposite.

With each step his animosity grew. He remembered being locked in that room when he first arrived and banging on the door to get out. He also remembered the laudanum, and Chelsea staying home from church that first day, when everyone else had left the house.

And how convenient that her mother had been turning a blind eye to all their lovemaking. When he'd asked Chelsea about it, she changed the subject.

She had been lying to him and using him from the beginning. He *had* been their prisoner here, and that lying, false-hearted viper had been using him for one thing and one thing only.

She had wanted him for seed.

Chapter 14

Chelsea ran into her room, slammed the door behind her, marched straight to her bedpost and shook it. She was imagining that she was strangling her mother.

She was so angry she wanted to scream!

Pacing around the room, she bit back a number of oaths and debated what she was going to do. This whole situation had spiraled out of control—not just the state of her emotions, but her mother's ideas as well. The woman was determined to be the grandmother of the next Earl Neufeld, no matter what the cost. Now, it seemed that she was doing her mother's bidding instead of her own, and would not have the freedom to change her mind.

Well, she would if she wanted to. Damn right, she would.

Just then she heard her doorknob turn.

God help her. If her mother was walking in

here again without knocking, she didn't trust herself not to strangle the woman for real.

But it was not her mother. It was Jack.

He entered the room and slammed the door shut behind him—just as she had a few seconds ago—and with fists clenched, glared at her like a devil wolf.

"What are you doing here?" she asked, her heart suddenly pounding with fear. This was not the Jack she knew. This was a wild creature. "I thought you'd gone to bed."

A muscle flicked at his jaw. "Hoped, you mean."

She said nothing, for she seemed to have lost her voice. He took a few steps closer, and she backed up until she bumped into her chest of drawers.

Immediately she put two and two together. "Did you see what just happened between my mother and me?"

"I did."

He continued to glare at her until she could barely breathe. "It's not what you think."

"No? How do you know what I think?"

"I can see it in your eyes," she said. "You think I've been coming to your bed because she has been forcing me to."

"Isn't that's what's been going on? I heard what she said. She told you that you had a duty to perform for your family."

"Yes, but—"

He glanced up at the ceiling. "I remember you saying something like that to me once. You said, 'If I am going to be forced to be miserable while I do my duty for this family . . . ' "

He paced back and forth in front of her like a lion in a cage.

"What a fool I was," he ground out. "I didn't realize that *I* was the miserable duty. Does your cousin, Lord Jerome, even exist? Or was that part of your plot to get me to do what you wanted? You really are a very good writer, Chelsea, a grand weaver of lies. You have a most promising future ahead of you, contriving elaborate fictions. Or perhaps you would do better on the stage, for clearly you are a gifted actress as well. You could write your own productions."

"It wasn't a story," she insisted. "I *was* being forced to marry my cousin. I still am. I would show you the letter he wrote, but . . . "

"But what?"

"I threw it into the sea."

His voice deepened. "How very convenient."

She sucked in a breath. "Please, Jack."

"Please what? Forgive you? Or lift your skirts one more time?" He gestured behind him. "Up against the door? Would that be sufficient? Or would you prefer to be on your back? I suppose it's all the same to you, as long as you can get me to take my pleasure on the *inside*."

Feeling a sharp, piercing stab of panic, she stepped forward. "Let me explain."

"I am not a character in one of your stories," he said. "My life is not a fiction. I may have washed up onto your beach like a fish and remember nothing about my life, but damn you, Chelsea, I am a man, and I am real. I exist!"

She comprehended the anxiety in his voice and the rage burning in his eyes.

"I know that," she tried to tell him. "You are a real man who has been through a terrible ordeal, and I have not been completely honest with you."

She had lied to him from the beginning and used him.

But she'd also fallen in love with him.

There was a hard rap on her door and she jumped.

God, was it her mother? Please, not now . . .

"Who is it?" she shouted irritably.

"It's Sebastian."

Jack turned and glared at the door, then his fierce gaze shot back to her face. "Does he know what's been going on here?" he asked. "Does he know that you've been screwing your invalid guest, who has no identity and nowhere to go?

That you've been trying to provide this house with an heir, because he cannot fulfill that duty?"

"Yes," she replied plainly.

He stared at her long and hard, then turned around and strode to the door. He opened it, took one look at Sebastian, then swung back and punched him in the jaw.

"What are you doing!" Chelsea shouted, dashing across the room. She pushed past Jack to tend to her brother, who had been knocked clear across the hall, where he sank down to the floor.

Chelsea dropped to her knees beside him. "Are you all right?"

She was acutely aware of Jack standing over them with both fists still clenched, as if waiting for Sebastian to get up so he could hit him again.

She looked up at him. "You caught him completely off guard."

Sebastian pressed the back of his hand to his split lip, which was already swelling like a grape, then inspected the blood on his knuckle.

"I take it our guest knows what we've been up to," he said.

She sat back on her heels. "Yes, but there was no call for that." She stood up and faced Jack. "It was *my* idea, not his."

Jack looked down at Sebastian, who was rising slowly to his feet.

"But your brother agreed to it," Jack said. "Honestly, man," he said with disgust. "Your own sister."

"I deserved that," Sebastian replied, straightening at last. "This was an idiotic plan, and I should never have agreed to it. I should have put a stop to it."

"No, Sebastian," she said. "I wanted to be with him. You know I did. And Lord knows, I deserved, for once, to do what I wanted." Chelsea met Jack's eyes and spoke with bite. "You told me that was what you liked best about me—that I was a rebel."

"It doesn't change the fact that what I now like *least* about you is your self-seeking interest, your ability to use and deceive an injured man who has no means of escape from your venomous attentions."

"I seem to recall," she said, striding back into her room while Jack followed, "that you quite enjoyed those attentions, sir, especially when you knew there would be no consequences. I told you I was promised to another man, yet you went ahead and took your pleasure with me regardless. You could have said no. And all along there has existed the distinct possibility that you are already married or in love with someone else. So I will not hear your self-righteous babble about my self-seeking intentions. You were acting selfishly, too, using me because you felt alone and needed to prove your existence and value in the world. You cannot deny that."

Sebastian walked into the room and raised a hand, as if he were a referee in the middle of a boxing ring.

"Stop," he said. "There is a reason I am here, and it's not to break up your quarrel."

They both looked at him with impatience.

"What is it?" Chelsea asked.

He wiped his lip again. "We have visitors downstairs," he said. "They arrived a few minutes ago, after a rough journey across the Channel. I think you both might want to go downstairs and speak to them."

Chelsea shook her head. "Who would be arriving at this hour?"

Sebastian straightened his posture. "We have the honor of receiving Devon Sinclair, Marquess of Hawthorne, and heir to the Duke of Pembroke, and his wife, Lady Hawthorne, who happens to be a peeress in her own right. She is also the Countess of Creighton."

"Why are they here?" Chelsea asked as a shiver of apprehension moved up her spine.

Sebastian looked intently at Jack. "For good reason, it seems. The Duke of Pembroke's heir has come to collect his brother."

Chapter 15

J ack did not go rushing downstairs right away. Instead, he sank onto the upholstered bench at the foot of Chelsea's bed. "I have a brother."

No one said anything for a moment. They simply stood in Chelsea's room while the rain slammed into the windows and the wind howled across the rooftop.

"I won't know him," Jack said. "I don't even recognize any of those names. They are not the least bit familiar."

He became keenly aware of Chelsea approaching and placing her hand on his shoulder. "Maybe you will remember when you see him. It might all come flooding back the minute you do."

The compassion in her voice did not diminish his hostility or the sense of betrayal he felt over what had just occurred. He was still angry with her. This was not going to make him forget it.

And God, he felt like such a fool. He'd been

vulnerable to this family's schemes. For a while, in the mad distortion of his reality, it felt as if Chelsea was the only woman in the world, the only person who cared for him, and he had therefore exposed himself to unwise intimacies with her. He had let himself fall in love with her, while she was holding him captive and using him for her own corrupt purposes the entire time.

Now at least he knew he had a family of his own and a place in the world, even though he was finding it difficult to gain any comfort from the knowledge. The people downstairs would be strangers to him. He was certain of it.

And what if this alleged brother was an imposter? What if it was not true? After what just happened, he did not feel he could trust anyone. He still felt completely alone, now more than ever, after this unthinkable deception.

"Jack . . . " Chelsea was still standing before him. He lifted his eyes to look up at her—the woman who had taken advantage of his pathetic situation. He felt a deep and bitter loathing toward her, and an unspeakable disappointment.

"Don't call me that. It is not my name." He glared at Sebastian. "What *is* my name?"

"You are Lord Blake Sinclair," he said.

"The watch . . . " Chelsea said. "It is yours. The initials were B.H.S."

"You are third in line to your father's title of duke," Sebastian continued. "Besides Lord Hawthorne, you have two other brothers—one is Vincent, the other Garrett. You live at Pembroke Palace in England."

Blake digested all of this, then stood. "Where are they?"

"In the drawing room."

Chelsea said nothing as he shouldered his way past her, but he was very aware of her following close behind.

The timing of this could not have been worse, Chelsea thought wretchedly as she followed Blake down the stairs. She had not had time to explain herself to him, or convince him that she hadn't been completely mercenary in her actions over the past few weeks.

The truth was, she'd enjoyed every precious minute they spent together, both in bed and out. Even in the beginning, part of what inspired her to concoct the idea was her wild attraction to him. She'd wanted to share a bed with him, and probably would have done so even without the guise of duty.

Of course, if she had known it would turn out like this, she never would have suggested the idea to her brother in the first place. She would have simply gone to Blake's room in secret and given herself to him for no other purpose but pleasure and friendship.

Now, she did not care if she was fulfilling her duty. She owed nothing to her mother. There was only Melissa and Sebastian to think of, and her beloved sister-in-law's disappointment over losing all hope for a child of her own, now that Blake knew the truth.

They arrived at the drawing room, and Blake entered first. He did not even look over his shoulder to see if she was still behind him.

It was clear to her at that moment that he had sliced her from his heart completely. That is . . . if she'd ever occupied a real place there to begin with. After what just occurred, she might never know, and she certainly could not blame him if he hated her forever. What she had done was unthinkable.

With her stomach tying up in knots, Chelsea followed Blake and Sebastian into the room, where they stopped to greet the handsome couple standing in front of the fire.

Blake took one look at the man who had come to claim him as kin and knew instantly that they were brothers. Not because he recognized him or remembered anything whatsoever about his life, but because Lord Hawthorne was practically his mirror image. He was tall and dark with blue eyes and similar facial features—the same nose, same chin, same eyes. They could have been twins, born on the same day, mere minutes apart.

"Blake!" Lady Hawthorne said. Her face lit up with joy as she strode across the room toward him, her arms outstretched.

His eyes darted to the stunning red-haired woman with eyes as green as a lush summer forest. He was not prepared for such an emotional greeting—these people were strangers to him— and it was all he could do to manage her loving embrace without demanding to know why she was hugging him. He did not know her.

But he did, of course. She was his brother's wife.

As they drew apart, he was vaguely aware of his brother moving across the room slowly, studying him with great scrutiny.

Blake met the marquess's eyes, and despite the fact that in his broken mind they were strangers, he felt a connection. He believed this man recognized and understood not just his discomfort, but most of what he was feeling under these bizarre circumstances. Clearly, Lord Hawthorne was someone of exceptional intelligence and intuition.

"I'm sorry," Blake said. "This is difficult."

His brother's eyes narrowed with concern. "Lord Neufeld was kind enough to explain that you have been unwell. He said you do not remember how you came to be here, or even where you come from."

Blake noticed his sister-in-law backing away from him, as if she were only then coming to understand the strangeness of the situation.

"That is correct," he replied.

"Then you don't know us," she said.

He wet his lips. "I'm sorry . . . "

"Can you tell us anything about where you've been for the past month," Lord Hawthorne said, "or what you remember about your life?"

"I don't remember anything at all," Blake replied. "I was rather hoping you would be the ones to supply the information tonight."

The couple exchanged looks and seemed to speak to each other with their eyes. Blake could see straightaway that they were close.

"Why don't we sit down," his brother suggested.

Blake moved to the sofa. He was aware of Chelsea and Sebastian taking seats by the window. Part of him did not want them there, but they were his hosts and had saved his life. Despite what had just occurred, he would not ask them to leave just now.

"How did you find me?" he asked his brother.

"You've been missing for a month," Devon replied. "We have been searching everywhere for you, and two days ago there was a piece in the newspaper about a man who was found washed ashore here on Jersey. The description seemed to fit, and we had already ascertained that you set off for France with some acquaintances around the same time, so in our minds it was not improbable that the man who washed up onto the beach was you."

"Perhaps you could fill in some holes for us," Chelsea said, and Blake felt a sudden irritation with her. These were his questions to ask, not hers. "When I found your brother, he was gravely wounded."

"How so?" Devon asked.

Blake placed his hand over his abdomen. Sometimes he could still feel the bloody gash in his side as if it happened only yesterday.

"I was impaled somehow," he said.

"Impaled? Do you mean stabbed?"

"We're not sure what happened," he answered. "Were there any reports in London of ships run aground or lost at sea in this area? If there was such an accident, I could have gotten caught on a harpoon, for all we know."

"No, nothing," Devon replied. "Are you recovered now?"

"Yes, fully. These people were very . . . " He paused. "They summoned a physician."

Some of the tension relaxed in his brother's

rigid posture, so Blake decided to leave out the part about being locked in his room while they drugged him into a stupor.

At least for now.

"We owe you a great debt," Devon said to Chelsea and Sebastian.

A great debt indeed. Blake had to work hard to control his hostility.

"That is not necessary," Sebastian replied. "I am sure you would have done the same if you'd found yourselves in our position."

Lady Hawthorne tilted her head to the side. "My word, Lord Neufeld, your lip is bleeding."

Sebastian spoke with his eyes fixed on his shoes. "Yes, I walked into a door earlier."

She seemed to accept this explanation, while Blake could not help but wonder if they were terrified he was going to reveal their devious plot to his brother, who was heir to a dukedom. They were probably shaking in their shoes. And if they weren't, they certainly should be.

"So we still do not know how I came to be here," he said, forcing himself to forget about Chelsea and Sebastian for the time being.

His brother shook his head. "No, but we may find out eventually if we can locate the people with whom you were traveling. Vincent is searching for them in France as we speak."

"You know who they are?"

"Yes. We discovered that you recently became acquainted with a gentleman by the name of John Fenton. His father is Baron Ridgeley, who is the chairman of the London Horticultural Society. You went there to look into their affairs, and that's how you met the man's son."

Blake drew back slightly. "Do I have an interest in horticulture?" He could not imagine it.

"No," Devon flatly replied. "But our father does, and you had your reasons for familiarizing yourself with the society." He paused and looked across at his wife. "This is where the story of your life becomes rather out of the ordinary, Blake. I am going to have a hard time explaining this to you, but it cannot be avoided." He turned to Sebastian and Chelsea. "I do apologize, but would you excuse us? This is a family matter of a somewhat private nature."

"Of course," Sebastian replied. "We will be in the library." They both stood and walked to the door.

Blake did not so much as glance in Chelsea's direction as she moved past, but he could feel the intensity of her mood chafing up against his own. She was anxious and apprehensive, afraid of what he was going to reveal to his family when she was no longer in the room.

He was glad. She deserved to perspire a little.

"Do you have any memory of our home, Blake?"

Devon asked after the door closed behind them. "Do you remember Pembroke Palace where you were raised? Do you remember anything about our father, the duke?"

"No."

Devon sat back. "Then I shall be blunt. He is not well. He is growing old, and he is also . . . I am sorry to have to say this, but there is no gentle way to put it. He is going mad."

"Mad?"

"Yes. We have hired the best doctors, but there is nothing that can be done for him. All we can do is shelter him from the public eye and do our best to keep him as comfortable as possible."

Blake sat back and contemplated this news.

"I see," he said at last.

He wanted to know if he should be grief-stricken to hear this, because presently he felt nothing but a detached sympathy for the family. He did not know the man to whom Devon was referring. He could not summon any genuine, heartfelt sorrow, for he could not picture his father's face in his mind. There was nothing there—no images, no feelings, no wish to return home as quickly as possible to hold his father's hand and ease his burdens.

Only then did a true sense of mourning come upon him, as he realized he was as good as dead inside. He cared for no one. Nothing was important to him. Perhaps he would have been better off if he'd drowned on the night he was lost.

"I am sorry to hear that," he said nevertheless, aware of his brother staring at him and recognizing this appalling indifference that he could do nothing about. He was not that good of an actor. He could not pretend to be devastated when he felt only a disconnected regret for these people sitting across from him, and for the aging duke who was losing his mind. "Is there anything I can do?"

Devon's shoulders rose and fell with a sigh. "There is, actually. It is something we have all been asked to do—all four of us. You, me, Vincent, and Garrett."

When Devon did not elaborate right away, Blake frowned. "What is it?"

His brother bowed his head and pinched the bridge of his nose. "This is all so difficult to explain, Blake, but I will do my best." He looked up. "One of the most obvious symptoms of Father's illness is his stubborn belief that the palace is haunted and cursed. He believes that if all of his sons are not married by Christmas, a flood of biblical proportions will sweep everything away— the house, the gardens, everything."

"A flood? But that is madness," Blake said.

"Exactly. Unfortunately. Father had his wishes written in his will *before* he was deemed insane—

minus the part about the curse—and his solicitor stands by it. If just one of us does not marry, we will all be disinherited, so we have been forced to trust and rely on each other. If one of us fails to abide by the terms of the will, Father will leave his entire unentailed fortune to the London Horticultural Society. I will get the title and property, of course, but with agricultural prices at an all-time low, I will have a difficult time maintaining it. The rest of you will have nothing."

"Which is why I was visiting that particular organization," Blake reasoned.

"That is our assumption."

"But why did I go to France?"

"From the information we gathered, the baron goes there often with his son to bring back non-native seeds and bulbs, rare flowers and shrubs, that sort of thing. But we believe also that you might have been courting his daughter. Like us, you've been looking rather urgently for a bride, and no one would be more suitable in Father's eyes than a young woman with an interest in horticulture."

"Good God, have I proposed to her?" he asked.

"We're not sure. There have been no announcements about it, and we did not hear any news of that nature while we were investigating your whereabouts. From what we gathered, you were closer to the young lady's brother, staying out late at night, drinking and gambling, but I suppose anything is possible."

Blake closed his eyes. "What is her name?"

"Elizabeth Fenton," Devon replied.

Blake cupped his forehead in a hand and whispered irritably, "*Christ.*"

"Do you remember something?" Lady Hawthorne asked, overlooking his unseemly oath and sitting forward in her chair.

Blake lounged against the seat cushions and tipped his head back to look up at the high, frescoed ceiling. "No. But I might have said her name once or twice in my sleep."

"Perhaps you are in love with her, then," she replied with a hopeful, somewhat romantic lilt in her voice.

He lifted his head and spoke to her icily. "I don't even know what the woman looks like."

Looking bewildered, she frowned at him.

Devon frowned also.

"What is wrong with you both?" Blake asked. "Why are you looking at me like that?"

Lady Hawthorne's voice was gentle but firm. "It is not like you to speak to me in that tone, Blake."

After everything he'd been through, he was in no mood for a scolding.

"My apologies, Lady Hawthorne," he replied. "I'll try to speak more courteously next time."

"You have always called me Rebecca," she said.

He turned his embittered gaze to his brother. "So let me get this straight. You expect me to return to England and do my duty for you—and two other brothers I don't recall—and marry someone by Christmas. Possibly a woman I have no memory of."

"Well . . ."

"What if I say no?" he blatantly asked.

They both looked at him the same way again, as if two horns had just sprouted from the sides of his head.

"What is the problem?" he asked.

Rebecca cleared her throat. "I beg your pardon, Blake, but when you first disappeared, some suggested that you might have run off and deserted us as an act of rebellion because you did not wish to marry, but then we decided that that couldn't be possible, because it is not *you*."

Devon picked up the thread of what she was saying. "She's right. Out of all of us, you are the most responsible. You've always been the voice of reason and harmony at the palace. You smooth out everyone else's problems and quarrels. I don't think any of us have ever seen you lose your temper."

"Are you sure you are not mistaking me for the brother you lost?" he asked. "Because I assure you, ever since I woke up without any knowledge of who I am, I lose my temper quite often."

"I make no mistake," Devon replied.

Blake turned his eyes toward the window. "Then maybe the brother you knew died on those rocks down there."

Looking deeply concerned, Devon leaned forward. "Let me tell you a little something about the man you are. Over the past three years, you have remained steadfast at home, taking care of everyone and everything tirelessly, while I have deserted the family to spend time abroad, and while Vincent has lived a wild and reckless existence in London. As far as Garrett goes, we don't even know where he is, perhaps on a sailboat writing poetry somewhere in the Mediterranean. He doesn't keep in touch. You, on the other hand, have always been the rock in our family. You have always done what is necessary to hold us together."

Blake sat forward also. "So what are you trying to tell me? That you expect me to do what you ask, because it is in my nature to be helpful and agreeable?"

By the looks on their faces, they were both growing increasingly sick with worry.

He scoffed. "Are you absolutely sure I am the brother you think I am? Because I sure as hell don't feel dutiful or agreeable toward *anyone* right now. What I'd really like to do is walk out of here and go find . . . What did you say his name was? Garrett? Yes, I have half a mind to tell you all to go to hell with your duties and expectations, because all I want to do is walk out of here this instant and start the hell over with my life."

"Good heavens," Rebecca said.

An uncomfortable silence ensued until his sister-in-law rose to her feet, crossed over the carpet and sat down beside him. "I understand this must be very difficult for you to hear," she said. "You've been through a terrible ordeal, Blake. But may I offer you some advice?"

"If you feel you must," he replied.

"You are a very fortunate person to have been born into the Pembroke dynasty, and I am not just referring to your family's wealth, power, and property, but to the devotion and loyalty of loved ones who would do anything for your happiness. Might I suggest you consider that? In the past, you have always honored that loyalty in return."

He glanced at his brother, who merely inclined his head in agreement.

"So your message to me," Blake said, "is that if I want the benefits and protection of my influential family, I have to do what you tell me to do."

"It is not quite like that," she replied. "We do not wish to force you into anything."

"The brother I grew up with," Devon said, "would want to do it of his own free will."

Blake studied Devon's eyes. "Did you marry *her* because you had to?"

He hesitated. "Yes, as a matter of fact I did. But as you can see, it worked out very well."

"Yes, obviously. Are you the only one who has done his duty thus far? You said Garrett is out of the country. What about Vincent?"

"He was just beginning his honeymoon when you were declared missing. His bride waits for him at home."

"They are deeply in love," Rebecca added. "As we hope you will be one day."

"One day . . . " he repeated. "You mean before Christmas. That rather puts the pressure on, does it not?"

Neither of them gave any response, so Blake decided it was time to end this conversation. There was another rather pressing one that required his attention.

He rose to his feet. "If you will both excuse me, I must go and speak to my hosts. But first I would like to know when you plan to return to England."

Devon paused. "That depends."

"On what?"

"On whether or not you intend to come with us, because we will not leave here without you."

Blake stood still for a moment, pondering what he now knew about his life and his future, while he regarded two very determined individuals who promised him an insurmountable family loyalty.

He could not deny he was curious about the other particulars of his life. He wanted to see the place where he was born and raised. His mother and father. He needed to know who he really was.

"I am eager to go home," he told them. "Perhaps seeing the palace will help me remember everything else."

"Then we shall leave in the morning," Devon replied. "At first light."

"So it seems the rush has already begun."

"It began quite some time ago," Devon somberly replied, "when our father began talking to ghosts."

Chapter 16

Blake strode into the library where Sebastian, Chelsea, and Melissa sat in chairs, each with a glass of brandy.

"We need to talk," he said to Chelsea, then turned to the others. "If you will excuse us."

Melissa stood and hurried out, but Sebastian was reluctant. "I will not excuse you if you are still inclined to hit things."

"Hit *people*, you mean." Blake was feeling impatient, and did not want to dally there while dancing around the point he intended to make. "No. You already satisfied my killer instincts sufficiently well, thank you. I'm quite over it now."

"It's all right, Sebastian," Chelsea said, touching her brother's arm. "I'll be fine."

Her brother rose and crossed the room, stopping beside Blake to deliver a warning glare. "If you lift one finger to harm her . . . "

They stared at each other for a moment, then Sebastian walked out.

"Your brother is quite adamant, suddenly, to be your heroic protector," Blake said as soon as the door swung shut behind him. "Too bad he's so selective in that regard, and didn't come to your rescue when I was helping myself to your virtue. If you could call it that. I doubt you know the meaning of the word."

Chelsea swallowed the rest of her brandy and set the glass down on the end table. "Must you be so vulgar?"

"I don't see why I shouldn't be. Ours was a vulgar affair from the beginning. It's not as if there was any affection between us. You said it yourself, we were using each other."

He saw her throat bob as she swallowed. "What did you want to discuss with me? I take it you're leaving."

"Yes, first thing in the morning, and you are coming with me."

"I beg your pardon?"

"You heard me." He paced around the room, fighting to keep his animosity under control, when so little else was within his power. Ever since he woke up on this godforsaken island he'd felt completely lost, with nowhere to go and no one to trust except this woman—and that turned out to be a bloody, ridiculous sham.

Now he was again finding himself plunked down upon a road not of his choosing, with a family who claimed they would do anything for his happiness, while they were dragging him back to England in a mad dash so he could marry someone—*anyone*—before the year was out.

All this to protect their inheritances.

His anger rose to a boil and he spoke harshly. "You could be carrying my child in your womb, Chelsea. Perhaps even a son."

"And if I am? What will you do?"

Recognizing the anxiety in her voice, he continued to pace the room. "If that turns out to be the case, we will be married and the child will be heir to my fortune and property, which evidently is quite substantial." He stopped, looked up and met her shocked gaze head on. "You didn't actually think I would allow a child of mine to be raised by false, charlatan parents, did you? And scheming ones at that."

"What if I don't want to go with you?" she asked.

"Then I will take you by force," he replied. "I will tie you up and . . . How did your mother put it? Oh yes . . . I will drag you by the hair if I have to."

"You wouldn't dare," Chelsea spat.

"Try me."

Her lips tightened into a pucker, while she sat

visibly furious, pondering her options. "What if we discover I am not carrying your child? What then?"

"Then I will ship you back here faster than you can blink your pretty little calculating eyes, and we will never see each other again."

She rose from her seat and went to pour herself another brandy. "So this discussion is not a proposal of marriage?"

"Hell no. At least not yet, for I will not condemn myself to a lifetime of misery with a scheming vixen like you, unless such a course of action is absolutely necessary. I will need to know your condition first."

He chose not to let her in on the fact that he was in urgent need of a wife before Christmas, for he was not ready to give up the possibility of being rid of her if she was not with child.

She laughed bitterly and faced him. "You expect me to agree to that, when you are treating me so appallingly, giving me no choice in the matter of my future?"

"You brought this on yourself," he said. "Besides, you couldn't possibly prefer for me to get down on bended knee and promise you hearts and flowers for the rest of your life. That would be a bald-faced lie, and neither of us would believe it. My suspicion is that you are praying your little heart out that you are *not* carrying my child, and that you will not have to marry me, because Lord knows, I will be the farthest thing you can imagine from a loving husband. You'd probably be better off with your ancient cousin."

She shivered noticeably.

"No? You don't think you'd be better off? Good. Then we are agreed." He started for the door. "Go pack your things. I don't want to be kept waiting in the morning, because I don't think I'll be able to tolerate one more minute than I have to on this god-awful island prison."

With that, he walked out and went straight upstairs to the guest chamber he had occupied for the past fortnight, and wondered where the hell he had been for the other two weeks he'd been missing.

"You have no choice now," Chelsea's mother said ten minutes later, as she barged into Chelsea's room and shut the door behind her. "Sebastian has informed me that Lord Blake knows of your deceitful scheming, and that he is not pleased you used him for stud."

"Mother . . . " Chelsea sat up on the bed.

"Hush! I should never have agreed to it. I have indulged you over the years, Chelsea, and this is my punishment. It appears there is nothing to be done now but to control the damage. The child—if there is one—can no longer be hidden or passed off as your brother's, therefore you must go to Lord Jerome instantly."

"I beg your pardon?" Chelsea rose to her feet.

"You must leave here tomorrow morning and marry your cousin straightaway. Let him have you in his bed as soon as it can be arranged—before the ceremony, if you can manage it. If you bear him a child, no one will ever know the difference, not even us. We will never speak of it again."

Chelsea frowned in dismay. "Mother, I cannot."

"You can, and you will. I will not tolerate any more rebellions from you. You will do as I say, whether you like it or not."

Chelsea's blood began to pound through her veins. "No, I will not do as you say." She strode to her dressing room and spotted her trunk. "I have already agreed to go to Pembroke Palace with Lord Blake." She dragged the trunk through the doorway to the edge of the carpet.

Her mother stopped pacing. "What? He has proposed to you? Surely not. He is the son of a duke. I don't believe it."

Chelsea flicked the latch, lifted the heavy lid, and flung it open. A damp, musty smell wafted out, causing her to recoil in disgust. How long had it been since she'd traveled?

"Not exactly," she explained, turning her face away. "He wishes to know if I am carrying his child, and if I am, we will be married and the child will inherit his fortune."

It was the truth. Some of it, at least.

"And if you are not?" her mother retorted in horror, following her back to the dressing room.

"Then we will part ways," Chelsea plainly said. "I will come home." She reached for two gowns, folded them over her arms and carried them back to the trunk.

Her mother's cheeks flared bloodred. "You expect me to agree to that? To allow you to go off on your own with no chaperone, nor any guarantee that you will be taken care of? That *we* will be taken care of?"

"Lady Hawthorne will be there to act as chaperone."

"But he will *wait* to decide if it is necessary to marry you? This is preposterous! What gentleman of good breeding would ever suggest such a thing? I am appalled, Chelsea, and I will not allow it. You will go to Lord Jerome. He has already offered to give you his name. It is a certainty."

Chelsea shook her head and returned to the dressing room. "You cannot hand me over to whomever you favor at any given moment, Mother. I have agreed to go with Lord Blake to Pembroke Palace, and I will not break my word. I've already engaged in enough unscrupulous behavior as it is. It's time I did the right thing for once. I will not make matters worse by trying again to pass off one man's child as another's."

"But this is no different from what you originally planned," her mother argued. "You were going to lie to Lord Blake and never reveal the truth to him. What has changed?"

Chelsea stopped in the dressing room doorway. "I suppose *I* have. I've discovered my conscience, Mother, as well as my heart. I had no idea it would be like this—that I would come to care so deeply for Blake—and I want to do the right thing. I want to be able to sleep at night, knowing I did not wrong an innocent man."

"The right thing? What if he jilts you and sends you home? What will you do then?"

She tossed two more gowns into the trunk and stood for a moment, thinking about her future.

"I will live out my days with my self-respect, at least." She glanced up at her mother. "If, on the other hand, I am carrying his child, you will be able to bask in the splendid knowledge that you will be grandmother to a ducal heir. Blake is third in line to the title. Our son would be fourth. That ought to cheer you up, Mother. Maybe if you say your prayers every night, all his older brothers will expire from illness or accident."

Her mother's eyes darkened. "That is uncalled for."

"Is it? I was under the impression you valued

a title above all else, including the happiness of your only daughter."

She returned to the dressing room, but her mother did not follow. When Chelsea came back out with her nightgown and undergarments draped over her arm, her mother was standing by the door with tears in her eyes.

Chelsea halted as a powerful wave of emotion washed over her. All she wanted was for her mother to understand what was important to her, and to respect her decision. She had not expected this. She had never, in all her life, seen actual tears in her mother's eyes. Was the woman finally experiencing a pang of conscience?

Still uncertain of her mother's true feelings, Chelsea took a step forward and softened her tone. "Have you never wished you had done something differently, Mother? Have you never regretted anything? Because I don't want to ever look back on this day and regret my actions. I don't want to live out my life ashamed of what I did."

For a long time her mother said nothing. She stood in front of the door watching Chelsea fold her belongings, when it was her maid's task to do so, and she was making a terrible mess of it.

"Go with him, then," her mother said. "Do what you must to ease your mind, if it means that much to you. And if he sends you home . . . " She paused, then cleared her throat. "If he sends you home, we will find a way to manage. I will be here waiting, and together we will decide what must be done for both of our futures." She started to turn away, but stopped in the doorway and waited there a moment. "I will pray that you have a safe journey."

Then she turned and walked out, leaving Chelsea to sink into a chair in a shocking and most unexpected state of astonishment, for her mother had finally begun to listen to what she had to say.

And perhaps she, too, was discovering that her heart was not impervious.

Melissa sat down on Chelsea's bed and began to weep. "Oh, Chelsea, I am so sorry. How could it have come to this? It is all my fault for agreeing to it. We should never have let you do what you did."

"It is not your fault," Chelsea told her as she went from wardrobe to dresser, searching for more undergarments, and continuing to throw everything haphazardly into the trunk. "It was my idea, remember? I wanted to do it, and not just to give you and Sebastian a child, but because I wanted some pleasure for myself. I was infatuated with him. You know I was."

"But surely you're not infatuated with him now, after he has treated you so severely."

"I can hardly blame him," Chelsea admitted. "I

lied to him and took advantage of his situation. We all did. He has every right to despise me." She stopped suddenly in the middle of the room with her hairbrush in one had, her mirror in the other, and looked across at her sister-in-law. "I am just sorry that you will not have the child you hoped for. Despite my selfish impulses, I truly did want to make you happy."

"You mustn't think of me," Melissa said, rising to her feet and wiping away her tears. "We will be fine. I accepted quite some time ago that my life was unfolding as fate intended it to. If I am not meant to be a mother, then so be it. I am not going to argue with God."

Chelsea walked to the window and looked out at the dark sea. The rain was coming down in sharp pellets that struck the glass in front of her face. She tilted her head forward to rest against it as a wave of melancholy washed over her. It seemed all she had done lately was argue not only with God, but with the people closest to her heart. Blake more than anyone, and now she was leaving her home and family to venture back into a world that had shunned her seven years ago. She felt as if she were standing on the edge of the cliff, teetering in the wind, about to fall into the sea at any moment.

In the window's reflection, she saw Melissa approach.

"I'll be honest," Melissa said. "I am surprised you did not put up more of a fight about going with him, because if you wanted an escape, we would help you. You could go somewhere on the island and hide. You do not have to do this."

Chelsea chuckled cynically. "How very theatrical that sounds, but no thank you. I believe I will take my medicine, no matter how bitter the taste." She turned around, leaned on the windowsill and sighed. "And I must confess something private to you, Melissa—something you may find surprising."

"What is it?"

She tilted her head back and marveled at how this outlandish situation had unfolded, when she had entered into it believing she was in full control of her emotions and her destiny. How wrong she'd been.

"As strange as it sounds, deep down there is a part of me that hopes I am carrying his child, and that he will be forced to marry me."

"Why?"

Chelsea suspected her sister-in-law already knew the answer to that question but wanted to hear her confess it.

"If that happens," she explained, "I will at least have a chance to earn his forgiveness and try to make him happy. Somehow."

"Chelsea—"

She did not let Melissa continue. "I cannot forget all the joys I have known since he came here, and how happy I was over the past few weeks. The hours I spent with him cannot compare to anything I've ever experienced in my life. I have come to realize I was living in a bubble, not really living at all—until he arrived and I fell completely in love with him."

Melissa took hold of her hand.

"Despite our quarrel tonight," Chelsea continued, "and despite the fact that I know he hates me now—and rightly so—I still want him. I want to go with him. I could not bear to marry Lord Jerome after knowing what it is to be with someone you love."

"Do you think he is capable of forgiving you?"

"I don't know. Right now it seems impossible, but I must at least try to make things right. Perhaps there is a chance."

"I suppose," Melissa said, "if that is the way you feel . . . "

"It is."

Her sister-in-law straightened and nodded. "Then clearly you have an important journey ahead of you." She glanced down at the sloppy state of Chelsea's trunk. "And I, for one, will not allow you to arrive at a duke's palace with all your gowns wrinkled. Come. Let us get you properly packed."

Chapter 17

❧

The waters across the Channel tossed the ship like a weightless toy, and Chelsea was unbearably ill. She had stepped aboard hoping that once they got under way, she would find an opportunity to speak to Blake privately and tell him she was sorry for everything.

She did not know if he would even be willing to hear her out, but she was at least determined to try.

She was not well enough to rise from her bunk, however, much less leave her cabin, so all her grand intentions were dashed onto the shoreline as soon as they broke away from the Jersey coast.

Sadly, after only a few hours at sea, she had no strength or energy left in her body to even wish otherwise. All she could do was lay like a stone in her cabin with a bucket on the floor beside her, accepting the fact that this was another form of punishment, which was certainly justified, while she dreamed of the blessed moment they would reach dry land.

"I think she's sick," Rebecca said to Devon as she approached her husband on the sloping deck of the ship. Cold spray flew up over the weather rails as the bow plunged down the trough of a massive wave. She held onto her husband's shoulder to keep her footing.

"Have you done anything for her?"

"Not yet," she replied. "I only heard her moaning in her cabin as I passed by. I knocked and asked if everything was all right, and she said it was, but I don't think she was being honest with me."

The wind blew Devon's thick black hair away from his face as he looked out at the raging water. "According to Blake, the woman has a deficiency when it comes to honesty."

"Yes." She was quiet for a moment. "But I find it so difficult to believe she actually did what he claims. To use a complete stranger in order to bear a secret child for her brother. It is beyond all ethics and propriety. I just cannot imagine it."

"It is shocking, indeed. Perhaps that is why I am so worried about Blake. I am troubled by his actions and his state of mind. Not only has he lost his memory, but he is dragging this woman back with us like a dog on a chain. It's not like him, and I'm surprised he even wanted her to come. After all he's been through, to be taken advantage like that, one would think he'd want to leave her behind."

"Perhaps it's not so strange," Rebecca replied. "She could be carrying his child, and it would be equally out of character for him to walk away from that responsibility." She glanced over her shoulder at her brother-in-law, who was standing alone on the other side of the ship, his cloak whipping in the wind. "Besides, he insists she has come willingly and that she understands his intentions—that he may or may not marry her when we arrive at Pembroke. So perhaps he did not actually *drag* her. And who knows? She might very well be pleased by this outcome, if she is the scheming type, for he is a Pembroke, and by any woman's standards a brilliant catch."

Devon sighed. "Whether her reputation was tarnished before or not, wouldn't it have been better to leave her at home with her family until her condition could be ascertained?"

"But Blake was adamant."

"I suppose we cannot blame him. How could he ever trust the Neufelds to tell him the truth?"

She shook her head sorrowfully as she watched Blake. "Oh, Devon, what has happened to him? He is not the same man, and I do not understand why he seems to resent us so much. All we did was tell him where he comes from and who he is. He seems so angry."

"Perhaps it is not *us* he resents, but the situation in general. He must be very frustrated about his memory loss, and angry over whatever happened that night, not to mention what happened after he was found—to be used and deceived in such a reprehensible way by his hosts and caregivers. And then we arrive and tell him he must marry by Christmas because Father has ordered it in his will."

"If only we knew what happened to him," she said. "Do you think he will ever remember? What if he does not? What if he remains a stranger to us forever?"

Devon watched his brother for a long time as the ship sailed over the waves and the spray flew up over the bowsprit. "Perhaps John Fenton will be able to shed some light on the events when we find him."

"If we ever do find him," she replied. "Despite all your searching, you and Vincent have not been able to find any trace of the family."

"Perhaps Vincent had better luck in France," he said. "I have already sent word to him that we have located Blake, so he will soon return to Pembroke, and then we will discover what he has learned."

A giant wave crashed thunderously against the

hull, and the captain called out a command to his crew to trim the sails.

"In the meantime," Rebecca said, as two young sailors contended with the rigging behind them, "what shall we do about our seasick travel companion?"

Devon's expression softened as he touched his wife's cheek. "Despite her past conduct, she is without her family and therefore under our protection. So why don't you go and see if there is anything you can do to make her more comfortable."

Rebecca nodded, then turned to go below deck.

Chelsea was just beginning to think her life had come to a cruel yet deserving conclusion when a knock sounded at her cabin door. She did not have the strength to answer. All she could do was lie there in her swirling bunk and stare up at the dizzying wooden beams over her head.

"Lady Chelsea, it's Rebecca. If you will let me in, I will see if there is anything I can do to help you."

Perhaps you can throw me overboard, she thought.

Five minutes later—or perhaps it was an hour, she had no idea—a key slipped into the lock, the door opened, and a steward held it open for Lady Hawthorne, who walked in on unsteady feet. The ship pitched and rolled, and she stumbled forward and grabbed hold of the bulkhead. The steward backed out and closed the door behind him.

"You poor dear." Lady Hawthorne removed the bucket and set it outside the room, then went to the porcelain washbasin, dipped a towel into the water, and returned to wipe Chelsea's face.

"Thank you," she managed to say. "You are very kind, but I would give one thousand pounds for something to drink. Some of that water, perhaps?"

"I am not sure I can recommend the water on board this ship," Rebecca said, rising to her feet, "but I will see what I can do."

"If you think the water might kill me," Chelsea replied, "then fill a jug to the brim and hurry back."

Rebecca gave her a funny look, then left the cabin. A few minutes later she returned and helped her sit up, then tipped a glass of something cool and tart over her lips.

"It's lemonade," Rebecca said, "straight from the captain's private reserves. Not too much, Chelsea. You must keep it down."

She swallowed a few sips, then lay back on the pillow.

"I suppose he's pleased I am feeling so poorly," Chelsea mumbled as she laid her forearm across her eyes.

"Do you mean Blake?" Rebecca held the remaining lemonade on her lap.

"Yes. He's quite angry with me, as I'm sure you must know, and I can hardly blame him. I can't imagine what you and your husband must think of me."

Rebecca said nothing for a long moment, then looked down at the glass of lemonade. "It is not my place to comment."

"But surely you want to say *something* to me," Chelsea replied. "I can sense it. Please feel free to be honest, even if you want to call me a wicked, scheming hellion who deserves the worst. It would only be the truth."

Rebecca reached for the towel and wiped her face. "So it *is* true, then. I wasn't sure. I thought perhaps there had been some mistake or miscommunication."

Chelsea shook her head. "No, there was not. I did what he said I did. I cannot deny it. I wanted to give my brother and his wife a child. They can't have one of their own, you see, and since I had no future to speak of, I thought it would be a very simple thing to do, and a very generous gift on my part." She sighed heavily. "I realize now that I was living a very sheltered life on that island, and was perhaps disconnected from the real world and the realities of the human heart, for I thought my own heart and conscience would stay out of it."

"But they did not?" Rebecca asked matter-of-factly.

"No, they did not. And I feel terrible about it now, Lady Hawthorne. I hope you can believe that. If I could take it all back, I would, if not for the fact that I would never have known the most wonderful two weeks of my life, nor would I be coming with you to Pembroke. I would have had to say goodbye to him and marry my cousin, and I am at least glad that I am still with you, because I care for him very much."

Rebecca looked at her with confusion. "Have you told him this?"

"No. I thought I would try to say these things when we set sail, but unfortunately I cannot move."

Rebecca slowly stood up and went to the washbasin. She rinsed out the towel and hung it on a hook, then returned to the bunk. "Blake has been through a terrible ordeal, Chelsea. Clearly, he feels very alone and angry, and all I want is for him to be happy again. So when we reach port in Southampton, I hope you will tell him what you just told me, even if it takes time to make him listen. I believe it would help him to know that whatever happened between you was not completely without feeling."

Chelsea nodded weakly. "You are a kind woman."

She paused and took a deep breath. "As I said, all I want is for Blake to be happy again."

"Whether you believe it or not," Chelsea replied, "I want the same thing."

Chelsea stared dizzily at Rebecca's red hair and striking green eyes, then placed her hand over her roiling stomach and said a silent prayer that she would survive the rest of this journey. Because if she was going to make amends, she would not only require calmer waters, but a much calmer stomach as well.

Chapter 18

❧⟋⟍❧

By the time the ship docked on the mainland, Chelsea had recovered enough to rise from her bunk, change her clothes, and wash up. She even ate some porridge and managed to keep it down long enough to consider it digested.

The world was much calmer at port, she discovered when she stepped up onto the deck of the ship and at last breathed in some much needed fresh air. She felt more awake and alive now, and stood still, taking in the atmosphere of the London dockyards – the sailors loading wooden crates onto wagons, the thick scent of coal smoke in the foggy air, mixed with the stench of dead fish. Voices swelled as streams of people rushed along the docks to wherever they were going, stepping around heavy coils of rope and large crates of cargo. In such a hurry they all were.

Chelsea closed her eyes and recalled the life she had once known here in London, the sound of her heels clicking along Regent Street, the colors of the fabrics in the shops, the hats, umbrellas and parasols, and the sensation of bumping elbows with someone at the flower market. She had forgotten all of that during the past seven years. She heard only the sounds of the sea and knew intimately the many shades of the sky. She would have never given London life another thought if she hadn't found Blake in the cave that day and boarded a ship to follow him back to the world that had once been her home. Now she was here again, returned to this bustling life.

A bell rang in the distance, and she adjusted her footing as the ship bobbed and tapped gently against the dock. She took one step forward, then another, tipped her head back and looked up.

The sky appeared ready to dump buckets of rain at any moment. Swirling gray clouds hovered low overhead, casting a heavy shadow over the ships tied up at the dock. She could smell rain.

She had not forgotten the stories she'd read in the papers about England enduring the wettest spring in over a century, and hoped the foul weather would at least hold off until they reached Pembroke. The last thing they needed was to have their carriage swept away in a mud slide. She did not think she could bear any more wild careening movements on this journey.

As she made her way down the gangplank

behind Rebecca and Devon, she searched the busy dock for any sign of Blake, who might have disembarked first. She had not seen him since they boarded the ship in Jersey.

He was not among the crowd, however. It was as if he had deserted her, and wanted nothing more to do with his family either.

Much later, when a porter hoisted their bags onto the roof of the coach, he finally appeared on the ship's deck and disembarked. He spoke to Devon briefly, then without a word assisted Chelsea and Rebecca into the coach. He waited for Devon to have everything arranged before he climbed inside and joined them, mere seconds before the coach rolled off.

They traveled mostly in silence, though Devon and Rebecca did spend some time revealing details about the palace and Blake's mother, the duchess, and his sister, Charlotte. Devon told him stories of their childhood—how they used to play in the subterranean passages of the great house and frighten their sister with spiders and ghost stories. Blake remembered none of it.

Late in the afternoon, they stopped at a coaching inn to change horses and get something to eat. Blake went straight to the barkeep and ordered a mug of ale, while Rebecca and Chelsea found a table and ordered wine.

"I think I will go and see if Devon needs me,"

Rebecca said, rising from her chair. "And I will tell Blake to come over here and sit with you."

"He won't want to," she replied. "He has not spoken a word to me since we left Jersey."

"You just need some time alone with him." She spotted her husband walking into the taproom. "Devon and I might be an hour or so, as we will be taking our dinner privately upstairs."

Chelsea watched the marquess pass Blake at the bar and say something in his ear, then he joined his wife. They headed upstairs together.

Blake turned and met her gaze. She raised an expectant eyebrow at him, and he rolled his eyes before picking up his ale and striding across the room to her table.

"My brother informs me that it is not acceptable for me to allow you to eat alone," he said, "when there are so many disreputable characters lurking about." He glanced about at the other patrons.

She picked up her wine. "As you can see, we are surrounded by cheerful travelers not unlike us, so you may relax. I am more than capable of taking care of myself."

"Mm. You're probably right, because by the look of things, *you* are the most disreputable character in the room."

She kept her eyes leveled on his. "You're right, I will not deny it. I am a wicked person. In that case, maybe *you* are the one who needs protection.

I can't blame you if you are afraid to sit with me. I would be, too, in your position."

He regarded her coolly, then pulled a chair out and sat down. Lounging back, he stretched his long legs out into the aisle between the tables and fixed his attention on the front windows.

Chelsea took a sip of wine. "You're going to have to talk to me at some point."

"Do you think so?"

"Yes," she replied.

"And why is that?"

"At the very least, you'll need to know whether or not I am carrying your child. Unless you intend to have a messenger go from my room to yours with the necessary correspondence on the day I receive my courses. *If* I receive them."

Still, he did not turn in his chair to face her. "That's not a bad idea, actually. My brother tells me I'm rich. I'll hire someone for that purpose alone. He'll sit outside your door day and night, waiting for news." He glanced over his shoulder at her. "Or how about this idea? He could do double duty, and stand guard while you are locked up in your chamber. We shall call you 'the Pembroke prisoner.'"

"Now you're being ridiculous."

She expected him to say something, but he merely turned his cold eyes back to the front windows.

The server came and took their orders for supper. After she left, Chelsea tapped her fingers on the table. This was not going well. She was finding it extremely difficult to apologize and grovel when he was treating her with such frosty disdain.

She took a deep breath and let it out in resignation. "Blake," she said, "we cannot continue like this. We really need to talk about what happened. I didn't get a chance to explain myself the other night. What you saw between my mother and me . . . it was not what you thought it was."

"You were using me for stud, Chelsea. I don't need to know anything else."

She wet her lips and steeled her resolve. "But there is so much more to it than that. It was never that simple. Or perhaps it was at first, but . . . When you heard me tell my mother that I did not want to go to your bed that night, it was not because I didn't *want* to."

He took a drink. "Try to make sense when you talk."

"I am trying, but it's difficult."

He glanced over his shoulder again, and she became distracted by how handsome he was. That perfect, chiseled jaw, the soft lips, and those dark, arresting eyes made it almost impossible to think. She took a deep breath and felt completely defeated.

"I didn't want to go to your bed that night," she said, digging deep for resolve, "because I was confused and frightened. When I started out on this twisted path to conceive a child, I didn't realize . . . "

Uncertain how to put it, she paused.

"You didn't realize what?" he asked. His hateful tone did nothing to relieve her anxieties.

"I didn't realize how much I would come to care for you. We enjoyed each other's company. You know we did. And that night I was . . . " She swallowed. "I was afraid I was falling in love with you, and I didn't know what to do."

For a long moment he stared at her, but she could read nothing from his expression. There was no change. He still appeared completely indifferent to her discomfort.

He looked out the window again and took another drink.

"Will you not say something?" she asked. "Please, just say anything. I am telling you the truth. That night, my mother was making everything sound so crude and sordid, asking me distasteful questions I did not wish to answer, and I was angry with her. That's why I resisted going to your room, because she was telling me I had no choice."

"And we both know how much you despise doing what you're told."

"You feel the same. Don't pretend otherwise."

He glared at her. "I never deceived you."

"You called me by another woman's name."

His expression darkened. "We're back to that, are we? I told you I had no control over that. You knew I remembered nothing from my life, and still I do not. You also knew what you were getting yourself into, obviously, because you never intended for it be anything more than just sex for one purpose."

She slumped back in her chair. "Indeed, that's what I intended at first, but please understand what I am trying to say. It became more than that, because I developed feelings for you." She glanced around the room and lowered her voice. "I loved everything we did together, not just in bed, but the walking and talking and writing and sketching. If you had any idea how guilty I felt about what I was doing—"

"Yet you continued doing it."

She sat forward again. "I wanted to stop, but I couldn't resist seeing you. And I wanted to tell you the truth, but I was afraid you would be angry, and I didn't want to disappoint my brother and sister-in-law, or spoil the time we had left together, because I didn't know how long it would last. I was living in constant fear that one morning you would wake up and remember where you came from, and you would simply disappear.

I didn't want that to happen. I wanted you to stay. It was all so much like a dream that I couldn't believe it was real. I still cannot believe it."

He made no reply. All he did was stare straight ahead, but at least he appeared to be listening.

"I would have told you the truth eventually," she said, "but I didn't get the chance. You discovered it yourself in the most dreadful way, and now all I can do is beg for your forgiveness. I hate what I did. I was so stupid and—"

"Yes," he said, turning in his chair to face her, and slamming his glass down on the table. "You were stupid."

Chelsea was shaken by his sound admonishment. It was agonizing to see him look at her with such hatred and disgust.

She lowered her gaze.

"All I can do now," she said, "is tell you how sorry I am. If I could take it all back, I would. Except that if I did, I would never have known what it felt like to be in love. And that part, at least, was heaven."

She could not bring herself to look up at him, though she could feel his eyes on her face, staring at her with fiery intensity. It was as if the space between them was exploding with the heat of his bitterness.

After a few excruciating seconds, he relaxed and sat back in his chair, picked up his ale, and swiveled around to face the windows again. She had to fight hard for the courage to look up.

The server brought their dinners then, set both plates down on the table and quickly left.

For a brief time Blake did not acknowledge the supper. Neither did she. Then at last he stood.

"I think I'll take mine at the bar," he said.

He picked up the plate and walked off, leaving Chelsea to sit alone and stare down at her unappetizing food while she struggled very hard not to cry.

Chapter 19

By the time the coach rolled up the long, winding hill to Pembroke Palace, Blake was ready to throw open the door and leap out of the moving vehicle.

Chelsea had not spoken one word to him since they left the coaching inn. She sat across from him in moody silence, clearly angry with him for not accepting her apology. Or was she legitimately hurt and heartbroken? He did not want to consider that—he did not want to *feel* anything—so he steered away from the notion. Perhaps she was merely insulted over the fact that he had not remained at her table to eat his dinner. Or maybe it was all an act.

The workings of her mind were a mystery to him, and he was not inclined to analyze any of it. He did not want to try and guess at what she was feeling, because he had no idea if what she'd said at the inn was true. She had done nothing but lie to him from the beginning, and he did not trust her. He trusted no one.

Nor did he want to feel any compassion for her. He did not want to care if she was afraid or lonely for her home and family. He was not going to let it bother him, because if she felt that way, it was her own fault.

Bloody hell. How did she think *he* had felt, waking up on a strange, remote island, half dead, his body unexplainably impaled? He certainly felt lost and forsaken then, and what had she done? She'd used him for her own perverted ambitions. She tricked him into becoming her stud, and if he had not discovered the ruse for himself the very night his brother came to collect him, he might never have known. Years could have passed without him ever knowing he had a child—conceivably a boy, the future Earl Neufeld!

It sickened him to think of it, made him seethe with disgust and disbelief.

What if one day in the future, not knowing the young man's true identity, his own daughter or niece met the young man and fell in love with him? Or wanted to marry him? His family might very well have permitted it.

He slammed his fist down on the windowsill, attracting the others' attention. They stared at him with questioning eyes, but he ignored them and looked out the mud-splattered window as the coach rumbled heavily up the crest of a hill and moved through the entrance archway to Pembroke Palace.

He sat forward to inspect the massive house in the mist—the place where he had been born and raised.

Sadly, nothing was familiar. He had not recognized the grounds or the lake during the approach, nor was there anything familiar about the house itself, which stretched across the rain-drenched land like a great royal city. It boasted ornamental statues, a massive, grand portico, and a wealthy abundance of columns and finials with flags flying triumphantly in the wind.

It was a palace to rival any other. That much he understood, even without the benefit of his memories. It was a testament to what Rebecca had said to him the other night—that he was a very privileged member of a powerful and renowned English family. He should be thankful.

He reached into his pocket for the watch Chelsea had found on the beach. He checked the time, but still did not recognize the damn thing. He slipped it back into his pocket.

When at last they rolled up to the wide steps at the front entrance, he climbed out of the coach and, without a word to encourage Chelsea or make her feel welcome, offered his arm to her.

He glanced at the clock tower overhead as

he escorted her up the steps behind Devon and Rebecca, and felt a strange rush of dread in his core, which he did not fully understand. Was it simply because he knew his father was losing his mind, and that he must marry before Christmas? It didn't feel like that was the source of it. Perhaps somewhere in the deepest recesses of his mind he *did* remember other things, and now that he was home again, it would all come back to him, as Chelsea had suggested . . .

They passed through the front door and entered the great marble hall, adorned with portraits, clean white columns, and impressive statues and busts. He looked up at a high frescoed ceiling— a scene of warrior angels battling their enemies against a vivid blue sky, dotted with white clouds. It had been painted by a gifted artist. The colors were subdued, yet vibrant, and the details were well-thought-out. All the noise and action was there for an appreciative art lover to admire. He was, in a word, mesmerized.

When at last he tore his gaze away, he noted that his brother was watching him intently.

"It was painted in 1612 by Ramon Junius," Devon said. "And there is another of his great works in the chapel."

"It's very impressive." Blake looked up again, but his attention quickly darted to a woman standing under the keystone arch to a gallery beyond the main hall. She stopped and placed a hand over her heart, then picked up her skirts and dashed toward him.

Devon leaned in and whispered, "Your mother, the duchess."

He was grateful for the clarification, for he would never have guessed this beautiful, golden-haired woman was a day over thirty-five. She was slender and lovely, with youthful blue eyes and an ivory complexion.

But how could any man not recognize his own mother?

"Blake, my son." She wrapped her arms around his neck and wept into his shoulder. "I thought you were dead."

"I'm perfectly fine," he assured her, even though it was not entirely true.

Drawing away from him, still half weeping with joy, she acknowledged Chelsea at his side.

"Mother," Devon said, stepping forward—and again Blake was grateful for his brother's helpful interruption—"this is Lady Chelsea Campion. She found Blake in a sea cave in Jersey and saved his life."

The duchess's eyes warmed instantly. "Oh, my dear. How can we ever thank you?"

"That is completely unnecessary, Your Grace," Chelsea replied. "I only did what any person would have done in such circumstances."

Hardly, Blake thought.

"I will want to hear everything," his mother said. "I must know what happened to you. Every detail."

Just then a lanky, elderly gentleman marched out of nowhere, startling all of them with his harried gait and panicked expression. His frizzy white hair flew about in all directions, and he wore nothing on his feet—no shoes, no stockings, nothing.

"This is your father," Devon quickly said. "Say not a word about your memory loss. Pretend you know him."

"Where the devil have you been?" the duke demanded as he came to a halt in front of Blake. "Did you find Garrett?"

"No, I did not."

The man's wild eyes darted to Chelsea. "Is this your wife?"

"No."

"Why not?" His gaze traveled from her face to the hem of her skirts. "She's pretty enough."

To his surprise, Chelsea smiled and curtsied. "Thank you, Your Grace."

Blake was not charmed, however. Turning to her, at his side, he spoke in a cool tone. "She is just a guest."

The duke examined her with a critical eye. He circled around her, looked down at her hips and backside, and squinted closely at the back of her head.

Blake took an assertive step forward to intercede, for he did not like any man's eyes on her that way, but Devon stopped him with a hand and discreetly shook his head.

"She would make a good wife," the duke said, coming around to her front again. "Why won't you have her? What's wrong with you? Are you blind? Or too fussy?"

Blake wasn't sure if he should laugh or hit something. This was completely absurd.

"We are just acquaintances, Your Grace," Chelsea said. "We met only recently."

"Ah," the duke said, winking playfully at her. "Well, perhaps you will win his heart yet, my young beauty. Stranger things have happened, when lovers meet at Pembroke." He lowered his voice and leaned in closer. "We have secret passages, you know, from room to room. That's why our shooting parties are always so popular. The gentlemen go out with the guns during the day, and bring them out fully loaded again at night, if you grasp my meaning."

The duchess cleared her throat and took her husband by the arm. "Come Theodore, it's almost time for dinner. You must go and get ready. We're having beef tonight."

"Beef you say?" He seemed to forget what they

had been discussing, as well as the fact that his son had just returned after being missing for a month.

Blake glanced down at Chelsea.

"What an interesting man your father is," she said. "He has a sense of humor."

Rebecca smiled at her. "He certainly has his moments, but we do love him."

"No doubt," Chelsea replied.

Blake could only shake his head. "Where are my rooms?" he asked, because he needed to get the hell away from all these people he did not know.

That night, Blake sat up in bed and shouted into the darkness.

His gaze darted from the unlit fireplace to the window, then back and forth between the various pieces of heavy furniture adorning the room. Where the hell was he?

It took him a moment to remember that this was Pembroke Palace and he had returned to his home that very day, and this was his own private bedchamber. He had slept here since he was a boy.

The dream flashed again in his mind.

Tossing the covers aside, he leaped out of bed and strode to the table in the far corner of the room, where all his sketches were strewn about in a disorganized pile. Moonlight shone in through the paned window. It provided sufficient light to see the papers, which he sorted through with frantic hands, searching feverishly for the one he wanted.

At last he found it—the sketch he had done of Chelsea that first day, when she took him down to the beach to sit on the rocks.

He held it up to the moonlight and focused on the first thing he had drawn when a pencil found its way into his hand—the emblem in the corner. The octagonal shape he somehow knew but could not explain.

A sudden, violent rage erupted in his gut, and he clenched his jaw, resisting the urge to snarl like an animal and throw this bloody table out the window.

But why was he so angry? Why did he want to grab someone by the throat and squeeze? If only he could remember . . .

Or had he already strangled someone?

He dropped the sketch as if it had caught fire, and turned his hands over to look at his palms. Terror gripped his mind, and he backed away from the table and bumped into the bedpost.

He put a fist to his forehead and shut his eyes, straining to remember something. Anything. But all he could think of was Chelsea. He wanted her here, close to him, even after all that had passed between them.

He turned and started for the door. He had no idea what room she was in, but he had to find her. He needed her calm presence. He needed to talk to her about the dream and see her familiar face, smell her hair and hold her.

He stopped himself.

Looking back at his disheveled bed, he rummaged around inside his mind for composure, and cursed this wretched yearning. Bloody hell, it was like some sort of addiction! She was the only person in the world he knew intimately, the only one who was familiar to him, especially now that he was in a strange place again.

That alone was why he wanted her, he told himself. There was no other reason.

Blake shut his eyes and remembered that he had a life of his own now, which included a great home with three brothers and a sister, and a duke and duchess for parents.

He did not need a scheming vixen he could not trust, except for the fact that she might be carrying his child. If not for that, he would have left her behind in Jersey without a single glance over his shoulder.

Breathing slowly, he tried again to calm the unexplainable wrath he still felt from the dream, and tried instead to focus on what it meant. He returned to the sketch on the table, picked it up and looked at it in the bluish moonlight. All he saw, however, was the portrait of Chelsea, which he had drawn while sitting on the rocks, the day after they made love for the first time. He could almost feel the sea breezes of Jersey blowing through the room. He could smell the salt in the air, hear the eternal hiss and roar of the ocean, and the seabirds calling out to one another.

Still fighting his stubborn desire to see her, he picked up his pencil and began sharpening it, then settled down on the bed to put the images he saw in his mind down onto paper. He hoped it would be enough to satisfy him.

Chapter 20

The following morning dawned with a thick and heavy humidity, and a fine mist blotted out the horizon. After staying up all night to sketch a number of portraits of Chelsea, Blake felt both spirited and restless. He put the sketches into a box on the table, rose from the bed, dressed and ventured outside to the stables, looking for a horse to ride.

The groom informed him which one was his favorite—a black gelding by the name of Thatcher—and in short order he was trotting out of the stable courtyard on Thatcher's able back and heading in the direction of the lake.

It would do him good, he decided, to explore the estate and see if he recognized anything. Perhaps an image from his childhood would materialize in his mind. Or something from more recent times.

He rode down the lane and crossed the stone bridge. Thatcher's hooves clopped steadily as he cantered along the west side of the lake. Blake could not help but admire the lush green landscape and revel in the peaceful sounds of nature—the ducks quacking on the still lake waters, the birds chirping in the treetops.

It was nothing like the wild ruggedness of Jersey, with the constant thunder of the surf as it pounded against the steep cliffs, and the amazing force of the wind, blowing through the shrubs and trees and grasses. It was a very different world.

He came to the far end of the lake, where it narrowed to a river, and followed a gravel path into the woods. He soon reached a whitewater cascade, where the noise of the rushing river drowned out the tranquility of the forest. He stopped for a moment to listen to its impressive roar—which to his great annoyance reminded him again of Jersey—then urged his horse onward, only to pull Thatcher to a halt when he encountered another early morning explorer making her way gingerly along the path on foot.

Chelsea . . .

She, too, stopped in her tracks.

His horse skittered sideways at the unexpected presence of another person. *"Whoa, now,"* he said, to ease the animal's agitation.

He had not wanted to see or talk to her this morning, or even think about her, so he simply tipped his hat.

She curtsied. "Good morning."

He promptly turned Thatcher around to head back in the other direction.

"Wait, please!" Chelsea called after him with a hint of desperation, which made him stop again. *Damn*. He closed his eyes.

When he turned around, she was walking toward him. "Please don't go. I've lost my way."

He took in her appearance. She carried her notebook at her side, and her skirt was smeared with mud.

"Did you lose your footing somewhere?" he asked.

She glanced down at her dress. "Yes. I came from that direction." She pointed behind her. "I had to cross over what turned out to be a steep mud slick. I've been following this river for an hour, you see, and I don't know how to get back to the palace. It's not the same when you can't hear the sea."

Thatcher anxiously sidestepped on the path, while Blake observed the clear note of distress in Chelsea's voice. Tossing a leg over the saddle, he hopped down, took hold of the reins and led Thatcher toward her.

"Are you hurt?"

"I'm fine," she assured him. "It was clumsy of me, that's all."

He looked down at the dark mud ground into

her skirt and knew that she could not possibly have come through such an accident unscathed.

Reaching carefully for her hand, he lifted it and turned it over to examine the chafed skin on the heels of her palms.

His eyes lifted. "This looks painful."

She pulled her hand away and hugged the notebook to her chest. "It's nothing."

"The palace is this way." He gestured in the opposite direction. "I'll take you back."

"That's not necessary. I don't want to interrupt your ride. Now that I know which direction is the right one, I'll be on my way." She started along the path, but he could see she was working hard to hide a limp.

"Don't be stubborn," he said.

She kept walking. "I'm perfectly fine, Blake."

He followed with his horse in tow. "No, you are not. Let me take you back."

He caught up with her. At last she stopped and faced him.

He glanced down at her notebook and made an effort to distract her from her impenetrable pride, which clearly was keeping her from accepting his assistance. "Were you writing?"

"I was trying to, but the words wouldn't come. It's so quiet here, and strange. Nothing feels right."

"I know what you mean." Then he realized for the first time that he might as well have been born on that bloody island a few weeks ago. It was all he knew.

"I'm accustomed to the sound of the sea," she continued. "And the smell of it, the feel of it in the air. It's difficult to explain, but I feel quite . . . *displaced*."

He felt displaced himself. He had felt that way since he saw her mother dragging her up the stairs that final night.

"Let me take you back to the palace," he said again, struggling with the weight of his concern for her welfare and the genuine grief he felt, seeing her lost like this, when he was still so angry with her for what she had done.

He had not forgotten. He would never forget. But he could not bear the idea of her falling and hurting herself.

She turned away from him again and looked off in the direction of the wooded glen behind them. "This is not what I expected," she said. "I wanted to come here and be formidable, and try to make things right between us, but I'm not sure I have the stamina for this."

"For what?" he asked irritably, worrying that she might want to leave, when she had agreed to stay until they knew her condition.

"For the waiting," she replied, meeting his gaze. "I don't know how long we will go on like this, and I feel very lost. There is no one I can talk to—no one who is close to me. Your sister-in-law, Rebecca, has been very kind, but I feel like such an interloper. I am ashamed of my reason for being here, and I know everyone is suspicious of me. I cannot even look your mother in the eye, because she is such a lovely woman and she knows what I did. It's not easy."

He had promised himself he would not feel sorry for her or sympathize with her situation—not after what she'd put him through—but try as he might, he could not help it.

"Please," he said, still laboring to keep a hard edge to his heart. "Allow me to take you back." He held out a gloved hand.

She stared at it and considered her options.

Or perhaps she was thinking of her choices in the past . . .

Finally, she placed her hand in his and let him assist her up into the saddle, the bridle in his other hand as he held the horse steady. When she was comfortably situated, he touched her ankle.

"May I?"

She nodded.

Standing below her, he lifted her skirts and discovered a mud-stained stocking. He followed it up to a chafed and bloody thigh.

"Chelsea . . . "

"Yes, it hurts," she finally admitted. "But I will not have you fussing over me."

He lowered her skirt and covered her leg, then led Thatcher down the wooded path. "When we reach the palace, I'll send the housekeeper to see you. She's very good with cuts and scrapes."

"How do you know that?" Chelsea quickly asked. "Do you remember things about her?"

He felt his eyebrows pull together with surprise. "Yes. Somehow I do. I know this one thing." A flicker of hope alighted in him. Perhaps in time he would remember more.

He reached into his pocket and pulled out the watch. He looked at the gold hands and black Roman numerals, but still, it was unfamiliar. He slipped it back into his pocket.

"Have you seen the Italian Gardens yet?" she asked. "Because I believe that is what you pictured in your mind that day on the beach. You mentioned mud puddles and a fountain and statue. When I looked out my window this morning, that is exactly what I saw."

He shook his head. "I have not seen it. The garden is below your window, you say?"

"Yes. Your sister mentioned it to me last night. She said your father moved all the flowers and shrubs to higher ground because he believes the palace is cursed and a flood is coming. It is a symptom of his illness. So that explains the mud puddles you saw in your mind, and why you thought it was depressing. It was a true memory, Blake, and that is good news."

Indeed it was.

They made their way through the woods to where the river widened into the lake.

"Did you sleep well last night?" she asked.

"Not a wink. I woke up in a cold sweat again." He glanced over his shoulder. "And you should be thankful you were not there, because if you had been, I probably would have thrown you to the floor in typical fashion and attempted to strangle you. It would have felt quite good, too, I suspect."

The horse plodded along slowly. A blackbird fluttered out of a leafy tree as they passed.

"Was there no candlestick handy to bludgeon me with?" Chelsea asked. "Because that is, after all, your weapon of choice in such situations."

"There's only a rather cumbersome lamp next to my bed."

"Well, that wouldn't do at all."

He found himself chuckling, and was quite certain it was the first time he'd smiled since he arrived at the palace.

"Did you have another dream that caused you to wake up in that state?" she asked.

He was glad he was walking ahead of her, and therefore did not have to look into her eyes.

"Yes."

"What was it about?"

"I wish I knew. All I remember is waking up in a rage and wanting to brawl. And then I recalled that strange emblem I drew on the beach that day." He glanced behind him. "Do you remember? You asked me about it."

"Yes, I remember exactly. Do you still have the sketch?"

"I do."

"You should show it to your brother. Maybe he will recognize the symbol."

"I will do that when we get back."

They walked around the lake and crossed over the bridge, then started up the lane toward the palace at the top of the hill.

"You have an extraordinary home, Blake," Chelsea said. "I do believe there is nothing in England to compare."

"I am a fortunate man."

"Yes." She was quiet for a long time. "But I must ask . . . Have you given any thought to what I said to you at the coaching inn?"

He felt his insides seize up, but fought not to let it show. "Which part?"

"The part where I told you I was sorry. I am, and I hope that one day you might be able to forgive me and believe that I do care for you. No matter what happens between us, whether I am with child or not, I want us both to at least have fond memories of each other."

He kept walking, and wished she were not in the habit of speaking so openly.

"I'm not very good at memories," he said.

"Not the old ones, but maybe the new ones will have a better chance of staying with you."

He looked down at his boots while he walked. The horse ambled along behind him, his head bobbing as he clopped up the lane.

"I predict they will," Blake finally said, for he could not imagine he would ever forget those early days of this new life.

They passed under the entrance archway that led to the cobbled courtyard, and reached the front steps at the main door. Blake reached up, put his gloved hands around Chelsea's tiny waist, and assisted her off the horse. Her skirts billowed as she landed softly on the ground. He stood for a moment, not quite ready to let go.

"Thank you," she said. Her voice was quiet and vulnerable.

"I'll send the housekeeper to your room."

Still, neither of them made a move to step apart.

"Blake," Chelsea whispered. She wet her lips and gripped his forearms. "Please believe that I regret what happened. And I miss you. I want what we had before. I can't bear this."

An enormous part of him wanted to speak the same words to her in return—*I miss you, too*—but he could not do it. He could not bring himself to trust that what they'd had in Jersey was real, or that *any* of this was real. This world around him still felt like a fiction, because he did not *feel* it. The only past he had was with her, but that had been a sham.

He lowered his hands to his sides and backed away from her, and without another word took hold of Thatcher's reins and headed back to the stables.

Chapter 21

⟨∿⟩

C helsea sucked in a breath and bit her lip the instant the cloth touched her bloodied thigh.

The housekeeper, Mrs. Callahan, drew back and tilted her head to the side. "I'm very sorry, my lady," she said. "I know it's painful. It's a terrible scrape, but I must make sure there is no dirt in the wound. We wouldn't want it to fester." She dipped the cloth into the bowl of water and squeezed it out. "I'll try to be gentle."

"And I will try to be brave," Chelsea replied.

Sitting back, she squeezed the mahogany arms of the Chippendale chair and remembered how brave Blake had been that first night, when he watched her stitch up his wound, which had been far worse than a silly scraped leg.

A knock sounded at the door. Mrs. Callahan stopped what she was doing, rose to her feet and crossed the chamber to answer it. "Lady Charlotte . . . "

"I hear our guest took a tumble," Charlotte said. "I came to see if there is anything I can do. It's not life-threatening, I hope." She peered in at Chelsea, who was sitting in front of the unlit fireplace.

"Please, come in," Chelsea said. "You can distract me from the perils of my treatment."

She had met Lady Charlotte the night before, at dinner, and afterward they spent time chatting in the drawing room when the family gathered to read and play cards. At twenty-three, Charlotte and her twin brother Garrett were the duke and duchess's two youngest children.

From what Chelsea had gathered, the entire family, except the duke, now knew the actual reason for her presence here—because Blake was waiting to establish her condition in order to determine if a wedding would be necessary.

Now, Charlotte entered with a friendly countenance, and Chelsea found it oddly disconcerting that the members of the family were so at ease with the circumstances. They appeared perfectly content to wait for her courses to begin—or not begin—as if this sort of thing happened at Pembroke all the time. They might as well have been waiting for a simple change in the weather.

"May I ask what happened?" Charlotte laid a hand on the back of her chair. "I heard you were walking by the river. It's very dangerous in certain places this time of year, with all the recent rains. You really must be careful."

"Don't worry, I learned my lesson," Chelsea replied, trying not to wince as Mrs. Callahan washed the dried blood from the most tender part of the abrasion. "It was foolish of me. I became lost, and crossed over a ridge that turned out to be a river of mud on the other side."

The color drained from Charlotte's face. "Oh. I know the spot, exactly."

"You do?"

"Yes, there was an accident there three years ago. A young woman died when the horse she was riding slipped and plummeted down the hill."

Chelsea was aware of Mrs. Callahan's noteworthy pause. The housekeeper lifted her eyes briefly, before continuing to wash the wound.

"I'm sorry to hear that," Chelsea said. "Blake didn't mention anything—" Then she realized what she was saying and looked down at her lap. "But no, I suppose he wouldn't remember it."

"Well," Charlotte said in a more cheerful voice, "I'm just glad you were not seriously hurt. How is she faring, Mrs. Callahan? Will she suffer any permanent damage?"

The housekeeper sat back on her heels and dropped the bloodstained cloth into the bowl. "By the looks of things, she'll recover. It's a bad scrape, to be sure, but not deep. Nevertheless, you'll be sore for a few days."

Chelsea tossed the hem of her skirt over her leg. "I believe I can tolerate a little pain. Thank you so much for your kind assistance, Mrs. Callahan."

The woman spoke with caring. "You must let me know if there is anything else you need, my lady. Anything at all. I will do my best to make sure you are well taken care of." She picked up the bowl of water and left the room.

"She likes you," Charlotte said after the door closed behind her.

"I can't imagine why," Chelsea replied. "I've done nothing extraordinary, outside of falling on my backside and giving her more laundry to do."

She chose not to mention the fact that she had deceived Blake when he was most vulnerable.

Charlotte walked to the window. "I'm afraid I must disagree."

"How so?"

She pointed outside. "Just look out there. What I see is my brother Blake, sitting on a bench in the garden, drawing a picture. A picture!"

Chelsea stood also, and limped across the room. She looked out at the famous Italian Gardens, which could hardly be called "gardens" now, since the duke had dug everything up. She realized that Blake must have gone there immediately after he delivered her to the palace door.

"And drawing a picture is remarkable ... why?" she asked.

"Because he has not sketched anything since he was a boy. It used to be a wonderful pastime for him, and he took lessons from some established artists. He had a distinctive talent. We all knew it."

"What happened?"

She shrugged. "He simply grew out of it. When he was sixteen or so, he took on more responsibilities here on the estate, and Father came to rely on him and appreciate his assistance. Blake became the shining example of what the others should aspire to. We all began to forget about his creative talents. Whatever did you do to make him feel artistic again?"

Chelsea looked outside. "I don't know. I gave him a piece of paper, I suppose."

"It must have been more than that. He's had access to a great many sheets of paper over the years, but he has never drawn a single thing."

Chelsea sighed as she remembered those lazy days on the beach and in the woods, when she wrote her romantic stories and he drew pictures of their surroundings—and of her. "Perhaps it was because, while he was convalescing, he had nothing better to do."

Charlotte looked at her profile. "I think it was your artistic spirit that inspired him. You were contagious, in a good way. He tells me you are a writer, and that you like it best when you can write outdoors."

"Yes," she said, "that is true."

But she hadn't been able to write a single sentence this morning in these strange surroundings. All she'd managed to do was get herself lost.

"I think what my brother needed to do," Charlotte said, "was simply break out of the confines of this place we all call home. Despite its many rewards, it can be oppressive sometimes." She smiled warmly at Chelsea. "Maybe one day he'll discover that getting washed up onto your beach was the best thing that ever happened to him."

Chelsea laughed bitterly. "I doubt that."

"Why?"

She paused, wondering how much she should say, then decided she would say what she wanted, because Charlotte and everyone else already knew what had happened between them and why he brought her here.

"Because I lied to him," she replied. "I know you know it, Charlotte. I pretended to be a woman of loose morals when I was in fact quite innocent, and now I have stolen his freedom to choose his own future."

"To choose to marry another woman, you mean."

"Yes."

Charlotte frowned at her in dismay. "But Blake is not like my other brothers."

"What do you mean?"

"He is not a Don Juan or a Casanova. Vincent, on the other hand, has had many women, and recently when he was forced to become betrothed, he simply chose a lady he knew Father approved of, but jilted her in the end to marry his mistress, who had already born him an illegitimate child."

"Really? There must have been a terrible scandal. How did he avoid it?"

"He didn't. It's the talk of the town at the moment, as he married Cassandra less than a month ago." She lowered her gaze. "I don't think my brother and his wife will be accepted anywhere for quite some time."

"I'm very sorry," Chelsea offered. "How dreadful for them. Where is she now?"

"She is at the house they just purchased in Newbury, settling in and choosing furniture. But it is not dreadful for them, not at all." Charlotte spoke with optimism. "And that is my point, you see, and the reason I am telling you this. They don't care one way or another if they are accepted in society. They are deeply in love, and thankful just to be together, when it had seemed impossible not so long ago.

"Besides," she added, looking out the window again, "Cassandra had already been an outcast after bearing his child out of wedlock, so it truly makes no difference to her. They are talking about going abroad for an extended honeymoon—possibly to Egypt or the Orient—until the dust settles."

"If it ever does," Chelsea warned. "I'm afraid I have some experience in that regard."

"Oh, yes," Charlotte replied, speaking with some fascination. "I heard about your shocking elopement seven years ago. What a daring woman you are, Chelsea. I quite admire you."

More than a little surprised by the young lady's liberal mind-set, Chelsea felt inclined to speak responsibly. "That is very kind of you to say, Charlotte, but don't be too quick to mark me as a hero. I've been hiding away in exile on the other side of the English Channel for the better part of my adult life. My experiences these days are hardly what I would call daring. My life has been very quiet and dull."

"Until my brother arrived."

She sighed despondently. "Yes, until your very handsome brother arrived and upset everything."

"Do you have any regrets?"

Chelsea looked down at Blake, still sitting on the bench in the devastated garden, sketching the statue of Venus in the center of the fountain.

"No," she replied. "No matter what happens, I will never regret those weeks we spent together."

"So you are in love with him, then?"

There was no point in trying to hide the truth. She had already ventured outside the lines of propriety in so many ways.

"Yes, I am. And I would do anything to earn his forgiveness. I'm just not sure it's possible."

"Oh, anything is possible," Charlotte replied. "I've just witnessed the nuptials of two very rakish brothers—both of whom no one ever believed would succumb to marriage, much less love—and they are happier now than they ever imagined they could be. Vincent especially. So do not lose heart. Think of what he overcame, by marrying his mistress, and consider that your circumstances are no worse. Just continue to be the woman you are, and win him back."

Chelsea looked out the window. "I just wish I knew how to go about it. Whenever I apologize, he walks away from me. If you have any advice . . . "

Charlotte thought about it. "I wish I could offer you some, but it's been a long time since I've had any personal experience in such matters. One thing I can share with you however"—her voice became animated—"is a marvelous Pembroke secret that has resulted in numerous marriages over the centuries."

"What is it?"

Charlotte took her by the hand. "Come with me." She led her across the room, pulled the corner tapestry aside and pointed down at a small door cut into the wainscoting. "This will lead you into a network of passages, some of which go straight down to the ancient foundations of the old abbey."

"What old abbey?"

"The building was a monastery before my ancestor accepted it as a gift from the monarchy and transformed it into its present grandeur. The east courtyard was the old cloister." She reached down and flicked the latch. The door swung open.

"This looks like another good way for me to get lost," Chelsea said.

"Yes, it most certainly is, but you will not lose your way this morning, because I am going with you, and I will show you exactly how to get to Blake's rooms . . . " She grinned mischievously. " . . . in case you ever decide the time is right for a private conversation."

She took Chelsea by the hand and led her through the secret door.

Blake looked up from his sketching when, out of the corner of his eye, he saw the butler coming down the stairs from the house, his gait swift and determined.

"Good morning, my lord," the butler said, slightly out of breath when he stopped in front of the bench.

Blake lowered his sketch.

"You have visitors, my lord."

"Visitors," Blake repeated. It seemed strange that he would have guests, when he still felt like a guest here himself.

"They are waiting for you in the green drawing room."

Blake slipped his pencil into his pocket and stood. He crossed the garden and climbed the stairs energetically, taking two or three steps at a time to the top, while the butler followed at a distance. When Blake walked through the door, however, and found himself standing in the back hall, he looked uncertainly left and right.

The butler entered behind him.

"The green drawing room is . . . ?" Blake pointed to the right.

"It's this way, my lord," the butler helpfully answered, gesturing to the left. "Allow me to show you."

Blake wondered how long it would take before he learned his way around this monstrosity of a house.

The butler led him through the long library, across another central hall of marble, and through two more drawing rooms, before they arrived at a third larger one, which boasted floor-to-ceiling tapestries on two facing walls and green floral paper on the others.

Seated on the sofa at the far end of the room was a young couple he did not recognize. Devon and Rebecca sat in two chairs opposite, engaged in conversation with them. Rebecca was pouring tea.

The moment he walked into the room, they fell silent.

Without a single idea about who these people were, he stood inside the door, waiting for someone to say something.

Devon stood. "Blake, you're here at last."

"I was sketching."

His brother cleared his throat and gestured to the others. "Allow me to introduce . . . " He hesitated, however, and looked down at the couple on the sofa, the young lady in particular. "I do beg your pardon. This must seem strange."

The lady's face flushed with color. She appeared to be fighting tears. "Yes, Lord Hawthorne."

Devon turned back to Blake. "I've explained to our guests that you lost your memories in the accident, so this is somewhat awkward—introducing you to people you already know."

Blake studied them both carefully. The gentleman was close to his own age, with blond hair and a taste for fashionable attire. The lady was younger—perhaps eighteen or so—with a quiet, oval face, a dainty, upturned nose, and shiny auburn hair.

He made every effort to remember them and hunted through his mind for something to grab hold of, even a tiny splinter of an image, but there were no recollections. None at all.

"I'm sorry," he said, shaking his head. "What my brother told you is true, and I apologize for what must seem to be rudeness on my part."

The gentleman squinted at him, as if trying to decipher if this was some kind of trick, while the lady's expression grew more despairing.

A heaviness settled in his stomach, while he stood locked in the young woman's emotional gaze.

"So you don't remember us at all?" the gentleman asked, still watching him skeptically. "You have no recollection whatsoever of our friendship, or your relationship to my sister?"

Blake tried to relax. He glanced questioningly at Devon, who stepped in at once to offer an explanation. He gestured toward the young couple. "This is Mr. Fenton, and his sister . . . " He paused, as if unsure what to call her. " . . . Elizabeth."

Devon allowed Blake a moment to comprehend the names. A horrible sensation of dread washed over him.

His brother continued. "Their father is Baron

Ridgeley, who is the director of the London Horticultural Society. They have recently returned from France, after a brief stop in Jersey shortly after we departed. They were searching for you, just as we were. Earl Neufeld informed them that I had arrived the day before and already brought you home. So here they are."

Blake regarded the young lady again. She was holding her chin high, but he could see she was also holding her breath. Her hands were clasped together so tightly, her knuckles were white.

"Rebecca and I," Devon continued, "have just learned that before you disappeared, you were traveling with the Fentons to France on their private sailing vessel, which I regret to say collided with another ship in a storm. The boat went down, but thankfully all the passengers were pulled from the water. All except for one."

"Me, obviously," Blake said, relieved at least to finally hear an explanation as to why he had spent a night thrashing about in the frigid waters of the English Channel.

They were all quiet for a long time, waiting for more of a reaction from him, perhaps.

"But there is something else," young Mr. Fenton said, sitting forward, still scrutinizing him, as if he were waiting for a slip that might reveal that Blake was lying, and was in fact in full possession of his memories. He did not seem able to accept that it was possible for a man to completely forget his life.

"Something very important," Devon added. "You might want to sit down, Blake."

"I prefer to stand."

Devon glanced uneasily at Rebecca, then at last offered the rest of the story. "The morning before you boarded the ship bound for France, you and Elizabeth were married under special license. She has the certificate to prove it, and even has a letter from our father, who evidently had written to give you his blessing and had sent you on your merry way."

Blake stared at his brother, baffled. "But he has said nothing about it."

"No, but his memory, I'm sorry to say, is worse than yours."

Blake frowned. This was all quite impossible to believe. He was married to this woman? *Married?*

"It's true, Blake," Devon said, standing up. "I've seen the certificate myself. Elizabeth is your wife."

Blake looked down at her. She maintained her composure for only a brief moment, then cupped her forehead in a trembling hand, bowed her head, and surrendered to a fit of weeping.

Chapter 22

~~~

Rebecca stood, which persuaded the others to rise from their chairs as well. "We shall leave you two alone," she said.

The next thing Blake knew, the door was swinging shut behind them, and Elizabeth—his wife?—was flying off the sofa and rushing into his arms.

"Oh, Blake," she sobbed. "You have no idea what I've been through these past few weeks. I thought you were dead!"

He held her in his arms and tried to comfort her while she shuddered and wept inconsolably onto his sleeve.

He was in shock. He could not embrace her the same way in return—with heartache and passion and wild desperation. He didn't know this woman. She was a stranger to him, and seemed no older than a child. He still could not accept that this was true.

And God . . . dear God! All he could think of

was Chelsea, and how he had made love to her so many times like a free man—a man who was at liberty to become intimate with a beautiful woman who'd offered her body to him willingly and eagerly, without consequences, mere *days* after he'd married someone else.

Allegedly.

Not only that, but he had let himself fall in love with her, even though he'd fought to control those emotions as best he could. On that final night, before he discovered her ploy, he wanted to marry her. He was going to journey out into the world to discover his identity for one purpose alone—to enable him to spend the rest of his life with her.

Now, at last, he knew the whole truth. According to what he was just told, he had not been a free man in Jersey, nor was he a free man now. He felt like he was being tossed about in those waves again, out of control, sucking in water as panic threatened to drown the life out of him.

When the young lady regained her composure, he took a step back, held her away from him so he could look at her face. Perhaps he would remember something. Even just a single, fleeting moment he had spent with her.

If he had married her, he must have been in love with her, or at the very least, admired her. He must have felt some affection or passion if he had gone to the trouble of securing his father's blessing, then spoke vows before God, promising her a lifetime of love and fidelity.

But when he looked into her eyes, he saw nothing familiar, and the only thing he felt was frustration and guilt for not knowing her.

"Perhaps we should sit down," he suggested.

"Yes, of course."

They sat on the sofa and faced each other.

"Do you have the marriage certificate with you?" he asked, needing to see it for himself.

"Yes." Her hands were trembling as she opened her reticule and pulled it out. "This is what I presented to your brother when we first arrived. He didn't believe it either."

He glanced up at her briefly before he unfolded the page and looked it over. This was indeed his signature. He recognized that, at least. All appeared to be in order.

He handed it back to her.

"I'm sorry," he said, while she slid it into her reticule, then withdrew a handkerchief and blew her nose. "This must be difficult for you."

She nodded and looked like she might cry again. He quickly engaged her in conversation to thwart another breakdown.

"Can you tell me how we met?" he asked. "Or what our wedding day was like?"

"We met by the orchids in the conservatory of the Horticultural Society. You were there to speak to my father and learn about the organization, because your father had placed a provision in his will to bequeath his money to the society instead of you and your brothers if you did not quickly marry."

"I told you about that?" They must have known each other intimately indeed if he had revealed such personal family secrets.

"You told my brother, actually," she replied. "You and he became good friends straightaway, and spent a great deal of time together at the clubs. He is the one who encouraged you to court me. He felt we would be a good match, and of course, I fell in love with you instantly."

But did I fall in love with you? he wanted to ask, but refrained, for he didn't wish to shine too bright a light on the fact that he felt absolutely nothing for this young lady now—nothing but confusion and regret for his lack of ardor, which surely must be breaking her heart if she was at all perceptive.

"Did I court you properly?" he asked instead.

"Yes, for a couple of weeks. We danced at some balls and went driving in the park. You seemed very determined to secure yourself a wife, and you secured me without the slightest dithering. You were very keen to have it quickly done because of your father's wishes."

It had been swift and to the point, then, without

a lot of wild and foolish passions, or insane, all-consuming desires.

She placed her hand on his knee. He looked down at it impassively, then she slowly withdrew it and set it back on her own lap. An awkward silence ensued.

"May I ask how old you are?" he inquired.

"I am eighteen."

"I see." Something churned inside his gut, and he looked away from her, toward the window.

"I was told," she said, "that you were injured when they found you in Jersey."

"Yes, I must have been wounded in the accident," he replied. "Perhaps I became caught in the rigging, or I might have been impaled on a sharp rock when I was washed ashore."

She lowered her gaze. "You would have been without clothes when they found you. I understand it was a lady . . . "

He watched her face go pale. "That's right." Then he thought about the boat going down.

Of course, of course . . .

"I had no clothes," he said, "because it was our wedding night."

"Yes. We were together in the cabin before the collision occurred. Water came rushing in very fast. There wasn't time for anything."

Had she been naked, too, when they pulled her from the sea?

"If only you could know how devastated I was," she told him, "when I regained consciousness on the other ship and you were not with us."

"I'm sorry you had to suffer through that," he said.

Eyes still lowered, she nodded, and another awkward silence surrounded them like a dense fog rolling into the room.

"Why did you not previously inform my family of the accident?" he asked, as he pondered all the particulars of his disappearance. "They had no idea where I was all this time. They were sick with worry."

At last she looked up. "My father wanted to tell your family in person, rather than send a letter with such devastating news, and we were holding out hope that you might have survived and we would find you."

He was not satisfied with this. "I was missing for a month. Could you not have told them the truth, so they could help in the search?"

She seemed somewhat frustrated with his lack of understanding. "The only reason they were worried about you was because your father did not tell them where you were. If they had been informed that you were bound for France on your honeymoon, as we thought they were, they would never have spent a single minute worrying. They would have been rejoicing."

"And no one would have ever found me."

"*We* would have found you," she insisted, "for we, too, saw the piece in the paper, as your brother did. We were only a day behind him."

Still, he was not pleased to know that they had kept his disappearance secret from his family all this time.

Deciding he would let the matter drop for the time being, he sat and listened while she told him about their wedding ceremony and other details about his friendship with her brother, John—none of which he remembered.

Then she posed a question. He suspected she had been waiting for just the right moment to ask it.

"When we arrived in Jersey," she said, "they told us you brought the lady home with you—the one who found you on the beach. Is that true?"

"Yes."

"And is she here now? At the palace?"

"Yes."

She studied him curiously. "May I ask why she accompanied you?"

Blake took great care in deciding how he should reply. Would it be best to tell her the truth?

As he looked into her youthful brown eyes, however, he decided that no, he could not do that to her—at least not until he knew what he was going to do about all this.

"My family felt beholden to her," he explained, "so my brother offered to show her Pembroke Palace."

"She came without a chaperone?"

He paused. "She is of an age that didn't require . . . " He hesitated, and began again. "Her family felt that Lady Hawthorne's presence was enough."

"So she is an older lady, then?" Elizabeth asked, seeming happy to hear it.

"Not terribly old." He did not want to talk about it. Perhaps she sensed it, for she asked him if he would like a cup of tea. He declined, but she leaned forward to pour some for herself.

Another prolonged silence followed, while they both looked away from each other. She stirred her tea and set the spoon down in the saucer with a noticeable *clink*.

"You mentioned earlier that you were sketching," she said cheerfully, sitting up straighter and seeming relieved to have thought of something to talk about. "May I ask what you were drawing?"

"The statue of Venus, down in the garden," he replied, wondering if she had an interest in art.

"Is that what you like to draw? Statues? I suppose they are easier than people, because they don't move."

"I sketch many things," he said, "including people."

She raised her teacup and held it in front of her mouth as she spoke. "Gracious, I had no idea you liked to draw. I wonder . . . " She set the cup down in the saucer again and appeared somewhat perplexed. "What is the point in it, if you are not going to earn a living from it, which clearly you would not do."

How could he possibly explain why he did it? The truth was, it fed his soul—a soul he suspected had been starving in this repressed and dutiful life he had been living. But he was not at ease saying that to her.

"I do it because I enjoy it."

"Do you paint the pictures as well, in order to add color? Or are they just pencil drawings?"

Just pencil drawings . . .

"No, I have not painted my sketches, but I am told I used to paint with oils when I was a boy, and that the canvases are at the London house, buried somewhere in the attic. I may very well try it again one day soon. I feel rather inclined."

She shifted uncomfortably. "I see." She giggled. "I don't think I could draw a flower without it looking like a sun. But of course drawing is for children."

He drew his head back.

"Except in your case, of course!" she stammered. "I only meant that the pictures I would draw would look like the work of a child, because I am not artistic. I cannot even embroider anything without a pattern." She took another sip of tea. "I like to sing, though!" she added, almost desperately.

They sat in silence again, while he looked toward the window, feeling bewildered by the man he was before he'd been lost at sea. What was it about this woman that had stirred his soul? Anything? Would he discover it eventually? Or perhaps his soul had been dead and buried, and he had not thought it would ever live again. Perhaps that is why he'd simply done his duty and obeyed his father's wishes.

A knock sounded at the door. "Enter!" he called out, grateful for the interruption.

"Have you had a chance to become reacquainted?" Rebecca asked as she entered the drawing room with Devon and John.

"Oh yes!" Elizabeth replied, wiggling in the seat. "We have indeed, and everything is perfect now. I am so happy."

He turned to look at her—she seemed so very young—and felt only a deep sense of dread for what lay in his future, for he did not know how this situation was going to play out. There were two women in his life now—one he felt passionate about—for he both desired her and was infuriated by her—and one for whom he felt nothing at all but guilt and obligation.

Chelsea, however, could be carrying his child.

But so, also, he supposed, could this woman. She was his wife. They had been together on their wedding night.

Before he had a chance to think about what he was doing or what he *should* be doing, he was on his feet.

"Where are you going?" Devon calmly asked. "To see Father, I hope. He's still waiting for you, and has probably become impatient."

He was not waiting, and they both knew it.

Blake let out a deep breath. Thank God he had someone on his side. Devon—his brother—who somehow understood so much about him, without ever being told a thing.

"I'll go and see what he wants," Blake replied.

He politely excused himself, left the room, and headed up the stairs to see Chelsea, because she, more than anyone, would need to understand the situation.

Chapter 23

C helsea tried not to bump her head as she bent to pass through the tiny doorway in the wall, which led into her own room. She had just spent an hour with Charlotte, who took her on a tour of the secret passageways through the palace, even down to the dark, damp, subterranean cavities beneath the ground. Charlotte had shared with her a number of ghost stories—which she said still haunted the palace today—about monks being murdered in the abbey, not long before the monasteries were dissolved by King Henry VIII.

Evidently, Charlotte's very own ancestor, the first Duke of Pembroke, was the illegitimate child of a murdered monk, and according to the duke, that monk's ghost was still roaming the corridors at night.

It was a good thing she didn't believe in ghosts, Chelsea thought now, or she might not have the courage to sleep alone while she was here.

Entering her room through the secret door, she straightened and pushed the tapestry aside. There, standing over her bed with her pillow to his nose, was Blake.

"Where were you?" he asked irritably, dropping the pillow onto the bed and striding around the foot of it.

Chelsea moved to the center of the room. "I was exploring the passageways."

"But I needed to speak with you."

She frowned. "Well, I'm very sorry, but I am not going to sit here all day in my room, simply waiting for you to come and talk to me. I am not a servant, here at your beck and call. I must find ways to amuse myself and pass the time."

"So you went snooping around the palace?" he replied. "Did you go into my room without my permission?"

She cleared her throat. "Charlotte showed me where it was."

"And did you go in?" he asked, infuriated. "Did you look through my things? My drawings?"

"No," she answered, wondering about the root of his anger. He had been quite calm when they parted outside earlier that morning. "That would have been an intrusion of your privacy," she declared, then glanced at the pillow he had just been sniffing. "And what is your excuse?"

He turned away from her. "I have something important to discuss with you. It could not wait."

"What is it, then?"

He strode to the window, and with hands clasped behind his back, looked out at the lush green countryside. "There are visitors downstairs—one in particular, whose name you might recognize." He turned and faced her.

"Please do not keep me in suspense, Blake, for I am already stuck in a constant state of waiting. I don't wish to add more to the heap."

He continued to hesitate, while his eyes never left hers. "Elizabeth is here."

Chelsea took a few seconds to recover from her astonishment, then walked to the bed and sat down on the edge of it. "Did you know her? I mean . . . that is to say . . . did you recognize her at all?"

"No. Not in the least."

She let out the tight breath she had been holding, but quickly discovered that her relief was premature, for it was instantly squashed by his next words.

"Which is unfortunate, considering the fact that she is my wife."

Chelsea closed her eyes and pinched the bridge of her nose. "Dear God."

Blake wandered listlessly into the center of the room. "It's not as if we hadn't known this could happen. We knew it was a possibility, yet we both went ahead and did what we wanted to do. So we have no one to blame but ourselves."

She looked up. "I am relieved at least to hear that you are willing to share the blame with me."

He acknowledged her comment with a nod, then paced around the room, looking down at the floor, shaking his head and thinking about everything.

"I just didn't *feel* like a married man," he explained. "There was not one single emotion or suspicion inside of me that suggested I might love someone or aspire to be faithful. All I felt was complete freedom, and I wanted to celebrate it. It was a hunger I cannot even describe."

Neither of them spoke for a long time.

"Does she know about me?" Chelsea asked. "And that I am here?"

"She knows you saved my life and that you returned with us, but she does not know the whole story. I could hardly tell her that we were lovers."

"No, of course not." She regarded him with subdued curiosity. "What is she like?"

Though in all honesty, Chelsea was not sure she wanted to know. She did not want to hear that his Elizabeth was beautiful and accomplished, charming and witty. Or that he had just fallen in love with her all over again, the moment he laid eyes on her, and that he regretted what he had done.

She remembered the moment he spoke his wife's name—when he was aroused in his sleep by her own mouth on his body. Had Elizabeth put her mouth in those places, too?

He stopped and looked at her. "I don't really know what she is like."

"But you must have spoken with her."

"I did. She showed me the marriage certificate." He stared at her impatiently, as if frustrated and annoyed by what he was about to tell her. "She asked me what things I like to draw."

He sounded baffled, incredulous, aggravated.

"Did you tell her?"

"Yes."

"And what did she say?"

"She said she thought drawing was for children." He paused. "She seems very young."

"How so?"

"She looks young. Acts young. She doesn't understand . . . "

"Understand what?"

"Why a person might want to draw or write."

Chelsea wet her lips and swallowed. "Perhaps she is simply not a creative person. They say that opposites attract . . . "

Why was she doing this? Trying to convince

him of why he might have loved this woman in the first place?

Then she remembered what Charlotte had told her earlier that morning—that Blake had left his artistic soul behind years ago when he took on more mature responsibilities on the estate.

He shook his head, turned away and walked back to the window. But there were still so many questions she wanted to ask.

"So your family knew nothing of your marriage?" she said. "Or how long you and she have been . . . ?"

"It's quite a story," he said. "We were married by special license the very day I went missing, which made it our wedding night. We were bound for France on our honeymoon when the ship went down."

His wedding night?

She lay back on the covers and stared up at the ceiling. "That is why you had no clothes on when I found you."

If only she had known. Instead, she'd thought it was some magical story, like something out of an ancient folk tale, or one of her own romantic stories of adventure and love.

"I have been such a fool." She dropped her wrist over her eyes. "I have been living in the world of my imagination. I've been exiled for too long and have lost touch with reality."

"There is nothing wrong with imagination."

She lowered her arm to the bed and looked up at him. She had not heard him cross the room to stand over her.

He was so handsome—so tall and dark and mesmerizing—and she desired him, still. She could not forget all those moments in his bed at her family's mansion by the sea, when she had listened to the waves pounding up onto the rugged coastline while he made love to her in the afternoons. It *had* been magical, every last second of it—even when he burst into her room to confront her after the scene with her mother. Even then she'd been filled with passion and fascination, and so had he.

She was filled with passion now. She could have wept from the intensity of her desires and the heartache over the fact that he was no longer hers. He belonged to another woman. He was married. There was no more hope for forgiveness and a happy ending. Everything they'd shared had been sordid and wrong. She would never forgive herself. She should have been more cautious.

"So what are you going to do?" she asked, rising up on her elbows and feeling as if she should cover her eyes, because she was looking into the brightness of the sun.

"Clearly, I cannot marry you," he said, "even if you are carrying my child."

"And what if I am?" she asked. "What will we do? Will you let me go home to my family? Will you let me keep the child?"

But dear God in heaven—she did not want him to release her. There was a bond between them now. She loved him.

But he was married.

What was she to do, then? Give the baby over to Sebastian and Melissa, as they'd originally planned? She'd never be able to do it, not now, when everything was different, when she had discovered the real world again and the undeniable forces inside her heart.

It would be *her* baby. *Hers*. No one else's. No matter what anyone thought.

"Or would you try to take the child away from me?" she asked suddenly, with challenge, as she sat up.

"I don't have those answers, but I do know this—I would not allow you to pass the child off as your brother's."

She frowned at him. "I would not want to. I could not do that now. The child would be mine."

"And mine."

She was strangely out of breath. "But that would not be possible." Then she remembered what Charlotte had told her about his brother, Vincent, who had just married his mistress, who bore him an illegitimate child. He had jilted his fiancée to do so.

But that was different. A fiancée was not a wife.

"If you tried to take the child away from me, I wouldn't let you," she said. "I would scream at the top of my lungs and cause the worst scandal your family could ever imagine."

"And I would put my hand over your mouth," he practically growled.

She stood up, horrified. "You wouldn't."

"I dragged you back here, didn't I?"

"You were able to do that only because I wanted to come."

He lifted his eyebrows in surprise. "Are you sure about that? You wanted to leave the safety of your home to follow a man who despised you and promised you nothing?"

"I had nothing before I met you."

"You had your freedom."

"And that is a valuable commodity, is it?" she asked, her temper reaching dangerous heights. "I'm afraid I must disagree, because I had it for seven years, yet I was completely unfulfilled."

"That is not what you told me. You said you were happy there. You were able to write."

"I was happy until you came. *Damn* you!"

"And damn *you*!" he shouted in return, glaring

down at her with rage and passion that blazed so hot it was beyond her comprehension.

Then suddenly his mouth was on hers, crushing her lips as he scooped her up into his arms. He moaned in despair as he kissed her, as if the world were coming to an end.

He was strong—too strong for her—and she could not push him away. Eyes wide, she voiced an angry protest, then bit down hard on his lip. He pulled back, and she shoved him away. She pushed him so hard, he had to grab onto the bedpost to keep from falling onto the floor.

"What in God's name are you doing?" she demanded, tasting his blood on her lip. "You're married! Your wife is downstairs! You cannot touch me. You shall never touch me again!"

He raked a hand through his hair and snarled. *"Damn my life! I don't know who the hell I am!"* He started for the door. "Do not leave this room," he commanded in a deep and threatening voice. "Unless your courses arrive in the next five minutes, you still belong to me."

With that, he stormed out of the room like a tempest, and Chelsea sank back onto the bed in disbelief.

Chapter 24

A shiny black coach behind four black horses thundered out of the mist, crossed the stone bridge, and traveled up the drive to Pembroke Palace. Hooves clattered noisily as it passed under the entrance archway into the cobbled courtyard and finally pulled to a halt in front of the wide steps.

The liveried footman hopped off the page board at the back and hurried to open the door. Out stepped Lord Vincent Sinclair, dressed in a long black overcoat with fur trim. He climbed the steps with brooding impatience, removing his gloves as he went.

Once inside the great entrance hall, he tossed his coat and hat to the butler. "Tell Lord Hawthorne I have returned. I'll be waiting for him in the study."

The butler hurried to do his bidding. "Yes, my lord."

A short time later Devon entered the room where Vincent was lounging back in a chair with a brandy cupped in one hand, his long booted legs stretched out on the desktop, crossed at the ankles. He was staring up at the ceiling.

Upon Devon's arrival, he sat forward and dropped his feet to the floor. "Your letter said you found Blake, but my driver has informed me that he remembers nothing about anything."

"That's right." Devon walked in and poured a glass of brandy for himself, then turned and explained the full situation to Vincent, including the recent arrival of John Fenton and his sister, Elizabeth—who was, to everyone's amazement, Blake's new wife.

But Vincent had already learned of Blake's marriage when he was in France. On the day he received the letter from Devon notifying him of Blake's location, he had found and met the girl's father, Lord Ridgeley.

At the time, Vincent was surprised to learn of his brother's hasty wedding, despite the fact that they had all been spurred into action by their mad father. Although Blake was dutiful to a fault, Vincent had expected him to be the last to comply, for it was not in his nature to act on impulse. He was highly prudent, and always thought things through very carefully.

"At least he is alive," Vincent said with relief,

sitting back in the chair. "Everything else can be dealt with, now that he has returned. That is all we wanted, after all—to know that he is safe. And here he is, home with a wife. That is one less thing to worry about, I suppose. Now we must only convince Garrett to return and do the same."

"By 'everything else,'" Devon replied, "do you mean his memory loss, or his new wife, who is a stranger to him because he does not remember her?" Devon strode to the sofa and sat down.

"All of the above, I suppose," Vincent uneasily replied.

Devon took a drink. "I regret to inform you that there is more."

"*More?*" Vincent lounged back in his chair again and waited for his brother to elaborate.

"A great deal more, because there is another woman here—the woman who found our brother on the island of Jersey and saved his life."

"A woman saved him? Then we are indebted to her."

"One would think so, but Blake has dragged her back here like a dog on a chain, believing she used him for stud."

"For stud?" Vincent let out a laugh. "Surely not. Is *he* going mad as well? You said he possesses no memories. First Father, now Blake?"

Devon shook his head. "It's not madness. The young lady has confessed to the scheme, and seems more than willing to be brought to some kind of moral justice. She came with us willingly, and seems to regret her actions."

Vincent frowned in disbelief. "So what are you telling me? There is a woman here who might be carrying Blake's child? Did she not know he was married?"

"Neither of them did. Incidentally, the lady is Chelsea Campion. Does the name ring a bell?"

"Campion . . . " Vincent tapped a finger on the desk while he toyed with the name in his mind. "Her father was an outspoken member in the House a number of years ago, if I recall correctly. Some thought he might rise to become Prime Minister."

"Until his daughter ran away with a fortune hunter and caused the scandal of the century," Devon finished for him.

Vincent's eyebrows lifted. He chuckled. "Blake has been sharing a bed with *her*? The willful runaway who disobeyed her influential father and ruined his political career?" He laughed again. "My God, what a lark. I cannot believe our younger brother—who does no wrong and is the perfect model for duty and decency—has been misbehaving." He continued to grin. "The cheeky bastard. I knew there was more to him than he always let on." He shook his head and downed the rest of his brandy. "Poor bloke—he's in a pickle now, isn't he?" Then he frowned. "What has Father said about it?"

"He doesn't know yet, and we are going to shield him from this just as we did with you and Cassandra, until we can decide how best to proceed."

"What a circus I came home to."

"Indeed."

Vincent stood. "Where is he? I must go and see him, and congratulate him for staying afloat in the Channel, not to mention for stealing a little pleasure for himself when he couldn't even remember his own name. Maybe he finally figured out how to live—by swiping all of us out of his head for a little while. Smart move. He always was the brilliant one."

Vincent started for the door, but Devon stopped him. "Be careful how you encourage him, Vin. Things may have worked out for you when you were juggling both a fiancée and a mistress, but it has gone beyond that for Blake. He is a married man now, and he doesn't possess your reckless nature."

Vincent scoffed. "You don't think so?"

"Vin . . . " His brother's dark tone held a warning.

"All right, all right," Vincent reluctantly replied. "I'll be as prudent as I know how to be. But remember, Devon, that I was in his position not long ago and I know where his head is. He's going to need some help sorting this out."

Devon simply nodded and let his brother go.

Blood still boiling in his veins, Blake stormed into his room, slammed the door behind him, and went straight to the window. He planted his clenched fists on the sill and shut his eyes to try and bring his body back under control, while he cursed this convoluted state of affairs which had his life in a stranglehold.

Why couldn't he remember anything? Would he ever recover those lost memories? More importantly, how could he have fallen in love with one woman while he was married to another? Why did the damn boat sink in the first place? Had the captain been a bloody imbecile? Had he not known how to handle a boat in a storm?

Blake turned around and looked at the sketches he'd drawn the night before when sleep eluded him. They were splayed out on the table, arousing his senses even now, for they were drawn from the most powerful and potent memories in his mind. They were sketches of Chelsea's nude form.

He wanted her still. He could not deny it. He had lost complete control in her room just now, kissing her with wild desperation and wanting to do so much more—mere minutes after he'd told her he was a married man. And after he'd just been reunited with his wife, who had recently thought herself a widow and was barely over her grief. She had wept on his shoulder, and he stood there, feeling nothing.

What the hell was he going to do?

A knock sounded at his door. He did not want to answer it. He wanted to be alone.

The visitor rapped a second time, and Blake could tell by the force of the knock that it was no servant or lady. It was someone with brawn.

Curious, he pushed off the windowsill and went to answer the door, then found himself, for a second time, staring at his mirror image. But it was not Devon. It was someone he had not met before, and his eyes were brown instead of blue.

"Vincent," he said.

The devious looking gentleman in the corridor inclined his head as if he were impressed. "They told me you wouldn't remember me."

"I don't." Blake gave him a shrewd look. "But clearly we are related."

"Yes, clearly," his brother said, seeming inexplicably amused.

"Is something funny?" Blake asked. He was not in the mood for this. He had no time for games.

"Yes, actually." Vincent smirked and leaned a shoulder against the doorjamb. "I just learned that you were taken in by a gorgeous hellion, who used you in the most appalling way." He placed a hand over his heart in mock sympathy.

Blake stared at his brother for a moment, then opened the door all the way and invited him to step inside.

Vincent sauntered into the room. He glanced at the nude sketches on the table but seemed unaffected. Evidently he had seen his share of naked women.

"What do you want?" Blake asked, feeling weary all of a sudden.

"I am in want of nothing," his brother replied, spreading his arms wide. "For I have just married the woman of my dreams, who incidentally is also a bit of a hellion, but that is why she is the only woman who exists for me. She's awaiting my arrival in Newbury, where we have purchased a quaint little house on a lake in which to raise our daughter, so I am going to have to make this quick and then be off." He looked around the room at the furniture, the pictures, then met Blake's gaze again. "I couldn't leave without seeing you in the flesh and satisfying myself that you are in fact alive and well, and let me be honest—I wanted to offer you some advice."

"You think I need advice?" Blake asked, unable to smother his frustration.

His brother looked him in the eye. "I think what you need is a friend—a friend who's been exactly where you are at this moment—minus the lost memories." He returned to the door. "Why don't we go amuse ourselves in a friendly game of billiards? The last time we played, you were the one offering me advice, so I think it's high time I returned the favor."

Blake followed his brother out into the corridor, where he paused. "Do I enjoy billiards?" he asked. "Or more importantly, am I any good at it?"

"You're exceptional," Vincent replied. "But the unfortunate news is, so am I, which means you only beat me half the time."

Blake felt some of the tension lifting from his shoulders.

"Let's go start a new game," his brother said as they set off down the hall. "And we'll see how much you remember."

Blake had to confess, he was anxious to find out.

Chapter 25

Dressed in black and white formal attire, Blake headed to the drawing room for a glass of champagne with the family and other guests before dinner. By some miracle, he arrived at the right doorway, but paused there a moment, perusing the room for Chelsea, because he was not entirely sure what he would say to her after what had happened in her room. Not only had he kissed her like a vile brute, he stormed out after informing her that she was his property and could not leave.

It was not likely she would wish to talk about the weather with him tonight. She was more likely to throw a glass of champagne in his face.

He did not see her with the others in the room, however. Instead, he locked eyes with another—his new bride, Elizabeth. She stood before the fireplace with her brother John, and held a glass of champagne in her hand. The instant she spotted him, she smiled.

Blake inhaled deeply. At least he felt more re-laxed since meeting Vincent, who had not told him what to do while they played billiards, but merely assured him that in time everything would work itself out. Vincent suggested that he simply continue along the path of his life until he could identify a proper course of action. Circumstances could change. *He* could change. Other people might reveal themselves in interesting ways, and all the pieces on the game board might very well move to new positions. In sum, Vincent suggested that he simply play it out and focus on one move at a time.

At present, his next move was to eat dinner with his wife, and reacquaint himself with her brother.

Crossing the room, he picked up a glass of champagne from a passing footman and ap-proached John and Elizabeth.

"Good evening," he said, bowing slightly at the waist.

John narrowed his eyes and looked Blake over from head to foot. "So bloody formal. You really don't remember a thing, do you?"

"We were not formal with each other?" Blake coolly replied. "Not even in a duke's drawing room?"

John looked around the room with a sneer. "We generally didn't frequent dukes' drawing rooms.

We preferred darker establishments, where the rules were a bit more lax."

Elizabeth's cheeks flushed with color and she lowered her gaze to the floor.

Her brother turned to her. "Don't be such a prude, Liz. You're going to bore your husband to tears before the honeymoon even gets started. Isn't that right, Blake?"

Blake looked down at the young lady who had still not lifted her eyes, then turned his own steely gaze to John. "How is it we became friends?" he casually asked. "I am curious to know."

The man waved his champagne glass through the air, and spilled a few drops onto the carpet. "I was there the day you came to the Horticultural Society offices. You were asking all sorts of questions about the daily operations. You wanted to know where your father's money would go, if you didn't get your hands on it."

"And you answered my questions?"

He squinted. "My father is chairman of the board, so I know how things work." He guzzled the rest of his champagne and set the glass down on the mantel. "I invited you for a few drinks, and we discovered we had much in common. My sister, for one thing, who was in need of a husband."

"John," she said with a note of pleading.

"What's the matter?" He picked up another glass of champagne when the footman came by. "You're a pretty girl. It wasn't hard to match you up with my new friend. Father was certainly pleased about it, under the circumstances." He tipped the glass back and swallowed the entire contents in a single gulp.

"The circumstances . . . ?" Blake inquired.

John stared at him intently, as if searching for some hidden truth in his eyes.

"You're the son of a duke," he said at last, with challenge in his own eyes, mixed with a note of disdain. "It was quite a conquest for our little Liz. Or did you forget about your rank, like you forgot everything else?"

Blake continued to watch John's face as he leaned an arm on the mantel and looked distastefully around the room.

"I lost my memories," Blake told him, "not my intellect. Did I do something to offend you, John?"

"No."

"Then I will respectfully suggest you tell me what is causing your foul mood."

John looked at him uncertainly. "You seem different, that's all."

"How so?"

"I don't know."

The duke entered just then, and began quacking like a duck and waddling across the room. Everyone fell silent until he straightened, pointed a finger at Devon and laughed uproariously. "You thought I was serious, didn't you? Look at your faces!"

The family chuckled uncomfortably, then the tension lifted, conversation resumed, and the duke picked up a glass of champagne and joined his wife.

Blake looked down at his own young wife, who had not lifted her eyes from the floor. "Would you care to walk with me to the gallery?" he gently asked.

"Yes, thank you," she replied. "That would be lovely."

He offered his arm and they excused themselves from John's company.

"Your brother is a curious fellow," he said, when they had left the others behind.

"I must apologize for his behavior. He can be rather uncouth sometimes, especially when he is drinking. We do not always get along."

"And yet I had become his close friend." He could not imagine wanting to spend time with such a man—which only added to his confusion about the man he had been before the accident. Nothing anyone told him about the old Blake seemed to match the person he felt himself to be now. Even John had just said he seemed different.

"He has a tendency to draw new friends into

his circle," Elizabeth said, "but he is not very good at keeping them there."

"So I would have eventually been shown the door?" Blake asked. "Or perhaps not, since we are now brothers. There is a certain permanency in that. Maybe that's what he does not like."

She gave no reply. She merely quickened her step. "What is it you wanted to show me in the gallery?" she asked.

"Nothing, really. I just wanted to walk with you."

"I see."

And walk is what they did, without saying much of anything else. When they reached the long gallery, they moved from portrait to portrait, but Blake could disclose nothing about any of the Pembroke ancestors in the paintings, for he was as good as a stranger here himself.

At one point he commented on an area he did know something about—the effect of the brush strokes and colors used—but Elizabeth merely nodded, while glancing restlessly around the room. It was clear the artistry of these great masters held no interest for her.

He knew that Chelsea, on the other hand, would have been enthralled.

When they returned to the drawing room, she was there at last, sitting at the piano, her slender arms moving gracefully over the keys as she played a quiet melody, which made him stop on the threshold.

He wished agonizingly to go to her and apologize for his behavior earlier. He also comprehended the notion that he might never touch her or hold her again. It was a wonder she was even here, joining the family for dinner tonight, after what had occurred between them. She could have packed her things and quit the palace entirely. It is what he would have done in her position. She was not without choices. She had a family to return home to.

But she was here. She had not left.

Elizabeth looked up at him. "What is it?" She glanced at Chelsea, then back at him again. "Is that the lady who saved your life?"

"Yes," he replied with deliberate indifference.

Elizabeth tilted her head to the side. "She is much younger than I imagined."

"She is five and twenty," he replied.

His wife said nothing for a long moment, then her face warmed with a quiet gladness he had not expected. "Quite so. Well, you must introduce us. I am your wife, after all, and surely I must thank the lady who saved your life and brought you home to me."

He breathed deeply and reminded himself of Vincent's wisdom, then escorted his very young bride across the room.

* * *

Chelsea finished her piece, thanked her audience for their kind applause, then rose soberly from the piano bench to meet Blake's wife.

The young woman was exceedingly pretty, with hair the color of chestnuts and big brown eyes that exuded cheerfulness and enthusiasm. She held out her hand, eager to meet Chelsea, who moved forward with some reluctance.

How was she ever going to hide her indignity from this lovely young lady who was not only attractive, but appeared to be pure of heart as well? She was an ideal choice for the wife of a respected son of a duke. Blake could take great pride in having her at his side. They would have a brilliant life together.

"It's a pleasure to meet you, Lady Blake," Chelsea said with a warm smile that ripped her heart out and took ten years off her life.

"And such a pleasure to meet you as well," Elizabeth replied. "You are a hero, Lady Chelsea. You saved my husband. Please, you must tell me what happened, and how you came to find him when he was washed ashore."

They moved to a quieter corner of the room, where they sat down on a small striped sofa and Chelsea described the events of that blustery day. She related how she had found the gold watch on the beach, then ventured into the sea cave and discovered Blake unconscious on the rocks. She told Elizabeth about the physician who came to examine him, and how Blake woke up remembering nothing about his life or how he came to be there.

Chelsea finally commented on what a relief it was to know at last what happened that night in the storm, for she and her family had spent many hours speculating about the circumstances.

When the butler stepped into the room to announce that dinner was being served, she wanted to drop to her knees in gratitude and thank him for ending this ghastly torture. She could not bear to look into the young woman's sweet, wide eyes for another excruciating second.

In the dining room, she accepted the Duke of Pembroke's arm to escort her to the supper table, hoping her moral debt to Blake and his family was now satisfied—because all she wanted to do was leave this place. There was no longer anything left to fight for. Anyone with any intelligence could see that the battle was over. She had no choice but to retreat.

His appetite gone, Blake sat beside Elizabeth at dinner and did his best to engage her in conversation about the food and whatever else he could manage, but most of his attention was fixed on Chelsea, who was sitting across from him, beside John.

He thought that her tête-à-tête with Elizabeth must have been difficult. Despite the fact that she had been warm and smiling, spoke well and made no mention of their affair, he saw the shame and regret in her eyes. He also heard it in her voice, because he knew her as intimately as a woman could be known. She was an open book to him. He had seen her at her best and worst. He knew her flaws and imperfections, and the depths of her shameful mistakes and failures.

Why then, he asked himself, did he still long for her in the most wretched way imaginable? Even now he wanted to push his chair back, go to her, and lead her out of this palace to start a new life. He wouldn't care if he didn't have a farthing to his name. They would manage somehow. They could go back to Jersey and he could paint or raise horses. They would find some quaint little cottage on the coast and dig a vegetable garden. They would raise the child she was carrying in her womb—*if* she was carrying his child—and then they would have a dozen more, because he would make love to her every single, blessed night of the year.

Realizing suddenly how long he had been drifting along upon these impossible daydreams, he looked to his left, and found himself the sole object of Elizabeth's concerted attention.

She smiled discreetly at him, but said nothing.

He thought of his brother's advice, and realized that time had indeed brought a certain degree of clarity, in one regard at least. He now knew which of these two women he truly desired. He wanted the one with all the flaws and imperfections.

This knowledge did not ease his mind or resolve things, however, because duty and honor could not be ignored. If it were not for that, he would follow his impulses, but life was not so simple. It was one thing to jilt a fiancée before a wedding, as Vincent had done. It was quite another to divorce a young lady who was in love with you. Not only would she be heartbroken, she would be socially ruined and scandalized.

Chelsea, on the other hand, was already ruined. And she had single-handedly devised her devious plot to become pregnant and keep it secret from him, and therefore brought this misfortune upon herself. He had promised her nothing, and he owed her nothing.

Elizabeth, on the other hand . . .

They finished dinner and concluded with dessert, then the ladies retired to the drawing room while the gentlemen remained at the table for port and cigars. His father, the duke, appeared as sane as any man could be, and conversed intelligently about the weather and current events without the slightest indication of madness.

The condition of his father's mind was a strange

phenomenon indeed, he decided as he leaned back in his chair and sipped his fine port, watching and listening to the others with profound interest.

He noted that Devon was particularly pleased to see their father behave with some normalcy. Devon spoke to him about politics and the condition of the fields after the rains, and could not seem to quench his thirst to converse with him.

His brother doted on their father. Clearly he adored him, which left Blake thinking about his conversation with Rebecca that first night in Jersey, when she tried to enlighten him about the privileges of being born a Sinclair.

He was beginning to understand it now.

Later, when they all gathered in the drawing room for the evening, Blake sat down beside his wife. He spoke quietly. "I hope you will not find this too disappointing, Elizabeth, but I think it best if I postpone coming to your bed tonight."

She frowned. "Why?"

He lowered his voice further. "Because despite the fact that we are legally married," he explained, "we are still strangers. At least in my mind, that is how I see it. I am very sorry for that, but if you will be patient, I would like to become acquainted with you again, in the way we must have been before the accident. I would like to court you, so to speak."

She smiled shyly and lowered her gaze.

It was not lost on him, however, that he had been more than ready to bed Chelsea without delay when they were strangers. There had not even been a bond of marriage to make it respectable.

"You always were such a considerate gentleman," Elizabeth said with a smile. "It is why I accepted you to be my husband."

He was relieved she did not require more of an explanation or push him to reconsider, for he did not want to argue the point.

At the same time, however, he questioned her polite, almost cheerful acquiescence. They had been torn apart by the most tragic of circumstances on their wedding night. She had wept for him on the rescue ship, believing him dead. One would think she would have been eager to welcome him back to her bed, to lie with him and assure herself that her happy marriage had been restored, and that she would not lose him again.

He looked away, wishing he could remember something from their wedding night, but alas, he could not. When he closed his eyes and tried to imagine himself making love to her, the only face he saw was Chelsea's. And he felt a great wave of sorrow when he recalled the heavenly scent of her skin.

Chapter 26

Chelsea slept very little during the night. She tossed and turned while she fought to block out the disturbing image of Blake making love to Elizabeth, as he must have done on their first night back together, reunited as husband and wife.

He must have gone to her bed and bestowed great pleasures upon her. He probably held her in his arms and promised never to leave her again, and assured her they would start fresh and settle back into the life he had promised her on their wedding day. Soon, he would become the man he had been before the loss of his memory and identity. He would convert back into the real Blake and leave behind the man she knew in Jersey, which in reality was nothing more than a fantasy. It was time for her to accept that.

The crowning glory of her sleepless night, however, came at dawn, when she was gifted with the unexpected arrival of her courses. She woke up with heavy cramps in her belly and discovered she was not going to be a mother. She was not carrying Blake's child. She had never conceived.

It was a wonderful thing, she told herself miserably as she rose from bed, then washed, dressed, and went downstairs for an early breakfast. Blake would certainly be relieved. There would be no need for any further contact between them. He would never have to tell his wife about his infidelity and break her heart in the process.

In turn, Chelsea would be free to leave the palace straightaway, and he would be able to forget they ever knew each other. He would move on with his life, as if his ordeal on the Jersey coast had never occurred. He would simply remember it like a strange dream, as would she. She hoped.

She ate alone in the breakfast room, and decided she would speak to Blake about her condition that very morning. But since it was too early for any such conversations and no one seemed to be up yet, she returned to her room to fetch her notebook, and made her way outdoors to write for a short while.

She exited the palace and walked to the Italian Gardens, which she imagined would be restored one day. She stepped carefully around a number of holes and piles of dirt, looking down at the muddy puddles and dead flowers lying on the ground with their roots torn violently from the soil.

It was a metaphor of her life, she supposed—torn apart and devastated. The color was all gone, replaced by bleakness and chaos. Only the statue of Venus remained in the center of the fountain, lonely and forlorn, as she looked out over this lifeless terrain.

She stopped and hugged her notebook to her chest while looking up at the goddess's melancholy expression, and remembered the colorful days in Jersey, when she and Blake went walking and riding on the beach. There had been so much passion and excitement. So much joy, laughter, and discovery.

She looked down at the desolated ground. One day all of this would come alive and grow again, and one day she would get over the shame of her actions, and these terrible feelings of loss. She would forget about Blake. She *must* forget him. There was no other choice.

Turning to find a quiet place in which to set her mind to prose, she ventured around the tall cedar hedge and arrived at a bench under a large oak tree. She sat down, opened her notebook, and withdrew a pencil from her pocket. She read over the last thing she had written.

"I thought I saw you come out here."

Chelsea jumped at the unexpected appearance of another person so early in the morning, when she'd thought the family was still sleeping. It was

Lord John, strolling toward her with his hands in the pockets of his fine, tailored overcoat. His blond hair seemed particularly light in the sunshine.

"Good morning," she politely said. Although in her mind she grumbled about his arrival, for she only wanted to write, and she would not be able to do that with him sitting here, trying to engage her in light conversation.

He sat down beside her. She closed her notebook.

"I'm quite glad I found you, actually," he said. "I wanted to ask you some questions."

"I'll do my best to answer them," she replied.

He seemed intent on trying to decipher what she was thinking, and she found it somewhat intrusive, like a spider climbing up her arm.

"Do you believe it's true," he asked, "that my brother-in-law remembers nothing about his life? I find it difficult to comprehend." There was suspicion and a hint of irritation in his tone.

"It is most remarkable," she said. "There is no question of that. But from what I understand, it is a true medical condition. It's called amnesia."

"What causes it?"

"No one really knows for sure, and I believe every case is different. From what I have learned over the past few weeks, some experts say it can occur from a blow to the head, which is what our physician concluded when he took into account the physical trauma Blake suffered in the storm. But I understand it can also occur due to shock or emotional trauma."

John squinted in the other direction. "Do the memories ever come back to a person who has lost them?"

"I believe so, in some cases," she said. "In other cases, no. The person simply begins a new life without ever remembering the old. That is what Lord Blake has been doing all this time—starting a new life. Even though he has returned to his home and family, he doesn't remember any of it. It is all new to him. He might never remember."

John looked down at his shoes as he spoke. "Is there anything that can be done to cause a person to remember? Another blow to the head, for instance?"

She thought about what she had learned from the doctor. "I don't think so. I certainly wouldn't want to try it."

He laughed. "No, we might end up killing the poor bloke."

She did not find the notion amusing, however, especially when he spoke of it so lightly.

For a few minutes more they sat on the bench, listening to the birds chirping in the treetops. John glanced at her sideways once or twice, and she felt some discomfort in the way he studied her eyes. She wished he would leave. She wanted to write.

"Enlighten me if you will," he said, turning his body more fully toward her. "What *really* happened between you and my brother-in-law in Jersey? Something tells me you did more than just save his life."

The presumption in his eyes unnerved her, but she did her best to hide the fact. "I don't know what you are referring to, Lord John."

He leaned back. "Come now, Chelsea. I didn't mention anything to my sister, but I do recall your tainted history. You're no innocent. You're quite a spitfire, if I remember the stories correctly. And Blake brought you back here without a chaperone. It's hardly what one would call proper. You were lovers, weren't you?"

She stood up and spoke with an aggression she could not suppress. "I don't wish to continue this conversation. Good day, sir." She walked away.

To her frustration, he followed. "Where are you going?" he asked. "Stay and talk to me. I'll be your friend."

"I don't need a friend."

"No? I think you do. Your lover is with his wife now, and you're on your own. Why don't you and I have a little fun? There's nothing standing in our way."

"Except my refusal of your offer." She reached the tall hedge and stopped. "And what you heard about me happened a long time ago. I am no longer that foolish young girl. I am not interested in any kind of 'fun' with you or anyone else, so if you will excuse me . . . "

She turned to go, but he grabbed hold of her arms and pushed her into the thick green branches. Her notebook fell to the ground.

"Don't be like that, you cheap little tart. Come here now. Stop that!"

She fought him with all the rage and fury that was bottled up inside her. After all that had occurred this week, she was overcome by it. She slapped at him and shoved him, and held nothing back as she screamed and kicked and pushed. "Let go of me, you animal! Don't touch me!"

Chelsea slapped him across the face, which only incensed him further and caused him to push her deeper into the hedge. A sharp branch scraped her cheek. Bits of green cedar broke off and rained down on her head while she struggled and fought and spit in his face. Then at last she pushed him hard enough to send him flying backward out of the hedge and onto the grass.

"You bitch," he growled.

"And you are a disgusting maggot," she replied, bending down to pick up her notebook. "Don't ever come near me again. Do you understand? If you do, I swear I will drive my pencil through your heart."

She turned and walked quickly around the hedge, found her way back to the Italian Gardens, and was soon running up the palace steps to safety.

Back at the hedge, John rose to his feet. He tasted blood on his lip and wiped it with the back of his hand, then reached into his breast pocket for a handkerchief and dabbed at the perspiration on his forehead.

He had thought she would be easier than that. If he had known she would be such a fighter, he wouldn't have made the attempt.

Then again, she had certainly aroused him with her grit. He liked spirit in a woman. Perhaps he would try again.

Feeling somewhat depleted from the struggle, he decided to return to the bench, where he could sit for a few minutes and wait for his lip to stop bleeding, but before he reached the spot, he noticed a dark figure peer out from behind the oak tree, then retreat out of sight.

Had someone witnessed what just happened? A servant perhaps? A member of the family who liked to rise early? That was just what he did not need.

Deftly, he made his way closer, then swung himself around the tree trunk to confront the unwelcome spectator. He had already made his mind up to persuade whoever it was to keep his or her mouth shut, no matter what the cost.

But it was no servant or member of the family, which helped him to breathe easier.

"What in God's name are you doing here?" he asked. "I suppose you saw what just happened."

"I did," his sister replied, looking none too pleased. "You are a monster, John. You always were. I should tell my husband what you tried to do to Lady Chelsea. You had no right."

He moved to the bench, sat down and dabbed his lip with the handkerchief. "Yes, you *should* tell him. If you were a proper wife, you would, but you won't, because if you did such a ludicrous thing, I would tell him all about *your* sordid circumstances, not to mention the root of our family's illustrious fortune—in particular Father's interest in wicked little plants. You wouldn't want that to happen, now would you?"

Her lips pulled together in a tight line. "Maybe I would. Maybe I would like to see you dig your own grave, John. Then at least you would get what you deserve."

She walked off then, striding past him in a huff and making her way back to the palace.

Chapter 27

Chelsea marched into Blake's bedchamber, slammed the door behind her and startled him from his sleep. "I will be leaving here today."

He sat up in a jolt on his elbows and shook himself awake. "I beg your pardon."

"I said I want to leave."

"No."

She gritted her teeth. "What do you mean, 'no'? You cannot keep me here against my will. I want to leave, so please prepare your coach. And I will need money for the train and passage across the Channel."

Tossing the covers aside, he rose from the bed in his nightshirt. "Tell me what has happened, and how you scratched your cheek."

She reached up and touched her face. Indeed, there was blood on her fingertips.

Blake went to fetch a handkerchief from his chest of drawers, dipped it in a porcelain bowl filled with water on the washstand, then offered it to her. While she dabbed at the blood, he pulled on his trousers and shrugged into a shirt.

Chelsea sat down in a chair.

"Now tell me what has happened," he said, buttoning the shirt before pulling on a waistcoat.

Finally managing to calm her breathing, she looked up. "Your brother-in-law just tried to ravish me in the garden."

A menacing thundercloud darkened Blake's expression. "Are you all right?"

"I'm fine, but maybe you should ask him if *he's* all right."

"Why? What did you do to him?"

"He was in bad need of a good thrashing. He ended up on the ground with a bloody lip."

Blake nodded. "Good girl. Where is he now?"

"I left him by the cedar hedge, on the other side of the Italian Gardens. I don't think anyone saw us. No one seems to be awake yet." She dabbed again at the scratch on her cheek. "I cannot bear to remain here, Blake." She passed the handkerchief back to him. "It's time for me to go."

"No!" he replied as he tied his cravat, seeming shocked she would even suggest it.

"Yes," she countered.

"I told you, until we know your condition, you cannot leave."

She looked down at the blood still on her fingertips. "That is the other reason why I am here," she explained. "There will be no baby. I am not with child, so we are free of each other."

She did not look up. She couldn't. She did not want to see the relief that was sure to be as clear as day in his eyes.

"Are you certain?" he asked.

"Yes. My courses arrived this morning."

She was aware of him crossing to the other side of the room in silence. "You don't have to leave right away."

"Yes, I must. You are with your wife now. It's not right for me to be here. We must forget what happened between us and put it in the past."

He faced her. "Maybe I don't want to forget."

Her gaze darted to his, and the hostility she had been working so hard to suppress finally exploded inside of her. "You have no choice in the matter."

"There are always choices."

"No, not in this case!"

They were both quiet for a moment, then Blake turned to face her. "I want you to go to the library and stay there," he said. "Promise me you will not move from there until I get back."

"Where are you going?"

"I am going to have a word with John."

"Will you give him a bloody nose for me?"

"Yes," he said as he headed for the door. "Then

I'll tell him to pack his things, because he is no longer welcome at Pembroke Palace."

"But he is your brother-in-law," she reminded him.

He stopped and pointed a finger at her. "Just go to the library and wait for me." The door slammed shut behind him before she could form a reply, let alone contemplate how she truly felt about the reality of finally saying goodbye to this man forever.

Elizabeth stood at her window, trying very hard not to cry. Everything that had occurred over the past few weeks had taken a toll on her spirits, and she was not sure she could bear one more day of this heartbreak.

What was she doing here? She did not belong. She was trapped.

And her brother was a snake and a rotter. She hated him. She hated her father. And Blake—dear, wonderful Blake—he was the kindest, noblest, most honorable man she had ever met in her life, yet she could not be happy here. She was miserable. She could not eat or sleep or concentrate on anything. All her smiles were artificial. Her laughter was untrue.

Just then her husband came into view below her window. She leaned closer to the glass to see him striding across the Italian Garden ruins, then disappearing behind the hedges. A few seconds later he reappeared, turning this way and that, searching for something, or someone.

Her brother, most likely.

She put a hand to her mouth. John would think that she'd told Blake what had occurred. He would be upset with her.

But she had *not* told her husband . . .

She watched in horror from the second story window as Blake spotted John still sitting on the bench under the oak tree, then strode toward him, grabbed him by the coat lapels and threw him to the ground.

John scrambled backward like a crab along the grass, then Blake stood over him, grabbed hold of his coat to hold him with one hand, and punched him repeatedly in the face with the other.

She covered her eyes. She could not watch.

When she looked out again, Blake's brother Devon was running across the lawn toward them, wearing nothing but a pair of trousers. No shoes, no shirt, no jacket . . . He must have dressed in a hurry after witnessing the brawl from his window.

Blake thrust John up against the tree and shouted at him—though she could not make out what he was saying. Devon grabbed hold of Blake's shoulders and tore him away. John crumpled to the ground and curled into a ball, clutching his stomach.

Blake said something to Devon, left John on the ground, and started back to the house. He walked quickly. Was he coming to see her? Would he want to know what she had witnessed?

But no, he did not know she'd been there. Someone else had told him what happened, and he'd responded like an enraged lover.

All at once, truth and clarity found a path to her mind.

She sank down into a chair and closed her eyes. For the longest while she could not move, then she lifted her eyes and said, *"Enough."*

A few minutes later she walked into Blake's empty bedchamber and closed the door. She searched frantically through his drawers and over his desk until she found the box with all his sketches.

I draw everything, he had said.

She took the box to the bed, climbed up onto it, and looked at every picture—the landscapes and portraits and all the beautiful, exquisite nudes—then came across a portrait of Chelsea with her father's secret insignia sketched into the corner.

Flopping back onto the feather pillows, she began to weep. They were not tears of sadness, however. They were the sweetest, most wonderful tears of joy, because everything was going to be all right now. Somehow, it was going to be all right.

* * *

"This just arrived for you, my lady," a footman said. He stood in the corridor outside the library, holding in his gloved hand a letter upon a silver salver.

Chelsea picked up the sealed letter, thanked him, then closed the door and returned to her chair. She recognized the seal and penmanship. It was a note from her mother, who must have sent it immediately after Chelsea left the island on that final morning.

Breaking the seal, she unfolded the heavy paper and sat down in front of the fireplace.

My dearest Chelsea, it began . . .

She read the entire letter, then lowered it to her lap and covered her mouth with a hand. She read the first paragraph again, and noticed how fast her heart was beating. Was it true? Could it really be true?

After instructing Devon to keep an eye on John so he would not flee the palace like the coward he was, Blake ran up the stairs to the library, praying that Chelsea would still be there. If she had gone to her room to pack her things, he would stop her. He would not let her go. Not now, when he felt such intense exhilaration and needed to describe it to her.

He had never imagined that thrashing a man

could feel so bloody good. He had certainly not felt such satisfaction when he clouted Chelsea's brother. That was different. Sebastian had deserved it, no question, but Blake had not enjoyed it.

This was odd. Yet somehow, it was not. There was an explanation for it. He had a suspicion.

Could he call it a memory?

He pushed through the door of the library, expecting to find the room empty, but Chelsea was there, slouching low with her head resting on the back of the chair, staring up at the ceiling, a letter dangling from her fingertips.

She looked at him with tears in her eyes, and he halted where he stood on the carpet. "What's wrong? Has something happened?"

"Yes," she replied, sitting forward and looking down at the letter she had been reading. "This was delivered to me while you were outside. It's from my mother. She had a great deal to say to me."

Blake strode forward carefully, waiting for her to elaborate, hoping she had not already decided to shut him out completely. He wanted to know what was happening in her life. He wanted to know why there were tears in her eyes, and to make them disappear if he could.

But then he recognized that they were not tears of sorrow, but something else, something much more profound . . .

"She has apologized," Chelsea told him. "She

said she was wrong to want to force me to marry Lord Jerome when I do not care for him, and that she regrets her actions on that final night, when we quarreled on the staircase."

"That is good news," Blake said, remaining a short distance away. "I am pleased to hear it, Chelsea."

She cleared her throat and wiped a tear from her cheek. "But there is more. She has confessed something else to me—that she has lived her entire life smothered by shame and regret because she trapped my father into marrying her, by arranging for them to be caught in a kiss at a ball."

Stunned, but curious, Blake moved closer.

"She knew my father didn't love her," Chelsea continued, "but she was in love with him and did it to secure a proposal. She has never told anyone about it, not until now, and has felt guilty about it all this time. But when she learned what I was trying to do with you, it made her feel less guilty, because suddenly she was not alone in her duplicity. Since I was attempting to do the same sort of thing, it made it seem more normal to her. But then when I refused to continue with the plan and admitted my remorse, she had to face her own as well. I left without saying goodbye, and she blamed herself for what she had forced me to do—because of her ambition and strategizing— all for the sake of a title."

Blake sat down in the seat opposite Chelsea. "What will you do? Will you forgive her?"

"Of course," she replied. "I must. She regrets her mistakes, and heaven knows, we all make them. I certainly have. And I do love her. How could I not? She is my mother. With all her faults and failings, I still love her."

"So she has changed her mind about forcing you to marry your cousin?" he asked.

Warmth filled Chelsea's eyes. "I believe she has, because of the regret she said she felt, and because there is more news. The morning we left Jersey, Melissa was terribly ill. She fainted and fell down the stairs. Naturally the doctor was sent for, and he discovered something wonderful, Blake. My sister-in-law is expecting a child. My brother is going to have a baby—an heir, possibly. She is more than three months along. The whole time you were with us in Jersey, she was expecting and none of us knew it. I am so happy for them." She smiled through her tears and covered her mouth with a hand. "Isn't it wonderful?"

"It is," he replied, as a feeling of euphoria flooded his heart. Chelsea's happiness was his own.

"But what about you?" she asked, folding the letter on her lap. "What happened when you went to see John? Did he plead for mercy? I hope so. And if he did, I hope you refused."

"Yes, he pleaded, and I refused him. Quite repeatedly in fact."

She smiled at him. It was the most mischievous and luminous smile he had ever beheld, and for a moment his heart stood still.

He could no longer deny the truth. Nothing had changed. Whether she was carrying his child or not, he loved her now as he'd loved her in Jersey— before he learned of her plan to use him to beget an heir for her brother. Despite all of his mistakes and her foolish, irrational schemes and decisions, they were connected, and there were no words for what he felt.

Except for love, but even that was not enough. It was beyond love. It was complete and total knowledge and understanding, and it was the most devastating feeling in the world, because she would leave him now. Her life in Jersey was no longer in jeopardy. She could return there without fear for her future.

More important, he was married to another woman, and he had to let this one go without argument or any contact in the future. He could not have her, and would never know paradise again. Not in this lifetime.

"You looked happy a second ago," she said, her own happiness draining from her face. "Now you look like someone just dropped a bucket of cold water over your head."

He was not sure what to say. She was exactly right.

But somehow he found words. "I think I remember something."

She sat forward. "What is it?"

"I remember thrashing John."

She inclined her head with a look of concern. "But that just happened, Blake. Are you feeling all right?"

He nodded. "What I mean to say is—I remember fighting him *before*. Every time I woke from a restless sleep and wanted to strangle someone, it was *him*. I think we were fighting each other when I lost my memory."

She shook her head as she tried to understand. "But they said you collided with another ship and the boat went down. When do you think you fought with him? Before that?"

"But did the boat really sink?" he asked. "Have there been any reports of such an event?"

"I don't know. What do you suspect? That there was no accident, but that he threw you overboard?"

"Possibly." He put his hand to his side. "I think he stabbed me."

She glanced down at his hand covering his abdomen.

"I remember . . . I remember fighting with him on the deck of the ship. It was raining and windy, and the boat was careening everywhere. I had no clothes on, and I fell back against the rigging. I was bleeding. The pain was excruciating."

He stood and paced around the room, searching through the chaos in his mind, remembering the brutal blows he had just delivered to John in the garden. He remembered the sensation of his knuckles connecting with the man's jaw, then he turned to Chelsea.

"He broke into the cabin where I was sleeping, and stabbed me in my bunk, then I chased him up onto the deck."

"Was Elizabeth there?" she asked. "Did she see this?"

"No, she wasn't there. I don't know where she was."

"Did he throw you overboard? Because that would be murder, Blake. If you remember it, you must send for the magistrate."

He shut his eyes and pressed the heels of his hands to his forehead. "No, there *was* a collision. I remember it now. We hit the other ship when I was still in my cabin. I woke up and there was water on the floor, and that's when John came in."

"But it makes no sense," she argued. "Why would he want to kill you when the boat was sinking?"

"Because he didn't want his sister to be married

to me, and wanted to ensure I went down with the ship?"

Chelsea stood up. "That makes no sense either. You are the son of a duke."

He faced her. "I hope it's true."

"You hope *what* is true?"

"That he does not want me as his brother-in-law—because if he or she wanted this marriage reversed, I would not quarrel. If I could turn back the hands of time, I would. I would never have married Elizabeth. Then I would be free. Free to marry you."

Her eyes filled with tears. "No one can turn back time, Blake."

Yet time seemed to be standing still.

"We've made too many mistakes," she continued. "We can't change that. What we had together was wrong. All we can do now is forgive each other. You're a married man, and even if you weren't, you have no obligation to me now. I am not carrying your child."

He strode to the door.

"Where are you going?"

He stopped, but kept his back to her. "I am going to speak to Elizabeth. Because if I can't have what I want, maybe I can at least have my memories back. And maybe I can have justice, too."

"I hope you can," she said. "You deserve a full and happy life, Blake. Despite all that has passed between us, I will never forget the time we spent together, and I will wish you well. Do what you must. Find out why John tried to kill you and make it right." Her voice filled with melancholy, but remained steady. "Then we will say goodbye and part as friends, because I wish to put this experience behind me. I want my dignity back, and I believe I will find it in Jersey."

He swallowed uneasily, then walked out to search the palace for his wife.

Chapter 28

Blake found Elizabeth in the Italian Garden ruins, staring up at the statue of Venus.

"Good morning, Elizabeth," he said. "May I speak with you?"

Looking almost delirious, she turned to face him. In her hand, low at her side, she held a sheet of paper.

He looked down at it as cold dread flowed through him.

"Where did you get that?"

"In your room. I had no idea you were so gifted, Blake. It just goes to show how little we know of each other."

He frowned. "You were in my room?"

"Yes. A short time ago, after I saw you beating my brother. I needed to know the truth. Now I do."

"Elizabeth . . ."

She made a feeble attempt to smile. "No, please,

don't apologize. There is no need. She's lovely, Blake. I thought so the first moment I saw her. She is your perfect match. It's there in the way you look at each other. It's as obvious as the sun in the sky."

She stepped forward and held the sketch out to him. It was the first picture of Chelsea he had ever drawn—the one with the unusual emblem in the corner, the symbol he had never been able to connect with anything.

He didn't know what to say. He didn't want to hurt Elizabeth. That's not why he came out here. He had come to ascertain if she knew what happened that night on the boat, and why John had tried to kill him.

"You don't love me, do you?" she asked.

He met her wet, teary gaze, and decided there was no need to say the words aloud. She knew.

She turned toward the fountain and looked up at Venus's face. "It's all right, I'm not hurt. Well, I am, but only because I was forced to marry you, just like you were forced to marry me. It has all been very difficult."

"We were forced?" he asked, a heightened frustration permeating his voice—a reaction to his persistent inability to remember all the things he needed to know. "By your brother? Or your father? Did I compromise you?"

She chuckled. "No, Blake, you are far too honorable for anything like that, which is why I hold such a high opinion of you. You were forced by *your* father. You had to marry someone to secure your inheritance, and my father wanted me to forget the young man I had fallen in love with."

"The young man?"

So there was another. She was in love with someone else . . .

Blake looked up at the clear blue sky and felt a wave of calm move through him. He took in a breath of fresh air and let it out, then went to Elizabeth, took her by the hand and sat down beside her on the fountain wall. She seemed so young—too young to be his wife.

"You were brokenhearted on our wedding day?" he asked.

She nodded. "Yes. I missed him. I still miss him now."

"Who is he?"

"He's a solicitor, the son of a clerk. But a match between us is utterly hopeless. My father would kill me first."

"I'm sure that's not the case."

"Oh, yes, it is. You don't know my father."

"Don't I? Surely I do."

She looked up at him with weepy eyes and laughed. "Poor Blake. You really need to recover your memories. You met him only once. That is all. On the day you asked for my hand."

"Obviously I made a good enough impression."

"Of course you did. You are a good man and a marvelous catch by any standards."

"But you don't love me," he said.

Tears spilled out of her eyes onto her cheeks. "I like you a great deal. You were very good to me."

For a long time he sat beside her on the fountain wall, holding her small hand in his and struggling to remember the night on the boat.

"After we were married," he said, "what happened? I remember being asleep in my cabin when our boat collided with the other, but where were you? Forgive me for being blunt, Elizabeth, but did we consummate the marriage?"

She shifted uneasily. "No. I left our cabin and went to the supper room to try and forget what I was leaving behind. You merely thought I was nervous, or perhaps you suspected the truth. I don't know. But you were very patient, and I was grateful for that."

"And that's when we collided with the other ship?"

"Yes. The storm was raging, and when we hit, we hit hard. Water came rushing into the supper room, and when I went back to our cabin to find you, you were gone. I didn't know where you were. By the time I found my way up onto the deck, the boat was already turning over on its side, and before I knew it, I was swimming in the

Channel. I don't remember what happened after that. I woke up on the other ship." She lowered her eyes. "You were not with us, and I was devastated. Truly I was."

"You weren't relieved to be rid of me?" he asked, hoping to make her smile.

She shook her head. "Of course not. I knew you were a good man, and I told myself that in time I would grow to love you. I'm sure I would have."

"And I you," he told her.

But they were living in the present, not the future, and they both loved other people.

"There is something else you must know," he said. "It is the reason I came out here to speak with you."

She looked up. "It has to do with my brother, doesn't it?"

He paused to give her a moment to prepare herself for the news it seemed she expected, but would nevertheless not find easy to hear.

"Yes, it has to do with your brother. I remember what happened that night on the boat. I was not simply lost overboard during the accident."

He watched her face go pale, and then her eyes revealed her understanding. "John tried to hurt you, didn't he?"

"He stabbed me in the cabin."

She stared at him in white-faced shock, then stood up. "He stabbed you?"

"Yes. And I am hoping you will be able to tell me why. I suspect it has something to do with the Horticultural Society and all the questions I was asking. And what is this emblem here?" He pointed at the sketch. "I drew it, but I cannot place it."

Looking faint, she sat down again. "What do you remember? What do you know?"

"I remember that I was concerned about my father leaving his fortune to an operation that was run by some questionable characters, and was curious as to how the organization could have the funds to own a ship and travel to France once a month to bring back rare flowers. And honestly, your brother hardly seems like the type who would enjoy botany."

"You are correct," she replied. "He does not. There is only one kind of plant that holds any interest for him and my father, and that is—"

"The poppy," he finished for her. He looked down at the emblem, and realized that's what it was. "Your brother is importing opium."

She stared up at him with shame. "Do you remember learning this? Did you have proof?"

"I don't know. If I did, it's lost now."

Then suddenly he remembered all the opium dens John had taken him to in the early days of their acquaintance, and how John had gambled like a man with bottomless pockets.

That was why he befriended John. He'd been seeking the truth . . .

A great flood of dark and filthy memories rushed into his brain, and he remembered the effects of the drug. He remembered taking it in order to keep John from suspecting why he had befriended him.

Then the doctor in Jersey gave it to him . . . No wonder he'd been so enraged. He had never wanted to become an addict. Thank God he put a stop to it when he had.

"This symbol I drew . . . " he said. "It identifies your father's activities, doesn't it?"

"Yes," she replied. "He stamps it on all his correspondence, and his associates in France do the same. It is how they know a letter is legitimate." She looked away. "John and my father must have known you discovered what they were doing. Although I believe at first they hoped you would join them. No doubt John realized eventually that you were too decent for that. He must have known you would blow a whistle, which is why he tried to harm you."

"It all makes sense now."

She stood and walked a short distance away. "I've had enough of my family's corruption, Blake, and their overbearing ways. I can get the evidence to expose my father and brother, and I am going to do it. Finally, I am going to do it. I cannot live like this any longer."

He stood up also. "It will cause a scandal."

"I don't care. I will have my solicitor to protect me. I know that he will. He is a good man, like you."

Blake approached her. "What do you want to do, Elizabeth? About us."

She looked him straight in the eye. "I want to do what is right, and what we both want. You are too much of a gentleman to say it, Blake, so I will be the one. I wish to seek an annulment. I want to be with the man I love."

He took hold of her hand. "I am sorry for all this."

"It's not your fault."

"I wish you every happiness," he said. "If there is ever anything you need . . . "

"Thank you." She covered his hand with her own and kissed it. "And I hardly need to wish *you* happiness," she added with laughter, "for I suspect you already found yours."

"Perhaps," he replied, not entirely sure that his happiness would be an easy thing to recapture, for he had been cruel to Chelsea since that final night in Jersey, and she seemed determined to leave here today and go home to her family, to reconcile with her mother, and be there for the birth of her brother's first child.

Chapter 29

Blake had to resolve matters with John before he could see Chelsea and talk to her about the future. He explained to Devon what he remembered from the night of the accident—how his brother-in-law had stabbed him in his bunk and left him to drown when the boat took on water and turned over in the Channel.

They sent for the magistrate before John could learn of Blake's recovered memories, and when the man arrived with three constables in tow, Elizabeth was at hand to offer her testimony—evidence that would expose her father's shady business dealings and ruin her family's good name forever. She had the support of the Pembrokes behind her, however, and did not waver in doing the right thing. All she wanted was her freedom, and the young solicitor she loved with all her heart.

A full two hours had passed since Blake left

Chelsea in the library, and when he returned, the room was empty, just as he expected it would be.

Trying not to lose hope, he went immediately to her guest chamber, but that, too, was empty—though her clothes and belongings had not been removed, which eased his concerns to some degree. From this it could at least be construed that she had not already dashed off to the train station, determined to put this nightmare behind her, now that she knew she was not carrying his child.

He stood for a moment in her room, looking at her bed and her belongings—the book on the table, the brush and the creams in little jars—and began to wonder if he'd left his heart outside in the garden. His insides seemed vacant and terrified. Terrified that he had spoiled everything and she would not forgive him for the way he'd treated her back in Jersey. Even before he knew he had a wife, he'd cut her out of his heart. He had dragged her from her home and left her here alone to wallow in her shame and uncertainty about the future.

He wished he could go back and do it differently. But what she said earlier was true. No one could turn back time. One could only go forward, and forgive.

But he wanted so much more than forgiveness.

He walked to the bed and picked up her pillow, raised it to his face and inhaled deeply. A maid entered just then with folded sheets in her arms. He set the pillow down.

"Have you seen Lady Chelsea?" he asked impersonally. "I must speak with her about an urgent matter."

"She went for a walk, my lord. She took her notebook with her."

"Did she say where she was going?"

"No. Only that she wouldn't get lost this time."

He went to the window and looked out, and had a sneaking suspicion he knew where she'd gone.

A short time later, after fetching Thatcher from the stables, he was trotting along the lakeside where he had met Chelsea the last time, after she fell and scraped her leg. But she would know her way around the lake this time, just as she had told the maid. She would not get lost again.

Ducks were quacking contentedly on the lake, and squirrels chattered in the treetops. A gentle breeze blew over the surface of the water, keeping the air cool.

He saw no sign of Chelsea. Then suddenly he remembered something. He *remembered*.

Chelsea had fallen down a hill. "A slippery mud slick," she called it. He knew exactly where it was. There had been a tragedy there a few years ago. A woman died on that hill. She was Vincent's fiancée.

He pulled Thatcher to a halt, stopped on the trail and thought back to the events of that day. His brother Devon had been responsible for the accident. He was with the young lady in the woods and was taking her back to the palace on horseback when they encountered the river of mud. The horse slipped and fell, and MaryAnn was killed.

Devon and Vincent became enemies after a lifetime of friendship, and both had withdrawn from the family. Devon went to America and Vincent lost himself in the worst watering holes and whorehouses of London.

Blake recalled that for three years he had run the estate on his own, while his father went slowly mad. He'd given up his youth and freedom and buried his artistic desires for the sake of his family and the interests of the dukedom and palace.

All of this explained the eruption of his passions in Jersey. He had once referred to himself as a volcano, and that's exactly what he'd been. He had needed to break loose and celebrate his newfound freedom. Chelsea helped him let go of his frustrations. She brought him out of himself and revived the artist inside of him.

All at once, something compelled him to reach into his pocket and withdraw the watch. For a long time he stared at the white face and black numerals, and then remembered something else.

Yes, he remembered . . .

His father, the duke, had given it to him upon his graduation from Cambridge. It was a gift to celebrate his homecoming and the recommencement of his duties and obligations at the palace. Blake remembered vividly how his father had embraced him with pride, and how in that moment, he felt as if he were suffocating.

In the very next instant, however, love had flowed through him like a great ocean wave. He had come home, because his family needed him.

Blake recalled the man his father had been in his younger days—vigorous, handsome, and dignified—and closed his hand over the watch. Holding it tight, he felt a swell of emotion in his heart. He would take care of this precious timepiece in the future, as he would also take care of his father.

Urging his horse on again, he rounded the bend and saw her at last—Chelsea, standing on the crest of the hill where she had fallen before.

He inhaled sharply. *"Be careful!"*

But there was no need to warn her. She would be fine. She had fallen before but would not fall again. She was merely looking at the hill, perhaps assessing where she had gone wrong.

She turned and spotted him. He stopped on the trail and waved. She waved back, then carefully picked her way down the safe side of the hill.

"Were you looking for me?" she called out to him. "Did you find out what really happened with John on the boat?"

He dismounted and tethered his horse to a branch, then walked to meet her. The sun was shining down on her lovely face, and her hair glimmered like spun gold. She held her notebook at her side.

"Did you have any luck writing today?" he asked, caring for nothing but her happiness.

She glanced down at the book. "No. I confess I have tried many times, but I haven't been able to write a word since we left Jersey."

He frowned. "Is it the palace? Have you been that unhappy? Does it crush your creativity?"

It had certainly crushed his over the years.

"No, it's not that," she replied. "It's very beautiful here. But I . . . " She paused. "I cannot pretend that I've been happy here, Blake. You know it as well as I do. I've not been happy with myself. And today, after reading the letter from my mother, I feel more displaced than ever. I need to go home, start fresh with my family and put this experience behind me."

He bowed his head. "Because of me. Because of the way I made you feel."

She sighed. "When I came here with you, all I wanted was for you to forgive me, but it seemed hopeless. And then Elizabeth arrived, and it only made me feel worse about what I had done."

He shook his head. "It was wrong of me to blame you for what happened between us. I was as much a part of it as you. I desired you from the beginning, and I seduced you just as much as you seduced me."

She kept her eyes on his face.

"Walk with me for a little while," he said, offering his arm.

Together, they strolled along the lakeside, breathing in the clean summer air and the fresh scent of all that was green.

"Do you think, then," she asked, "that you have forgiven me? I've not heard you say it, and I would like to go home knowing that you do not despise me. I once said that I wanted you to remember me fondly. I shall certainly remember you that way. I will never forget the time we spent together in Jersey. They were the most wonderful weeks of my life, because it changed me as a person. I know now that I must take responsibility for my future and learn how to live, instead of just imagining and writing about a life of adventure for characters that do not really exist."

He placed his gloved hand over hers, which was resting on his arm. "And I have realized something, too," he said. "I now know that life has not been easy for you. You've lived in exile on that island for seven years, and I believe that many of your passions have been repressed. I know it because I have experienced something similar myself. The only difference is that you used your art to keep yourself sane. I simply went a little mad."

She grinned up at him. "I thought it was your father who went mad."

"Oh, he's definitely mad. Nuttier than a fruitcake, for all the world to see. At least I *think* he is. As for me . . . " He paused. "I went mad on the inside, but no one knew it. Not even me."

"Do you still feel that way?" she asked. "It can't help matters when you are without your memories."

"But I have recovered some," he told her. He went on to explain what he remembered about the woman who died not far from where they were walking, and he described the years of strife between his brothers, and the precious memory of receiving the watch from his father.

"If you remember those things," she said, "perhaps it is only a matter of time before you remember everything else. Are you pleased?"

"Very." Then he stopped on the path and took both her hands in his. "But there is so much more to celebrate, Chelsea. I must tell you what happened when I spoke to Elizabeth. It was true, what happened between John and me. He did try to kill me on the boat, and she knew why. Both her brother and father have been involved in an illegal opium trade and were using the Horticultural Society to disguise and hide their crimes. I sent for the magistrate, Elizabeth has exposed them, and John has been taken into custody."

Chelsea stopped on the path. "How incredible. But there will be a scandal."

"Yes," he replied. "A gargantuan one. A scandal without equal, not to be surpassed."

She shook her head and chuckled, bewildered. "You seem to be taking this very lightly. What will happen? Elizabeth is your wife. John is your brother-in-law."

"Not for long," he replied.

"What do you mean?"

"We are going to have the marriage annulled. Elizabeth never wanted it. She was in love with another man from the beginning, and I was only doing what had become my habit. I smothered my own needs and desires for the sake of duty and honor and responsibility to my family. And while I still value honor and the well-being of my family, and I wish to continue being a devoted son and brother, I must also be true to myself and seek my own happiness. I did that when I was in Jersey. I began to sketch again, and I let my heart run where it wanted to run."

"Into the world of your art?" she asked.

"Into *you*."

She looked up at him with some caution. "What are you saying, Blake?"

"I am saying that I love you." He felt rather dizzy with excitement, and dropped to one knee on the path. "Please forgive me if I am doing this clumsily. I am still married to another woman, and have no ring to offer you, but I must make my feelings known. I love you. I cannot go on if I must give you up. You are everything to me. If it were not for you, I would still be that other man I was before I died and was reborn in that cave where you found me. I owe you my life. I owe you my happiness." He looked up at her with pleading. "Please marry me, Chelsea. Marry me as soon as I am free to walk down the aisle with you. Bear my children. Be my wife. Forever, until death do us part."

She gave him a dazzling smile, and he found he could not breathe. He was so desperately in love, it hurt.

"Don't speak of death," she said. "Speak only of life. I, too, came alive when I found you. You rescued me from a world that was not real. I had forgotten what it is to connect with another person, to love another person. Yes, I will be your wife if you can weather the gossip about being married not only to a young woman with a reputation, but to a writer!"

He laughed and stood up. "I wouldn't want you any other way. So it is yes, then? You will be my wife? You will forgive *me*, for if anyone should be asking for forgiveness today, Chelsea, it is I. I am so sorry for all that I have done wrong."

"As am I." She reached up and took his face in her hands. "But it is the future that matters now, not the past. Although it is a blessing beyond words that you are remembering your past—finally. Everything is coming around right, and all I see in the days and years ahead of us is joy."

He pulled her close into his arms, pressed his lips to hers, and pondered the extraordinary truth that this beautiful, imperfect woman belonged to him and loved him. They were similar creatures with similar pasts, and therefore shared the same dreams. He would never lose her again. Not while he had breath in his body.

Scooping her up into his arms, he carried her into the bushes and laid her down on the soft green grass to kiss her lovely eyelids, cheeks, and lips, and to listen to the birds and the ducks and the bees buzzing in the air—all the sweet sounds of nature, pure and true, surrounding him as he kissed her.

Epilogue

Jersey
Summer 1875

The sun was setting in great splashes of pink over the sea, while a glorious splendor of light outlined the thick, downy clouds that floated over the horizon. Blake, who was perched on a stool at the edge of the lawn—paintbrush in one hand, his palette in the other—reveled in the persistent call of the waves upon the rocks below, while he touched up the painting he had begun a few days before. Overhead, seagulls soared and dove down to the silvery surface of the water, and he watched them with the observant eye of an artist, noting the reflection of color and light upon their feathered wings.

Not far away, Chelsea was reclining on a teak lawn chair on the stone terrace. She, too, was listening to the call of the sea. Eyes closed, she ran her fingertips lightly back and forth over her swollen belly.

"You must come and feel this!" she called out to him, opening her eyes suddenly and lifting her head off the chair.

Blake set down his brush and palette, rose from the stool and walked across the lawn. He placed the flat of his hand on her belly.

"Do you feel him?" she asked.

"You say 'him' as if you're certain it's a boy."

"I am. I don't know why. I just feel it."

Her stomach jerked and joggled before their eyes.

"Did you see that?" Blake said, laughing. "*That's* how you know it's a boy. Obviously he has two gigantic feet, and he's as strong as an ox."

Chelsea laughed, too, and looked up at her husband with love.

"What shall we name him?" she asked. "We've not yet decided, and we only have a few more weeks. Have you given any more thought to Theodore, after your father?"

Just then Sebastian and Melissa emerged from inside the house with baby James, and crossed the terrace toward them.

"This just came for you," Sebastian said. He handed Chelsea a letter.

She swung her legs to the ground, sat up on the edge of the lounge chair, broke the seal and began to read the note. "It's from a London publisher," she told them, rising heftily to her feet. "They want to publish the story I sent them, and they want to see more of my work. They want to see everything I have written!"

Melissa, who was bouncing baby James in her arms, exclaimed with delight. "That's wonderful, Chelsea! I always knew we would see your stories in print. Congratulations."

Chelsea lowered the letter to her side and looked at Blake. "I can't believe it."

"It's true," he said.

She smiled. "I daresay it is. But I could never have sent them this story without your confidence and encouragement, Blake. Thank you."

He stepped forward and kissed her on the cheek. "It was your talent and imagination that won their esteem, darling. I had very little to do with it."

"You're going to be famous," Melissa interrupted.

"Well, I don't know about that," she replied, laughing at the idea. "I suggest we see how well my story is received before we make that claim."

"Who's going to be famous?" her mother asked, coming around the side of the house as she returned from her evening stroll. At her side was Dr. Melville, her fiancé. They had been walking on the beach, exploring the sea caves.

"Our very own Chelsea," Sebastian said with pride. "One of her stories has been accepted for publication."

"How extraordinary," her mother replied, but the initial excitement in her eyes quickly died away. "I hope you're not going to write under your own name. My wedding is only three weeks away. I can't possibly arrange it with another scandal looming. We only just tiptoed out from under the last one."

Chelsea took her mother's concerns quite seriously. "I do have time to think about it," she said. "But either way, you'll be married and gone off on your honeymoon by the time the book is printed. I predict your wedding day shall proceed without a single hitch."

Lady Neufeld looked up at Dr. Melville and smiled alluringly. "Only three more weeks, darling. Then we will be strolling the beaches of Monaco."

A seagull sang a shrill song over their heads, and the sun glowed like a great ball of orange fire in the twilight sky.

"Shall we go inside and dress for dinner?" Sebastian asked, addressing Melissa, who nodded and carried little James toward the door.

Later that night, after a quiet dinner with her husband and family, Chelsea lay in bed beside

Blake, warm and safe in his arms as they looked out the window at the full moon. "I am so glad I found you that day," she said softly. "Imagine if I had not gone walking . . ."

He kissed the top of her head. "You saved my life."

She snuggled closer to him, laid her hand upon his cheek and gazed into his eyes. "Just as you saved mine. I never knew happiness like this was possible, Blake, and now I have everything I ever dreamed of. I am so grateful."

And as he lowered his lips to hers and they basked in their feelings of love and completeness, the ocean waves surged and exploded onto the rocks outside their summer retreat, and their baby kicked his little legs in her belly, immensely eager to greet the world.

*Unforgettable, enthralling love stories,
sparkling with passion and adventure
from Romance's bestselling authors*

HOW TO PROPOSE TO A PRINCE   *by Kathryn Caskie*
978-0-06-112487-7

NEVER TRUST A SCOUNDREL   *by Gayle Callen*
978-0-06-123505-4

A NOTORIOUS PROPOSITION   *by Adele Ashworth*
978-0-06-112858-5

UNDER YOUR SPELL   *by Lois Greiman*
978-0-06-119136-7

IN BED WITH THE DEVIL   *by Lorraine Heath*
978-0-06-135557-8

THE MISTRESS DIARIES   *by Julianne MacLean*
978-0-06-145684-8

THE DEVIL WEARS TARTAN   *by Karen Ranney*
978-0-06-125242-6

BOLD DESTINY   *by Jane Feather*
978-0-380-75808-1

LIKE NO OTHER LOVER   *by Julie Anne Long*
978-0-06-134159-5

NEVER DARE A DUKE   *by Gayle Callen*
978-0-06-123506-1

At Avon Books, we know your passion for romance—once you finish one of our novels, you find yourself wanting more.

May we tempt you with . . .

- **Excerpts** from our upcoming releases.

- Entertaining **extras**, including authors' personal photo albums and book lists.

- Behind-the-scenes **scoop** on your favorite characters and series.

- **Sweepstakes** for the chance to win free books, romantic getaways, and other fun prizes.

- Writing **tips** from our authors and editors.

- **Blog** with our authors and find out why they love to write romance.

- **Exclusive content** that's not contained within the pages of our novels.

Join us at
www.avonbooks.com

AVON

An Imprint of HarperCollins*Publishers*
www.avonromance.com

Available wherever books are sold or please call 1-800-331-3761 to order.

FTH 0708